They walked together through an alien world, sur-rounded by danger, beset by enemies, and torn by the most deadly force of all—their desire for each other. . .

The city seethed.

The Senyas fire dancer should have been blinded and cowed by the display, but she was not. Her hair lifted, rippling like a golden river in freefall, tendrils reaching, seeking the invisible currents of energy that reshaped the city each instant. Lines of power burned on her skin, traceries of gold sweeping up from her hands to her face, across her shoulders, down her torso, dividing into a single slim line over each hip.

Her gray robe covered most of the lines, but her Bre'n mentor, Kirtn, could sense their heat. That heat disturbed him, awakening a desire for her that should have been dormant for several more years. She was too young to be his lover, too young to be sending out the subtle currents of energy that made him ache, too young to realize the danger of what she was doing. It had driven him into madness once before. Only Rheba's desperate skill and Fssa's ability to absorb energy had saved Kirtn and Rheba from burning to ash and gone.

He could not expect to be so lucky twice.

Turn the page to see what the world is saying about this very talented author. . .

Also By This Author

Writing as Ann Maxwell

Writing as Elizabeth Lowell

*Written with Evan Maxwell

ANN MAXWELL

DANCER'S LUCK

PINNACLE BOOKS
KENSINGTON PUBLISHING CORP.

PINNACLE BOOKS are published by

Kensington Publishing Corp.
850 Third Avenue
New York, NY 10022

Pinnacle and the P logo Reg. U.S. Pat. & TM Off.

First Pinnacle Books Printing: December, 1995

Printed in the United States of America

I

The ship came out of *replacement* in a soundless explosion of energy. Rheba checked the colored status lights, peeled away the pilot mesh, and stood stiffly. She wanted nothing more than sleep, but that was impossible. All around her in the control room were former slaves whom she had promised to take home. Behind them a city and a culture lay in ruins, burned to ash by a fire dancer's rage and slaves' revenge.

It would not be smart to stir such hatred again. The sooner the ex-slaves were off the *Devalon*, the sooner she would feel safe.

A questing whistle rose above the babble of languages around her. She whistled in return, looking over the heads of strangers for the familiar face of her Bre'n. Kirtn's whistle came again. His tall, muscular body pushed through the crowd of people. Around his neck, bright against the very short copper plush that covered his body, there was a snakelike being known as Fssa. Shy, vain, and astonishing, Fssa was both friend and translator.

"We can keep everyone alive and nothing more," said Kirtn, bending over her. He spoke in Senyas now, an uncompromising language known for its bluntness and precision. It was his native tongue, as it was Rheba's. The second half of their language was Bre'n, known for its subtlety and beauty. "The power core is good for two *replacements* and maybe four days of maintaining this many people."

Rheba looked at the slanted gold eyes so close to hers. Absently she rubbed her palm over the soothing suede texture of Kirtn's arm. "What does the navtrix show within two *replacements?*"

"Onan." His voice was carefully neutral.

"Onan," she said bleakly. A place she had every reason not to return to, having left behind there a gaggle of enraged Yhelle Equality Rangers, a burning casino called the Black Whole, and a sizable amount of money. She would not mind getting her hands on the latter, but the former she would gladly avoid. She looked at the people around her, overflowing the control room and tubular hall, packing the tiny galley and crew quarters, stacked breast to back in the exercise room until only tiredness kept them from turning on each other with snarls of outraged privacy. "Onan." She sighed and began to climb back into the pilot's mesh.

"Wait," said Kirtn.

Rheba's cinnamon eyes searched his. "More bad news." It was not a question.

Kirtn whistled a Bre'n curse. "Our navtrix."

"Yes?"

"It didn't recognize any of the planet names we tried on it."

"What? But—" She stopped, then turned her attention to the silver snake draped around Kirtn's neck. "Did you try languages besides Universal?"

Fssa flexed, taking time to create the proper internal arrangements to speak Senyas. It would have been less trouble to whistle Bre'n, but when Rheba's eyes sparked gold in their depths, Fssa knew that precision was preferable to poetry. "Where planet names could be translated into other languages, I did. The navtrix," he said primly, "was completely unresponsive. Onan is the only Yhelle Equality planet it acknowledges. Kirtn told me you programmed in Onan yourself, long after you left Deva."

Rheba whistled a sour Bre'n comment. Their navtrix had been made by her own people. It reflected the extent—and limitations—of their knowledge. On her home world of Deva, the Equality had not even been a myth. In order to take the slaves packed aboard the ship to their farflung homes, she would have to get her hands on a Yhelle Equality navtrix.

Fssa darkened as he mentally translated Rheba's whistle into its Universal equivalent. When he spoke again, his voice was coaxing rather than arch. "I'll keep trying, fire dancer. Maybe one of the new languages I've learned will help." Then he added, brightening visibly, "Twenty-three of the slaves want to get off on Onan."

"How many does that leave, Kirtn?"

His torso moved in a muscular Bre'n shrug. "I gave up trying to count at sixty."

"On a ship built for twenty and modified for two." She stretched, brushing against Kirtn. "Take us into orbit around Onan. I'll see if Ilfn needs help with the lottery." She scooped Fssa off Kirtn's shoulders. With a delighted wriggle, the Fssireeme vanished into her hair. Next to a live volcano or ground zero in a lightning storm, Rheba's energetic hair was the snake's favorite place to be.

As Rheba began to work through the people toward the tubeway, two compact brown forms appeared. M/dere and M/dur quickly cleared a path for Rheba. No one, not even the fierce survivors of the Loo slave revolt, wanted to antagonize J/taal mercenaries.

"Where are their clepts?" Rheba asked Fssa softly, referring to the J/taals' war dogs.

The snake's whistle was pure and startlingly sweet against her ear. "Guarding Ilfn and her storm dancer."

"Are they all right?" she whistled, concern clear in each note.

"Yes, but when I told M/dere how much the female Bre'n and the male dancer meant to you, she insisted on putting a guard over them. She's not at all happy with the slaves we took on. They're a murderous lot."

"They had to be to survive Loo," pointed out Rheba.

"And we'll have to be to survive them," the Fssire-eme added sourly.

She said nothing. She had given her promise to get those slaves home, and get them home she would. She did not need any carping from a snake to tell her that she might have cooked more than she could eat.

With a human sigh, Fssa subsided. He liked the energy that crackled through Rheba's hair when she was angry, but he most emphatically did not like to be the focus of that anger.

Ilfn and Lheket were packed into what would normally have served as a single bunk. The Bre'n woman, like all of her race, was tall and strong. Where Kirtn's body was covered with a copper plush, Ilfn's had a dense chestnut fur that was slightly longer than his. Like him, she had a mask of fine, metallic gold fur surrounding her eyes. Like him, she was totally devoted to the Senyas dancer who was her protégé.

As Rheba pushed against the bunk, Lheket's blind emerald eyes turned unerringly toward her. She touched his cheek, allowing some of the energy that was her heritage to flow into him. For an instant her hands brightened as akhenet lines of power flared. Lheket smiled dreamily, a child's smile of contentment.

Although he could not see, she smiled in return. He was the only Senyas besides her that she knew to have survived their planet's fiery end. Someday he would be her mate. But until then he was a blind, untrained dancer, one more burden on her shoulders.

As though she read Rheba's tired thoughts, Ilfn's hand protectively smoothed the boy's fine hair.

"Did the computer respond for you?" asked Rheba, looking up from the boy to his Bre'n mentor.

"Once I got the accent right," said Ilfn wryly. She was from the far side of Deva; her inflections were not precisely those that the computer had been programmed to respond to. "I gave each of the thirty-eight planets a number, stored them in the computer under a code word, and gave orders for the computer to be continually choosing among those numbers. When you say the word, the computer's choice will go on the ceiling display. Whoever belongs to that number goes home first. All right?"

"As good as any and better than most." Then, realizing how grudging that sounded, Rheba added,

"Thank you." She leaned against the bunk. "We have to go to Onan first. Power core and navtrix."

Ilfn touched Rheba in quiet sympathy. Although the Bre'n had never been to the Yhelle Equality's most licentious planet, she had heard about it from Kirtn. Rheba could expect nothing but trouble there.

Rheba pushed away from the bunk. As she did, she noticed a man watching her. He was her height, about the Equality norm for a man. He smiled at her, a smile of startling beauty. He twisted deftly through the press of people beyond the bunk until he was standing close enough to speak to her. He would have come even closer, but a grim-faced J/taal prevented him.

"Can I do something for you?" he asked in Universal. "You've done so much for us."

"Do you have a Yhelle Equality navtrix in your pocket?" asked Rheba dryly.

The man fished in his gray slave robe, then turned his hands palm up in apology. "Sorry," he said. "I don't even have the Equality coordinates to my own home world."

"You and every other ex-slave aboard," she muttered. She looked again at the young man with the engaging smile. He appeared closer to Lheket's twelve years than to her twenty-one, but it was hard to tell with some races. "Do you have a name?"

"Daemen." His smile widened, inviting her to share his good nature. "Actually it's *The* Daemen, but on Loo no one seemed interested in a slave's former rank. Daemen is what I'm used to now."

"Were you on Loo long?"

"Yes." His smile changed, cooler, like his voice and his rain-colored eyes. "And you?"

"No. It just seemed like it."

Daemen laughed, a sound too adult for his appearance. "My family—there were ten of us when we were kidnapped—kept talking about home, how beautiful it was under its single sun." His left hand moved in a dismissing motion. "Maybe it is. I barely remember its looks, much less its location."

Rheba felt a rush of sympathy. She, too, had lost her planet, had felt what it was like to stare at a night sky and know that not one of the billion massed stars was home. "We'll find it, Daemen. I promise you."

His smile returned, full of possibilities and silent laughter. "That's what he said."

"He?"

"The man who looks like her," said Daemen, indicating Ilfn. "Huge and fierce."

Rheba's smile was as much for her Bre'n as it was for the stranger in front of her. "Yes, he's all of that. He was one of the finest poets on Deva, as well . . . when there was a Deva and when he still believed in poetry."

She scratched the top of her arms absently. The new lines of power that had appeared when she fought her way off Loo itched unmercifully. She would have to get some more salve from Ilfn. But first, the lottery. Thirty-eight names, thirty-eight planets. Only one could be first. She wondered aloud who the lucky one would be.

"Me."

Daemen's voice was confident, yet not arrogant. She looked at him closely, trying to see beyond the charming smile and gray eyes. "You sound very sure."

"I was born lucky. That's the only way I survived Loo."

She smiled perfunctorily. He was neither obviously strong nor obviously gifted. Perhaps he believed that luck was responsible for his survival of Loo's various hells. "What's your planet's name?"

"Daemen."

She blinked. "Daemen? Just like you?"

"Yes. The oldest member of my family is always called The Daemen." His face changed, looking older than it had, almost bitter. "I'm the only one left. Whatever name I was born with, I'm The Daemen now."

The ship chimed like a giant crystal, warning its passengers that *replacement* was imminent. The masses of people shifted subtly, seeking secure positions. In the absence of nearby gravity wells, it was unlikely to be a rough translation.

Chimes vibrated up and down the scale of hearing until no known race could have missed the warning. There was a heartbeat of silence, then the ship quivered microscopically and *replaced* itself. It was a brief maneuver, accomplished with Kirtn's usual skill. The *Devalon* ran on silently, gathering speed in another direction, bringing itself into alignment for a final *replacement* in a far orbit around Onan.

Rheba whistled soft instructions to Fssa. The snake moved beneath her hair, changing shape to accommodate the needs of translation. Almost all of the former slaves understood the language of Loo. Many understood Universal. Those who understood neither usually did not survive. The Loos had not distinguished between ignorance and disobedience.

"While we maneuver for the next *replacement,* we'll have a lottery to decide which planet we'll stop at after we pick up supplies on Onan. The ship's computer is randomly scrambling the planets by number. At my command, the computer will display the number that is under its scanner at that instant."

Rheba spoke in Universal. Fssa's simultaneous translation into Loo was accomplished with a minimum of distraction. The snake could control its endless voices with such skill that words seemed to come out of the air above the crowd.

A buzz of speculation in many languages greeted the announcement as it was carried throughout the ship by the *Devalon*'s intercom. Fssa changed from a snake to a bizarre listening device of quills, spines, dishes and tiny spheres in every shade of metal from copper to blue steel. It was one of his more astonishing performances, but then he had rarely had the chance to hear so many new languages at once.

Rheba felt the snake sliding out of her hair, too intent on his listening modes to keep a secure position. She caught him before he hit the floor, then held him up to facilitate his reception of the various sounds. Out of the energy field of her hair, his weight quadrupled.

Whether it was the appearance of the glittering, changing shape over her head or the simple fact that the lottery needed no further discussion, people stopped talking and stared at the snake.

No longer consumed by the Fssireeme imperative to learn new languages, Fssa realized that he was the focus of attention. He darkened with embarrassment, cooling palpably in Rheba's hands. Being on display frightened the shy snake. He was convinced he was repulsive because he did not have legs.

"You're beautiful," fluted Rheba, using all the complex shadings of Bre'n to reassure Fssa.

Glints of metallic silver ran in ripples over his arm-length black shape. When a few gold traceries joined the silver, Rheba smiled and lifted Fssa back to her head. Immediately, he became so light that she did not notice his presence in her hair. She tilted her head and whistled an intricate Bre'n trill.

The computer responded with a single short tone that indicated that she had established access. Her lips shaped another Bre'n sound, a single command: Choose.

In the air over her head a number glowed, then the corresponding planet's name appeared.

Daemen.

Rheba felt a chill move over her neck. She whirled to face the charming stranger. He was gone, swallowed up in the seething disappointment of the former slaves.

II

Kirtn stared glumly at the hologram of the port city of Nontondondo. The view shifted as the *Devalon's* sensors responded to his curt Senyas instructions.

"Any Rangers?" asked Rheba.

"Not yet. Maybe they believed the name we gave them."

Her lips twisted skeptically, but she said only, "What's our OVA?"

He frowned. The Onan Value Account was established for each ship before it was allowed to touch down on the planet. It was one of Onan's less endearing customs. "Subject to physical verification of the gems, our OVA is eighty-thousand credits."

Rheba looked at the multicolored, brilliantly faceted jewels winking on the ship's sensor plate. She frowned. "On Onan, that's not much."

His whistle was eloquent of pained agreement. "A power core, four days' dock fees and some odd change."

"That's all?" she demanded. Her whistle flattened into a curse. "How much does a navtrix cost?"

He did not answer. She looked at him and felt her breath catch. His eyes were narrow, hot gold, and his lips were so tight that his faintly serrated teeth gleamed. It was the face of a Bre'n sliding into rage, and from rage into *rez*, the Bre'n berserker state that was almost always fatal to the Bre'n and whoever else was within reach.

She stroked his arm slowly, trying to call him back from anger. For a moment he resisted, then he sighed and stroked her hair until it crackled beneath his big hand.

"I can play Chaos again," she offered hesitantly.

His hand closed tightly on her restless hair. "No. If you're recognized they'll lynch you."

Rheba did not disagree. She had cheated at Chaos the last time she was in Nontondondo; in Chaos, cheating was not only expected, it was required. But for a stranger to cheat so successfully that she bankrupted half the players in the casino . . . She shuddered, remembering the riot that had ensued. She had been forced to burn down the casino in order to escape. Even if the Black Whole had been rebuilt, she had no desire to play Chaos in it again.

Together, Rheba and Kirtn watched the hologram of the seething city. In Nontondondo, everything had its price. It was the only place in the Yhelle Equality where everything was licensed and nothing was illegal. With money you could do anything.

But they had no money.

Absently, Kirtn fiddled the controls, zooming in on a street where people of all shapes, colors and races mingled. The scene enlarged until it filled the curved ceiling of the control room and merged crazily with the heads of the taller slaves. Suddenly, one of the depicted citizens screamed and began clawing at her neck. Just behind her, someone darted into the crowd, a stolen bauble glittering in his hands the instant that he vanished.

Kirtn and Rheba looked at each other for a long, silent moment. Because he was touching her, she could sense pictures and words from his mind, as he could from hers. It was a rare thing among Senyasi dancers and their Bre'ns, a thing that neither of them had found time to adjust to. The odd form of communication had come to them just short of death, on Loo.

"How many licenses to steal can we afford?" asked Rheba, even as her Bre'n asked the computer the same thing.

"Three-day licenses?" he muttered.

"That should be long enough. I hope."

The computer queried its Onan counterpart.

"Twelve," said Kirtn, deciphering the computer's response.

Rheba frowned. "I'll need protection. How much is a three-day license to kill?"

Kirtn whistled a query at the computer. Rheba winced at the amount that was displayed in answer. It was Onan's most expensive license. Buying it would leave nothing for lesser three-day licenses.

"How much is a one-day license to steal?" she asked.

A credit figure blinked into existence above Kirtn's head. She looked, added quickly, and decided. "One license to kill, three licenses to steal and two licenses to entertain on the streets. One day. How much?"

She held her breath. After they bought the power core—absolutely essential—and the most minimal ship supplies, they would have only 15,000 credits in their OVA. Dock fees were 1,500 credits per Onan day, and subject to weekly changes. That left only 13,500 for licenses.

The figure 12,750 shimmered in the air above Kirtn's head.

"Close," whistled the Bre'n, but the tones of the whistle said, "Too close," and many less polite sentiments.

"We don't have a choice, do we?"

He hesitated, then resumed stroking her hair, smiling as silky gold strands coiled around his wrist. "Will one day be enough?"

"It will have to be. Fssa, are you awake?"

The Fssireeme hissed softly. "Yesssss."

"Do your guardians' memories recognize any of our shipmates as coming from races of thieves? Nothing fancy—strictly swipe and run. Although it would be nice if they were so light-fingered that the victims didn't notice anything until they looked in a mirror."

"The J/taals," said Fssa simply. "They're very fast. Or the Yhelle illusionists. In an emergency, they can go invisible."

"And the rest of them?" she asked, waving her hand at the multiracial press of people throughout the ship.

Fssa sighed very humanly. "My guardians' memories are very old, fire dancer. Most of these races weren't fully formed then. They are as strange to me as they are to you."

She scratched her arms, ignoring Kirtn's frown at this sign that she had used her fire-dancer skills too recklessly on Loo. She had not had any choice then. She did not have a better choice now. She turned to the brown-furred, compact woman who was as inconspicuous and ubiquitous as her shadow.

As Rheba spoke, Fssa instantly translated her words into the language of J/taal. The process was so unobtrusive that both parties often forgot it was the Fssireeme who made communication possible.

"M/dere, we need money. Do you have any objections to turning thief? Licensed, of course."

M/dere smiled. "Licensed, unlicensed, no difference. You're our J/taaleri. What you command, we do. Although," she added matter-of-factly, "we're better killers than thieves."

There was little Rheba could say to that. She had seen the J/taals in action on Loo. They were better at killing than most people were at breathing.

"May I suggest?" said M/dere.

"Yes," said Rheba quickly. She was uncomfortable in her role as J/taaleri, focus of J/taal devotion. She did everything possible to shift the relationship to a more even footing. She failed, of course. J/taals were notoriously single-minded.

"The illusionists. They fight badly. Perhaps they steal well?"

Rheba scratched her arm fiercely. She was reluctant to ask the proud, aristocratic Yhelle illusionists to descend to thievery. On the other hand, they were wonderfully equipped for the job. "I don't know where—or as what—the illusionists are," she said finally.

"M/dur is bringing them."

Rheba realized that she had been neatly maneuvered into a position the J/taals felt confident of defending. If they were out stealing they could not protect her. Protecting her was their reason for living.

M/dur arrived with the illusionists in tow. The two J/taals exchanged a look.

Rheba knew that behind the J/taals' blue-green eyes information was being passed on. For an instant she envied them their precise, species-specific telepathy, a gift that had been both rare and prized on Deva. The few moments of mind dancing she had shared with Kirtn had made her appreciate the tactical possibilities of silent communication.

I'sNara, the feminine half of the Yhelle couple, watched Rheba with the patience long years of slavery on Loo had taught. Beside her stood f'lTiri, equally patient.

Rheba measured them, impressed by their altogether unnoteworthy exterior. Although elegant in movement, both of them were frankly drab in appearance, their exteriors a blank canvas on which their startling gifts drew a thousand forms.

As though sensing her appraisal, the illusionists stood without moving, their eyes unfocused, patiently waiting . . . slaves.

"Stop it," snapped Rheba. "You aren't like that. I've seen you mad enough to kill."

F'lTiri almost smiled. His appearance changed so subtly that Rheba could not point to any single alteration, yet the result was profound. Before her now stood a man of middle years, thin, worn and very proud. Beside him stood a woman who was equal to him in every way, slave no longer.

"We gathered," said f'lTiri, "that you wanted us for something. M/dur was polite but very firm."

"Ummm," said Rheba, scratching her shoulder absently, wondering how to put her proposition delicately. In Bre'n, it would have been possible, but the illusionists did not understand Bre'n. Universal was

a very bald language, rather like Senyas. "We need
money for a navtrix," she said bluntly. "Everyone I
asked suggested that you two would make crackling
good thieves. Would you?"

I'sNara's face twitched with smothered laughter.
F'lTiri looked pained, then resigned. Rheba waited.
They spoke between themselves quickly in their native
language. Fssa heard and understood; he also was
diplomat enough to save his translation for later.

"What kind of thieves?" asked f'lTiri neutrally.

"Ummm . . . ordinary," said Rheba helplessly.
"What other kind is there?"

F'lTiri's voice was patient. "Are we to be *yimon*—"

"—electronic thieves—" whispered Fssa to Rheba.

"—or *s'ktimon*—"

"—arm-breakers—"

"—or *mnkimon*—"

"—kidnappers—"

"Wait," said Rheba desperately, wondering what
kind of culture named its thieves so formally. "Kirtn
and I will do a little act on a street corner. When the
crowd gets big enough, you'll go through and take
whatever you can get your hands on while the crowd
is watching us."

"Pickpockets," summarized Fssa in Universal.

"*Liptimon*," said i'sNara and f'lTiri together.

Rheba muttered. Fssa did not translate her clinical
Senyas.

"Would this do?" said i'sNara. The air around her
dimmed, shifted, then cleared. A young, slightly grimy
child stood in her place, eyes wistfully appraising her
surroundings. She was the essence of innocence.

F'lTiri laughed. "That old cliché. You'd be spotted
in a second. Nontondondo is sophisticated. Some-

thing more like this, I think." His eyes narrowed and his face tightened as he concentrated on her.

The air around i'sNara shifted again. When reality settled back into place, i'sNara was a beautiful woman of apparent but not blatant wealth. On her shoulder was a fluffy, sharp-fanged animal.

Rheba realized that her mouth had dropped open. She had not guessed that the illusionists could project their gift onto another person. But it was f'lTiri's shrewd appraisal of Nontondondo's populace that really impressed her. He was right; an innocent child would be the first person suspected. Nontondondo did not believe in innocence.

"Can you hide jewels and OVA tabs beneath that illusion?" asked Rheba.

"Of course."

Rheba almost felt sorry for the people out in the streets. Almost, but not quite. Certainly not enough to change her mind. Anyone who came to Nontondondo knew what the rules were. "No stealing from licensed innocents," she said firmly.

"Of course not." I'sNara's tone made it clear that she was shocked even by the suggestion. "Thievery is an honorable profession, calling for fine judgments and skill."

Rheba swallowed hard and said only, "Then you'll do it?"

"Will you license us?"

"I can afford one day for three thieves and one killer to protect you."

"That's me," said M/dur. No one argued, even M/dere.

"Who's the third thief?" asked f'lTiri.

"Me," said a voice from behind Rheba.

She spun and found herself looking into Daemen's

rain-colored eyes. "You?" she said, her voice rising. "You're hardly old enough to be on your own, much less turned loose out there."

Daemen merely smiled.

"You're not as quick as a J/taal," said Rheba, her voice under control again, "or as strong as a Bre'n or as skilled as an illusionist."

Daemen's smile did not change. "I'm lucky, Rheba. Lucky is better than good anywhere in the galaxy."

Rheba made an exasperated sound and turned toward M/dere. In matters of strategy, she deferred to the J/taal woman's greater experience. "What do you think?"

Although Daemen had spoken in Universal, Fssa had quietly translated for the benefit of the J/taals. The mercenary looked at Daemen for a long, silent moment, an appraisal that few beings could stand without fidgeting. But Daemen merely stood at ease, smiling his uncanny smile.

M/dere turned toward Rheba. "He survived Loo's Fold?"

"I survived the Pit," said Daemen quietly.

Rheba shuddered. The Fold had been bad enough, but the Pit was beyond belief.

"He survived the Last Year Night rebellion?" continued M/dere.

"Yes," said Rheba.

M/dere's aged copper eyes stared at the young man again. "Then he must indeed be lucky, for he certainly isn't *good.*"

Reluctantly, Rheba agreed. Yet she had to look away from Daemen as she spoke, for it went against her akhenet grain to put at risk anyone who looked so vulnerable. "You're our third thief, Daemen. But if you get into trouble, I'll feed you to the clepts!"

"Be the best meal they ever had," he responded, smiling.

Despite her uneasiness, Rheba could not help smiling in return. She hoped that Daemen's victims would be similarly charmed, for she had no confidence in his skill, strength or judgment.

Grimly, she instructed the computer to trade stolen Loo gems for licenses to steal on Onan.

III

Nontondondo seethed. There was no sky, only a ceiling of energy shaped into words—demands, enticements, celebrations of every sin and pleasure known to the beings of the Yhelle Equality. The noise hovered on the threshold of pain for Rheba. Her eyes ached, assaulted by colors and shapes that she was barely equipped to receive.

She should have been blinded and cowed by the city, but she was not. Her hair lifted, rippling like a golden river in freefall, tendrils reaching, seeking the invisible currents of energy that shaped and reshaped the city each instant. Akhenet lines of power burned on her skin, traceries of gold sweeping up from her hands to her face, across her shoulders, down her torso, dividing into a single slim line over each hip.

Her gray robe concealed most of the lines, but Kirtn could sense their heat. It disturbed him, awakening a desire for her that should have been dormant for several more years. She was too young to accept him as a lover, too young to be sending out the subtle currents of energy that made him ache, too young to realize the danger of what she was doing. It had driven him into *rez* once before. Only her desperate skill and Fssa's ability to absorb energy had saved Bre'n and Senyas from burning to ash and gone. He could not expect to be so lucky twice.

Resolutely, he turned his thoughts away from the body swaying next to him, the delicate traceries of desire that bloomed innocently on her skin. Too soon. Too young. A net of energy uniting them, burning them, fire-dancer passion like lightning in his blood.

With an angry sound he pushed through the crowd, forcing a puzzled Rheba to run to catch up with him. He could have told her what was wrong, but did not. The passion that eventually bound Bre'n mentor to Senyas dancer was something that each Senyas had to discover. Most made the discovery in time, before a Bre'n went into *rez,* killed a Senyas protégé and died.

Most, but not all.

Kirtn's gold metal eyes searched the streets for the correct place to stage their act. He needed a corner where people were inclined to loiter, not one where they would be impatient at any delay. He rejected three possible places before he found one that had the right combination of space and relaxed pedestrians.

The act he and Rheba would perform required no props. Songs sung in Bre'n whistles had cross-cultural appeal. Rheba's ability to manufacture hot or cold fire out of the air also had an appeal that was not limited to single races or cultures. Together, Bre'n and Senyas made an unusual display. He hoped it

would be enough to excite the jaded tastes of Nontondondo's habitués.

The corner Kirtn finally selected was already occupied by a group of jugglers who were more numerous
than competent. Kirtn watched them for a long
moment, wondering which of the Equality's thirty-
one planets they called home. The longer he watched,
the less he believed they were any part of the Equality
at all. They somehow reminded him of the awkward
peoples he and Rheba had found on their flight from
Deva's death, cultures barely able to chin themselves
on their planet's nearest moon. Their worlds hung
like soap bubbles against the enormousness of space,
iridescent, fragile, quivering with life. And so alone.

"Kirtn? What's wrong?"

Rheba's voice pulled Kirtn out of his thoughts.
Bre'n discipline returned to him, holding him aloof
from all emotions . . . like a planet caught in darkness,
held in place by invisible lines of force.

"We'll use that corner," he said, turning to
M/dur, the male J/taal who had preempted the single
license to kill.

Fssa's translation was instantaneous, unobtrusive.
The J/taal mercenary slid into the crowd, followed
by three silver-eyed war dogs. Silence spread behind
them. J/taals and their clepts were well known in the
Yhelle Equality.

Kirtn never found out whether or not the jugglers
knew the language of J/taal. M/dur appeared on the
corner, pointed at the jugglers and then at the street.
The jugglers bunched up as though to contest the
eviction. Then the avid silence of the crowd warned
them. Quietly, quickly, they vacated the corner.

Rheba looked at Kirtn questioningly. He sent the
illusionists into the crowd. When the act began to

attract attention, they would return veiled in illusion. Then they would begin to steal.

Daemen also walked into the crowd, his slim body swallowed up almost instantly in the press of people.

"Ready?" asked Kirtn.

As an answer, Rheba began drawing on the currents of energy that laced Nontondondo's sky. Immediately her hair fanned out, swirling and rippling in vivid display. Less obvious, for she was not working hard, were the whorls of akhenet lines beneath her brown skin.

Energy blossomed at her fingertips, streamers of colored light that flowed into shapes. Kirtn's pure whistle slid through the street noise like sun through darkness. He gave the audience a simple song, a child's tale of hidden treasure, Fifth People and friendship in unexpected places.

The energy pouring from Rheba's fingertips took on the ghostly glimmering associated with the Fifth People, that category of intelligent life which was rarely glimpsed and then only out of the corner of one's eyes. Fifth People seemed to hover soundlessly around her and Kirtn as though waiting for the child hero of the song to appear.

A few people stopped to watch, called by the Bre'n whistle and held by the languid sliding shapes created by a fire dancer. As the tale progressed, more people wandered over and stopped to enjoy. By the time the story ended—replete with monsters, heaped gems and heroism—a small crowd had collected. Unfortunately, there were not enough people to safely rob more than one or two. For really effective stealing to take place, a much bigger crowd was needed.

Kirtn's song changed to a lilting work tune that had been popular before Deva's situation became so

desperate that its people forgot how to sing. Rheba's
Ghost figures solidified into Bre'ns and Senyasi working together, calling storms or sunny days, curing
sickness, lifting girders and force fields into place,
building and laughing and singing, always singing,
for Deva had once been filled with song.

The compelling rhythms of the work song drew
more people to the corner where Rheba and Kirtn
performed. The akhenet lines beneath her skin
pulsed more brightly now, responding to the
increased demands of her performance. New energy
forms appeared, cascading from her hands like supple gems, then condensing in recognizable Bre'n and
Senyas forms. It was hard work for her, much harder
than warming soup or lighting a dark hall. Not since
she had played Chaos in the Black Whole had she
tried to manipulate energy in so many distinct shapes.

Kirtn felt her hair stream out and wrap caressingly
around his arm. Currents of energy ran deliciously
through him, touching every cell. Desire flared—and
died instantly, crushed beneath Bre'n will. He looked
away from her, knowing that she had noticed neither
the caress nor his response. Her face was taut, still,
concentrated wholly on creating figures to people his
songs.

A second whistle joined his. Beneath Rheba's seething hair, Fssa was singing.

Slowly the song shifted, still melodic, still in har-
mony, but the words were different. The crowd did
not notice, for only a handful of living beings understood Bre'n. Kirtn, however, realized that Fssa was
trying to communicate without disrupting the act.
The Bre'n glanced over and spotted Fssa's opalescent
sensors beneath the shifting veil of Rheba's hair.

"I'sNara is in place and f'lTiri is working the crowd.

Daemen is out at the fringe," continued the snake, whistling in sweet counterpoint to Kirtn's song.

Kirtn looked over the crowd, but saw no one familiar. He did not have the Fssireeme's ability to make minute discriminations among solid shapes. The snake "saw" with everything but the wavelengths of energy that comprised visible light for nearly all the races of the Fourth People. The Fssireeme was a product of genetic engineering performed many Cycles ago, before the people known as Bre'n and Senyas had even been born. He was a perfect translator and predator, although the latter had not been planned by the men who had reshuffled the genes of Fssa's species.

"Daemen just brushed past i'sNara. I think he gave her something. Yes! Oh, it's lovely, a great long necklace that's cut into a thousand surfaces!"

Kirtn sang and peered at the spot where the snake's sensors were directed. All the Bre'n saw was the outline of a very rich woman watching the act. A second look assured him that the woman was indeed i'sNara, changed by f'lTiri's illusion. Nothing in her jewelry matched Fssa's description of what Daemen had handed over. Then Kirtn remembered that Yhelle illusions were limited to visible wavelengths of energy. The Fssireeme's methods of "seeing" were not affected by such illusions.

The song ended. Kirtn and Rheba bowed while she drew the outlines of a crowd throwing money to the two performers. Laughter rippled and coins from various planets rang against the stones at their feet. As Kirtn gathered the money, Fssa resumed his monologue in Bre'n. The lyric whistle helped to stem the flow of departing people.

"From what I can overhear, the act is nice but not

really exciting," whistled the snake. "Even f'lTiri is having problems getting away unnoticed, and he's in his invisible mode. You need something that will make the crowd overlook a hand in their pants."

Kirtn laughed shortly. "About the only thing that would be that interesting would be—how did our dead stage manager put it?—'a single dance of kaza-flatch.'"

Fssa made a flatulent sound. Dapsl's death on Loo had not been mourned by the Fssireeme. Yet—"He was right," whistled the snake on a series of descending, sour notes. "It worked."

Rheba's hand moved protectively on Kirtn's arm. The Loos' casual assumption that all furries were animals had infuriated her. Neither Fssa nor Kirtn needed Rheba's indignant whistle to explain her feelings.

"Dapsl *was* right," whistled Kirtn softly, resonances of laughter and regret in each note. "Appealing to Loo prejudices saved our lives."

"Public mating?" demanded Rheba incredulously. She whistled a Bre'n phrase describing intricate sex among thirteen cherfs.

Kirtn laughed. "I didn't have anything that complicated in mind. A simple love song . . . the Autumn Song?"

"I hate to soil its beauty for these swine," she muttered in Senyas.

"What they feel is their problem," he responded in the same language. "Ours is getting enough money to buy a navtrix."

"But they'll think it's sodomy!"

Kirtn tilted her head up until he could see into her eyes. At their cinnamon depths, gold sparked and turned restlessly. "Is it sodomy to you, little dancer?"

The question, asked in controlled Senyas, sliced into Rheba like a knife. Anger and orange fire swept through her simultaneously. Streamers of flame rushed out from her body, causing the crowd to gasp and step back. She was too furious to speak, able only to burst into flame as she had not done since she was an undisciplined child.

Suddenly her arms wrapped around Kirtn's neck in a hold that even Bre'n strength could not shift. He had an instant to regret goading her, then her mouth was over his in a kiss that made him forget the crowd, the navtrix, and—almost—his Bre'n discipline.

The fire that had leaped out from her changed into a lacework of gold surrounding her and her Bre'n. Like the lines on her body, the lines surrounding the two of them pulsed with energy. She did not know that she was building a cage of energy around the man who held her; it was a fire-dancer reflex as basic as breathing.

Kirtn knew what was happening, however. In a mature dancer the filigree of energy would thicken as dancer passion rose until finally the two lovers would be enclosed in a supple, incandescent world that was deadly to any but the Bre'n and Senyas inside. That much Kirtn knew from his past on Deva. What he did not know was what it felt like to be inside the cage, inside his dancer and the world around him hot and gold. Nor did Rheba know. Only a Bre'n could survive the full passion of a Senyas dancer; only a Bre'n could fully arouse it.

But Rheba had not been told that. It was something she must discover on her own. To tell her would negate the Dancer's Choice, the moment when Senyas dancer chose a Bre'n—just as once, in the danc-

er's infancy, a Bre'n had chosen a dancer. Without
that second choosing, the relationship of Bre'n and
Senyas was incomplete, and very dangerous to both
partners.

As from a distance, Kirtn heard the bittersweet fall
of notes that was the Autumn Song. Melancholy and
harvest, chill winds and a lover's warmth, fruition
and death sung by the inhumanly perfect voice of an
immortal Fssireeme.

Kirtn knew he should take Rheba's arms from his
neck, lift his mouth from hers, set her warmth at
arm's length. No dancer could make an honest choice
while held against a sensual Bre'n body, his hands
shifting her until she fit perfectly against him, his
arms holding her in a grip both gentle and unbreak-
able. He knew he should release her . . . but he did
not, not until the fact that she was trembling uncon-
trollably registered on him.

His body moved subtly, changing the embrace to
one of affection rather than passion. He was shocked
to see how thick the lacework of energy around them
had become. Silently he cursed the Bre'n sensuality
that had betrayed her trust, forcing a choice on her
that she was not old enough to make.

Rheba trembled between his hands, looking at him
with eyes that were half aware, half knowing . . . and
half frightened. She had neither Senyas mother nor
sisters to prepare her for full dancer passion. All she
had was brief memories of half-grown Senyas boys,
giggling pleasure under triple moons, simple release.
It did not prepare her for the feelings that heated
her now.

She tilted her head, sending her hair across his
face and shoulder in electric caress. Her smile made
him ache.

"*That's* how much I care what anyone thinks," she whistled softly. Then, wickedly, "You know, I rather like sharing enzymes with you."

Kirtn grimaced at her reminder of their slavery on Loo. When the Loos would have separated Bre'n and Senyas, he had lied, telling the Loos that he and Rheba were symbionts who would die unless they could share enzymes by kissing. "Do you?" he murmured. "Some day I'm going to remind you of that," he added, brushing her lips with his.

"It—it isn't wrong, is it?" she said in a rush, glancing away from him, embarrassed to ask him. But she had no one else to ask, no one else to tell her what was proper and safe behavior between Senyas and Bre'n.

Kirtn's hands slid into her seething hair, holding her so that she could not evade his eyes. "Nothing you could ever do with your Bre'n is wrong. *Nothing.*"

He felt the tension leave her body. Suddenly, mischief crackled in her eyes. She stood on tiptoe and ran her fingers around the rim of his ear, tickling him unmercifully. It was the only way she had had as a young child to get even with her huge Bre'n mentor. Much to Kirtn's despair, it seemed to be something she would not outgrow.

"Nothing?" she asked sweetly.

He caught her tormenting hands and said hastily, "Almost nothing. Tickling my ears is definitely a badnaughtywrong."

The childhood word made Rheba laugh. She leaned against Kirtn, smiling. "I'm glad you Chose me, Bre'n mentor."

Someday, maybe you'll Choose me, thought Kirtn, then realized by her sudden movement that she had caught his thought. He cursed the inconvenience of being so close to each other that minor mind dancing was possible—and so far apart that he could not tell her about her Dancer's Choice.

The lacework of fire dimmed to invisibility. Money rained down on them, startling them into an awareness of their surroundings. Fssa's clear whistle faded into silence.

"That was wonnnnderful!" whistled Fssa, bright with enthusiasm and the energy he had absorbed from Rheba's hair. "You should do it more often. Such *energy*." He expanded to twice his former length and size, luxuriating in the instant of not having to fold in upon himself to conserve warmth and energy. Then, as though noticing the charged silence, he subsided. "Well, *I* enjoyed it, even if you two didn't. Humanoids," he whistled sourly, "may have legs but they don't have much sense."

"Shut up, snake," said Kirtn.

Fssa darkened precipitously, quailing before Kirtn's anger.

"By the Inmost Fire," swore the Bre'n, seeing his friend go from bright to dark. "You're beautiful, snake," he whistled coaxingly. "You just have too many mouths for your brain to keep up with."

Rheba snickered and began collecting the money around their feet. It was soon apparent that she would need more than her two hands to hold the coins. Kirtn bent to help her, but even his hands were not large enough. With a gleam in his yellow eyes, he snatched Fssa from Rheba's hair.

"I just thought of a use for one of your big mouths. Open up."

Fssa squawked indignantly, but complied. He rearranged his dense molecules until there was an opening beneath the sensors on top of his head. His head was a matter of convenience, a conceit to make him more like the Fourth People he was among, for Fssireemes were almost infinitely plastic.

A stream of money poured into Fssa. He sorted the coins according to size and made suitable pockets inside himself. He made an odd, musical sound when he moved. Rheba snickered again. Fssa ignored her.

By the time they were through picking up money, Fssa was quite heavy. Kirtn saw a few of the less well-dressed city dwellers watching the snake with open greed. The amount of money inside Fssa was not great—probably no more than a few thousand credits—but to some of Nontondondo's inhabitants, a few thousand credits were worth killing for.

Kirtn smiled at the men staring at Fssa. The smile revealed slightly serrated teeth and frankly predatory intent. The men looked away quickly and faded back into the crowd.

Fssa made another mouth and hissed contempt. "You should have let them touch me."

"You aren't licensed to kill."

"I'm not a Fourth People, either. Onan's rules don't apply to me."

Kirtn looked toward Rheba in silent question. Her understanding of Onan's licensing system exceeded his.

"True," conceded Rheba, "but I'd hate to try to explain your exemption to the Equality Rangers. I don't think it would work. Onan's licensing system is efficient and profitable. When you've got a good game going, you don't let a wise-mouth stranger break the bank."

Fssa made a flatulent noise. Coins quivered in an unexpected musical echo. Then his head turned suddenly and his sensors brightened as he shifted energy into their use. From the rim of the crowd came an ugly shout. Rheba caught only the word "furry" and some random unpleasantries.

"Trouble," whistled Fssa.

The crowd dissolved away, warned by the uncanny sense of danger that was part of all Fourth People's survival equipment. Where the audience had been stood twelve hooded men. Nine of them were licensed to kill. Three wore circles broken in three places; they were licensed to do everything but kill.

In a blur of speed, M/dur and three snarling clepts came to stand between the hooded men and Rheba. The J/taal's license to kill shone clearly on his forehead. The hooded men paused, seeing first the full silver circle and second the nature of the man who wore it. They murmured among themselves, then began fanning out to surround Rheba and Kirtn.

"Snake," whistled Rheba urgently, "tell M/dur I take it all back. He can do whatever he has to however he can—just get us out of here!"

Fssa relayed the J/taaleri's revised instructions in a guttural burst of sound. M/dur heard, but the only sign of that was the clepts padding lithely toward the men who wore closed silver circles. Narrow-eyed, lethal, the war dogs glided closer to their prey.

On the fringes, the Equality Rangers closed in. Rheba looked up in momentary hope, then realized that the Rangers were not there to prevent mayhem, but to regulate it. She would not be able to use her dancer skills or Kirtn's deadly strength to help M/dur. They were licensed only to entertain, not to fight.

One of the hooded men spotted the Rangers. He called out a question. Fssa's translation of Nontondondo's gutter language hissed in Rheba's ear.

"Ranger! Have these animals been licensed?" called the hooded man, his hand sweeping around to point at the clepts.

Before the Ranger could answer, Fssa called out, "The man is J/taal. He is licensed to kill. Those animals are his weapons."

"Clever snake," murmured Rheba as his translation whispered to her from a separate orifice he had just created. "Will it work?"

The Rangers muttered among themselves, then shrugged. One of them answered, "He is J/taal. The clepts are weapons. His license to kill is valid and plainly displayed." The Ranger's voice was bored.

The hooded men hesitated, then pulled weapons out of their clothes.

Rheba's nails dug into Kirtn's arm. She began to gather energy despite her lack of license to do anything but entertain. She knew that if she broke Onan law there was nowhere else to go. Her navtrix could only take her back to the slave planet Loo, or to Deva, a dead world orbiting an unstable sun. She could not afford to break the law and help M/dur—but neither could she stand by and watch him killed because his J/taaleri had been too poor to buy weapons for him.

Her hair stirred in sibilant echo of the clepts' graceful stride. Beneath her skin, akhenet lines smoldered, waiting only her release to leap into deadly, illicit fire.

IV

Suddenly, another J/taal appeared in the center of the hooded men. It was M/dere. On her forehead a full circle shone with diamond brilliance. Shocked by the appearance of an enemy in their midst, the hooded men fired without thought. Beams of razor light slashed through the J/taal—*but she did not go down*. The men surrounding her screamed, caught in the fire from weapons across the circle of hooded attackers.

Instantly the J/taal vanished, leaving behind two dead men, two more wounded, and chaos.

Clepts and J/taal attacked the instant the hooded men looked away from M/dur. When M/dur was finished, there were no screams, no wounded men. Simply death, silent and incredibly fast, too fast for any eyes to distinguish details.

In seconds it was over. M/dur stood, swaying, deep burns down the left side of his body.

Kirtn swore in the rhythmic phrases of a Bre'n poet,

then leaped forward to catch the wounded J/taal. Rheba, remembering the J/taal tradition of committing suicide when badly wounded rather than living as a burden on their J/taaleri, shouted at Fssa, "Tell him to live! If he dies on me I swear I won't allow anyone to burn his corpse!"

There was no worse threat for a J/taal than being held in this life endlessly by an uncremated body. M/dur looked over at her with pain-narrowed eyes and made a weak gesture of agreement.

Rheba spun and watched the street, wondering if there would be trouble from the Equality Rangers. They were staring toward M/dur, still stunned by M/dur's speed and deadliness. It was one thing to know J/taals by reputation. It was quite another to see one of the mercenaries in action.

"Are you satisfied, Ranger?" called Rheba. "Or should I have my J/taal fight again?"

"Animal," said one Ranger loudly.

Though M/dur was smooth-skinned, everyone knew that the females of his race were furred. Onan permitted mating between furry and smoothie, but taxed it heavily. Only a license to murder cost more.

Rheba waited, hoping that the Rangers were honest enough to obey their own laws.

To her surprise, they were. Without another word they withdrew, checking doorways and alleys for the female J/taal who had come and gone so mysteriously. Rheba found herself doing the same, although she knew that M/dere would not have left the ship against the express orders of her J/taaleri.

Daemen sauntered out of a doorway. His coat was lumpy around his slender frame. She half expected to see M/dere following him, but it was only the Yhelle illusionists, appearing as themselves. She waited until they were close enough that no random pedestrian could overhear.

"Was that you?" she asked, gesturing toward the place where M/dere had appeared—or had *seemed* to appear.

F'ltiri smiled wanly, obviously exhausted. "A real person would have been killed in the center of all that fire. I merely projected M/dere's illusion, hoping to distract the hooded men long enough for M/dur to get out from under their guns. We were lucky, fire dancer. They weren't used to illusionists. They shot without suspecting that nothing was there, and killed their companions instead of their enemy."

"Lucky," repeated Rheba, her eyes wandering over to Daemen, whose smile was like sunrise. She shivered. "There are two kinds of luck. I hope we're off Onan before the other kind finds us."

Daemen walked forward, no longer smiling. "Don't think about that." His hands moved in an odd, sinuous gesture of warding off. "If you name the other kind of luck, you'll regret it."

Rheba stared into his gray eyes, level with her own. Unconsciously she retreated a step, bumping into Kirtn. The combination of corpses, Daemen's fey presence and the Yhelles' illusion was unnerving.

"Sorry," she murmured to Kirtn as she stumbled against him. "As much death as I've seen, it still . . . bothers me."

He caught her and gently set her on her feet. "Back to the ship," he said. "You need to rest before you work with fire again."

"But we're only licensed for today."

Kirtn shrugged. "Without a licensed killer, we're helpless."

Rheba looked at the wounded J/taal, who leaned

against Kirtn. M/dur's compact body was bloody, but some of the burns were healing even as she watched. It was a gift the J/taals had, part genes and part training.

"I won't be any good to you for two days," said M/dur flatly. "It would have been better to let me die."

"I value my J/taals."

M/dur's head moved in a gesture both proud and submissive. "I'm yours to kill or keep, J/taaleri."

"Remember that," she snapped. "None of you is to die without my direct permission."

Something that might have been a smile changed M/dur's face. "You're a hard woman. We're proud to be yours."

"You aren't mine."

M/dur smiled and said nothing. It was an old point of disagreement between them.

Rheba made an exasperated, untranslatable sound and turned to Kirtn. "Carry that unbending lump back to the ship."

When Kirtn picked up M/dur, the clepts made a menacing sound. They fell back at a gesture from the J/taal. The war dogs ranged themselves into a moving shield that broke a path through the crowded streets back to the spaceport.

Once inside the *Devalon,* the illusionists sighed and let their last illusions go. Kirtn, seeing the amount of loot they were carrying, whistled approvingly.

I'sNara smiled and began peeling off ropes of gems and purses of magnetic OVA tabs. "I'd like to take all the credit, but my really valuable stuff came from Daemen."

"Mine, too," admitted f'lTiri, dumping gems and tabs out of his pockets. "That halfling is uncanny.

Four times I was sure he was going to be caught, but each time his victim coughed or stumbled or farted or sneezed at just the right moment. I still don't believe it. I could steal more deftly with my right foot than he could with four hands—but he got away with it!"

Daemen smiled. "I told you. Lucky is better than good."

Kirtn gave M/dur to his J/taal mates and turned to face Daemen. "You ride your luck pretty hard."

"No." Daemen's face changed, haunted now, withdrawn. "It rides me." He emptied his inner pockets into Kirtn's hands. One of the items was a comb made of precious-metal strands studded with oddly carved gems. "This is particularly valuable," he said, handing it over with obvious reluctance. "It's—"

Fssa, who had been studying the growing pile of loot with his opalescent sensors, interrupted with a piercing sound. "Let me see that!" he demanded, using the idiom if not the visual organs of the Fourth People.

Kirtn held the comb out toward the Fssireeme. "This?"

In answer, Fssa began to change shape, going into a mode that would permit him to scan the comb with a variety of wavelengths. The coins inside him clanked and clinked. With a disgusted grunt he opened a long slit in his side and disgorged the money.

While Daemen and the illusionists watched in fascination, the Fssireeme went through a rapid shape-changing display, scanning the comb with all the subtle means at his disposal. Finally he held one shape, a bizarre fungoid imitation. It was the shape he often used to communicate with Rainbow, the

Zaarain construct that looked like a sunburst of multi-colored crystals.

Rheba recognized the shape and recoiled. Rainbow was the jeweled fragments of a library millions of years old. Unlike a true First People, Rainbow was not a living crystal independently conceived out of unguessable lithic imperatives. Rainbow was man-made yet . . . different. Fssa insisted it definitely was more than a machine. Rainbow vaguely remembered being built by the legendary technological genius of the Zaarain Cycle. It remembered wholeness and mourned its fragmented self. It was terrified of being further reduced by man or circumstance.

Rainbow's expression of that terror on odd wave-lengths was what had alerted Fssa to the fact that what looked like a grubby mineral matrix was actually a living being. Well, almost living, and certainly sen-tient. When Fssa told Rheba about Rainbow's nature, she rescued it from dismemberment at the hands of greedy slave children.

Once cleaned up, Rainbow proved to be gorgeous, a scintillant mass of colored crystals. There was only one problem: Rainbow was desperately lonely; but when Fssa communicated with it, the resulting energy exchange gave Rheba debilitating headaches. Thus, she watched the Fssireeme's fungoid imitation with premonitions of agony.

Kirtn's arms went around Rheba in a protective gesture that was as futile as it was instinctive. Fssire-eme-Zaarain construct communication gave the Bre'n a towering headache, but it was nothing to what Rheba endured.

Rheba bit her lip and moaned. Pain belled in Kirtn's head. She twisted in his arms and moaned again. With a curse, Kirtn lashed out at Fssa.

The blow was harmless to the dense-fleshed Fssire-eme, but it did knock him off balance. He changed back into a snake, a very dark, very embarrassed snake. He had promised not to speak to Rainbow when Rheba was within range. While what he had just done was not—strictly speaking—communication with Rainbow, the result was the same. Pain for the fire dancer who had befriended him.

A tremulous Bre'n apology hung in the air, sung by a chagrined Fssireeme. Rheba sighed, rubbed her temples, and whistled slightly off-key forgiveness.

"Is it part of Rainbow?" asked Kirtn, his voice harsh.

"I think so," said Fssa, taking the trouble to form organs for speaking Senyas. As whistling required only a flexible orifice, the snake normally communicated in Bre'n, but he wanted to apologize for his lapse, and so spoke within the confines of Senyas. "Probability to the twelfth on the green carved gem, to the ninth on the three yellow gems and to the eighth on the blues. I didn't have a chance to test the colorless crystals," he added, "but they have a *zigr* probability of—"

"Enough," whistled Kirtn sourly. "We won't sell any of the crystals until Rainbow has a chance to look them over."

Fssa was tempted to point out that Rainbow did not have eyes with which to "look" at anything, but decided that now was not the time to insist on Senyas precision—especially with an irritated Bre'n.

Rheba eyed the mounds of loot with distaste, wondering if any more of Rainbow was hidden within, a dead loss as far as buying a navtrix was concerned. There were times when she wished she had left Rainbow buried in the dirt of a Loo slave compound.

"I doubt if there are any more pieces of Rainbow,"

said Kirtn, guessing her thoughts. "With the whole galaxy to look in, it's incredible luck that we found any of Rainbow at all."

The word "luck" made Rheba flinch. "Maybe," she said shortly. "And maybe Rainbow was as big as a planet once and we'll be tripping over chunks of it every time we turn around."

Kirtn looked at Daemen. The young man stood silently, gray eyes fastened on the comb with peculiar intensity.

"Let's put the rest of this junk on the sensor plate and see what Onan's computer will give us," said Kirtn, scooping up the comb in one big hand.

It took several minutes for the computer to weigh, sort, describe and transmit information from its sensor plate to Onan's port computer. It took about the same amount of time for a tentative sales figure to come back—37,899,652.753 credits, subject to physical scrutiny by Onan's computer.

A gasp ran around the room as the figure hovered in the air above Rheba's head. She closed her eyes and then looked again, as though afraid the figure would disappear or diminish.

It did not. She cleared her throat and looked up at Kirtn, who was watching the figure with a fascination that equaled hers. Only the illusionists were not surprised.

"I told you," said f'lTiri calmly to the illusionist beside him, "that the braided cord of gems was a genuine MMbeemblini. It alone must have been worth eighteen million credits. What fool would wear something like that to a city like Nontondondo?"

"An unlucky son of a five-legged dog," murmured i'sNara, satisfaction resonant in her normally colorless voice. "May his right-hand wife conceive by his left-hand son."

A ripple of uneasy black ran through Fssa. The Yhelle curse was both obscene and vicious in the context of its culture. The fire dancer stared at the Yhelle woman, but asked no questions. Rheba had enough troubles with a hold full of vengeful former slaves; she did not need to rummage in their individual pasts to find more.

Her hands went out to the sensor plate. Within its energy field, her akhenet lines sprang into prominence. The plate flushed orange, accepting her identity, then cleared in anticipation of her orders.

"Ask the port computer if it knows of anyone in Nontondondo who has an up-to-date navtrix to sell," said Rheba, "and at what price."

There was a pause, then the plate went into colorful convulsions. When it cleared, a woman's face was staring out of the ceiling at them.

Rheba went cold, then her lines of power flushed hotly as she recognized the woman. She was one of the few people on Onan who could recognize the fire dancer who had illegally razed the Black Whole.

The woman's image suddenly became a hologram hovering at ceiling level. Black eyes, elongated and shining, searched the upturned faces until the woman saw Rheba. The woman smiled. Her teeth were silver, as shiny as the closed circle she wore in her ebony hair.

"Hello, Rheba. There are a lot of people who would like to see you again."

"Hello, Satin," said Rheba evenly. But she leaned against Kirtn, joined in minor mind dance as her thoughts rang in his: *I knew bad luck would find us, but I didn't know her name would be Satin.*

V

Satin's eyes continued cataloguing the multiracial contents of the control room. Either the illusionists, Daemen, or the three striped men behind him caught her interest. Her eyes narrowed to intense black slits. She laughed bleakly. "Of course. I should have guessed."

"What do you want?" asked Kirtn, his voice calm and hard.

"Curiosity. A weakness of mine," said Satin, her eyes returning to Rheba. "When newly licensed thieves are so spectacularly successful, I want to know their names. And when those same thieves want to buy a navtrix, little chimes go off. I own the only loose navtrices on Onan, you see."

Rheba muttered a Senyas curse.

"I don't see Trader Jal," said Satin, her restless glance probing the room.

"You won't."

Satin looked at Rheba with renewed interest. "Dead?"

Rheba remembered Trader Jal, the man who had enslaved her and Kirtn. She had last seen the Loo lord on his back in a spaceport light-years away. He was very dead, every last bit of heat drawn from his molecules by a Fssireeme, the galaxy's most efficient energy parasite. Drops of rain had frozen into a shroud over Jal's body. "Yes. Dead."

"Congratulations," murmured Satin. "There will be parades in Nontondondo." Her eyes watched Rheba, noting with particular intensity the hair that lashed restlessly. "Are there many more like you out there, beyond the Equality?"

Despite her control, Rheba's face echoed some of her memories of Deva burning, Senyasi and Bre'ns dying but not quickly enough, not before their flesh blistered and cracked and they screamed. "No." she said. "No."

"Ahhh, then you're alone, too." Satin's black eyes took in the many races, faces of every hue crowding around as word passed in the ship that something unusual was happening in the control room.

"No, not alone. I have my Bre'n." Rheba drew Kirtn's arms around her, warming herself against the cold of her memories.

"But he isn't your kind."

Silently, Rheba rubbed her cheek against the suede texture of Kirtn's chest. "He's Bre'n. I'm Senyas. That's enough."

Satin smiled, a gesture both predatory and oddly comforting. "Come to the Black Whole." At Rheba's surprised look, Satin's smile widened. "I rebuilt the casino after the fire. It's mine now. I claimed Jal's half." Her head turned quickly. The movement made her killer's circle gleam. "No one wanted to challenge me for it. Strange, don't you think? I'm such a small woman, not strong at all."

Kirtn laughed grimly. Satin looked at him, caught by the sound of Bre'n laughter.

"Come to the Black Whole," she repeated.

"No. Once was enough," said Rheba.

"If you want the navtrix, you'll come to the Black Whole."

"If I go there someone else might recognize me. I wasn't," Rheba added dryly, "very popular the night I left."

Satin made a dismissing gesture with her shoulders. "If you're worrying about the Equality Rangers, don't. Your last OVA covered fines and damages for unlicensed rioting. As for the dead"—she moved her shoulders again—"you were licensed to kill. I think you even have a few credits left over."

Rheba wanted to trust Satin, but did not. Satin and Jal had been partners; perhaps she had vengeance rather than business in mind.

"Bring your furry," added Satin.

"Furries aren't allowed in the Black Whole, remember?" said Rheba.

"New management, new rules. License him to kill and bring him along. Bring as many as you like—except don't bring *him.*"

An immaterial hand appeared. A jet-black fingernail pointed plainly at Daemen.

"Come to the casino now," said Satin, turning her attention back to Rheba. "If you wait, I'll be too busy to see you. If you wait too long, I'll be too angry to sell you a navtrix. Then you'll have to try your *luck* stealing from the Equality Rangers. I don't recommend it. They're psi-blocked and immune to illusionists. I'll expect you.''

Satin's hologram vanished, leaving only a visual memory of her narrow silver smile.

"You're not going to the Black Whole," began Kirtn. "I'll—"

Rheba made a flatulent noise that was an exact imitation of Fssa. Then she smiled tiredly. "Of course I'm going—licensed to burn, kill and steal. There's no other choice."

"Someone else might have a navtrix to sell," offered i'sNara.

Rheba hesitated, then shrugged. "I doubt it. If Satin says she has the only loose navtrices on Onan, I believe her. Besides, if we take time to check around and then discover that she was telling the truth, she might decide not to sell us one at all. You heard her."

Kirtn whistled intricate instructions to the computer. Two silver circles popped out the ship's downside connector and rattled into the receiving compartment. The Bre'n pinned one circle on Rheba and the other on himself. A weapon thumped into the compartment. He pulled out the gun and tucked it into his weapon harness.

"Where's my license to burn?" asked Rheba. "And to steal?"

His finger tapped her circle. "The lesser licenses are marked off on the major one."

She noted the darker lines dividing her circle and headed for the exit ramp without another word. Once on the ramp she paused. "What about Fssa?" she asked. She looked back to where the translator-snake lay curled around a colorful mass of crystals atop the pilot mesh.

"Satin speaks Universal," Kirtn said shortly. His

eyes reflected his anger that Rheba once more had been maneuvered into danger.

Rheba saw his uncoiling rage and was silent. Like all Senyasi, she knew when it was not safe to disturb a Bre'n.

The air was cold outside, spiced with autumn and Onan's sudden night. There was no darkness at street level. Advertisements and enticements flashed and beckoned in every color known to man.

Reflexively, Rheba drank the energy around her, storing up against time of need. Her hair lifted and quivered as though individual strands sought to touch the cascading colors of the night.

The Black Whole had not changed. The anteroom was still manned by a laconic killer. He glared at the Bre'n, but made no move to exclude him from the casino. Kirtn's slanted yellow eyes were never at rest. He saw Rheba's hair seethe and knew she was as edgy as he. Both would be glad to be off Onan, and delivering former slaves to homes they had never expected to see again. Only then would Bre'n and Senyas be free to comb the galaxy, looking for the few survivors of Deva's holocaust that might exist.

But to do that, the *Devalon* must have a navtrix.

Side by side, Bre'n and Senyas pushed through the velvet force field separating the anteroom from the casino proper. Sounds poured around them, prayers and imprecations in every language of the Yhelle Equality. Far off across the huge room was a glitter-blue spiral galaxy. Beneath it were the seats and stations for a game called Chaos.

Rheba shivered and looked away. She had no desire to play Chaos again. She had been lucky to survive the first time. She stood on tiptoe, trying to see past the sweep of gamblers and hangers-on, looking for a pool of darkness where Satin would be.

Kirtn lifted Rheba easily, holding her high. She spotted Satin across the room, sharing a small table with another gambler.

Rheba pointed the way, then followed as Kirtn pushed through the crowded casino. Some of the patrons took exception to being touched by a furry. Their protests faded when they saw Kirtn's size and the deadly warning he wore on his shoulder.

Satin looked up at their arrival. She gestured to empty chairs on either side of her, but Kirtn moved another chair so that he and Rheba would not be separated. The man across from Satin never looked up. He was obviously in difficulty, sweating and squirming unhappily. Despite the silver circle pinned to his square hat, he seemed afraid. He picked two gems from a small pile in front of him and placed them meticulously on the grid between himself and Satin.

Satin studied the move he had made for only the briefest moment. Languidly, her hand moved over the grid, setting in place three colorless gems. The grid chimed and changed shape. The man watched and all but groaned. He reached again for the diminished mound of gems in front of him. His hand trembled as he picked out five stones, then four more, and placed them on the grid.

Satin did not even hesitate this time. Her hand dove into the heap of gems in front of her, hovered over the grid, then deposited only three stones. There were almost no openings left, except at the center. Watching him, she put a single transparent stone in the center of the grid.

A chime sounded. The grid reformed. There were

more openings now, many more, far more than he had stones to fill.

"Your turn," urged Satin, her husky voice soft.

The man said nothing. With a savage gesture, he shoved his remaining stones into the center of the grid. Gems skidded and caromed off the raised edges of the table. He stood up and pushed into the crowd.

Laughing softly, Satin gathered the gems into a mound and began pouring them from her hand to the table as the grid chimed and changed again. Gems twinkled and stuck to the grid, held by force fields and rules wholly unknown to Kirtn and Rheba.

"Game?" asked Satin, smiling slightly.

"No. Just a navtrix," said Rheba, her voice neutral, her eyes fascinated by the gems sliding and winking across the table. She was careful not to show her impatience. If she let Satin know how much they needed the navtrix, their flesh and bones would be part of the price.

Satin looked from Rheba to the Bre'n beside her. The woman's black eyes were unreadable, her face utterly still. Gems flashed and fell between her slim black fingers. She made no gesture that Kirtn could see, but suddenly two Equality Rangers appeared and stood behind him.

Silently, Kirtn raged at the necessity that had driven them into Satin's lair. His weapon appeared in his hand in the same instant that Rheba's akhenet lines burst into flame. Satin noted the speed with which they had responded to the Rangers, and the sudden appearance of incandescent patterns on Rheba's skin.

Satin gestured from the Rangers to two empty chairs. "Sit."

It was not an invitation. Warily, both Rangers lowered themselves into the chairs.

"Are these the ones you saw earlier?" asked Satin, indicating Rheba and Kirtn with a tilt of her head.

"Yes. They weren't licensed to kill, then."

"Did they?"

"No. They're legal to the last credit."

"And their OVA?"

"Over thirty-seven million credits. All legal. No fines, complaints or judgments outstanding."

"Then they're in no way forbidden to own an Equality Ranger Scout navtrix?" Clearly, the Rangers wanted to say no. There was a long silence, punctuated by Satin's sudden laugh. "Answer me, Rangers. You're being recorded."

"I don't like the idea of a furry with a Scout navtrix!" snarled one of the Rangers. "If you give a furry your little finger, he'll have your whole arm."

Satin waited. The Ranger's partner sighed.

"They aren't Equality citizens," said the second Ranger.

"Neither am I. I own three navtrices." Satin's voice was husky, intimate—and dangerous.

Rheba shivered. She did not know what was happening, but she sensed danger coiling invisibly around the table. One of the Rangers turned to study her. She noticed for the first time the subtle signs of rank embroidered on his scarlet collar, and the lines of hard living engraved on his face. He exuded power the same way his partner exuded hatred of furries.

"Sell it to them," he said abruptly. Then, "We're even, Satin."

He tossed a hand-sized packet onto the table and walked off without a word. His partner gave a hard look at Kirtn, then followed.

Satin watched, amusement curling around the corners of her mouth; but in her hand, barely visible, was a lethal little gun. She put it away with a smooth motion and turned toward Rheba. "Thirty-five million credits. First and last price. Of course, you're licensed to steal. You could just take this"—she tapped the packet—"and run."

Watching Satin's easy assurance, Rheba sensed it would be very stupid to steal a single credit from the owner of the Black Whole.

Kirtn apparently reached the same decision. He put their OVA tab into a slot in the table, spoke briefly, and reached for the package.

"Or," continued Satin, "I could keep the packet *and* the credits you just transferred to my OVA."

As she spoke, her hands flicked out. The package containing the navtrix vanished as though it had never existed. There was an instant of shock when Rheba expected Kirtn to crush Satin between his hands, then a moment of even greater shock when Rheba realized that Kirtn was standing frozen, muscles rigid with effort, fighting something she could neither see nor sense.

She felt peculiar energies flowing into her from the point where her body touched Kirtn. The discordant energies made her world tilt and her mind scream. She felt her Bre'n's terrible struggle to right the canted world and quiet the psychic cacophony that was destroying him.

Rage burst over her. She sucked into her akhenet lines all the power coming from the casino's core. Games stopped, force fields vanished, lights died. In the sudden midnight, lines of pale lightning coursed from Rheba, shattering the gems on Satin's table. A warning.

"Let him go!"

As Rheba spoke, even her breath was incandescent—but not deadly, not yet. She did not want Satin to die until Kirtn was free.

And Satin knew it. *Satin was there, in Rheba's mind.* The fire dancer felt a cool brush of approval and laughter as the gambler withdrew.

"Turn the fields back on," said Satin, handing the navtrix to Kirtn. "You're frightening the children."

Rheba put a blazing hand on Kirtn's arm, sensed his rage and fear . . . and freedom. With a sigh she released her drain on the casino's energy source and damped her own fires. Except for the ruined gems, there was nothing to mark the moments of fire-dancer rage.

"Are there any men of your race around here?" asked Satin, smiling languidly as she stirred the hot fragments of her gems. "Men who can't be controlled?"

Rheba did not answer. The only male of her race that she knew of was a boy called Lheket, her only hope of children, of a new race of Senyas. But she could not tell Satin that; she did not want Satin to know anything at all.

As though guessing—or *knowing*—her thoughts, Satin murmured, "So few, then? Don't worry, I wouldn't take him from you. But I surely would like to borrow him from time to time," she said wistfully. "How about him?" she continued, looking at Kirtn. "I couldn't control him, either. Kill him, yes, but not control him." She switched her attention back to Rheba. "Is he any good lying down?"

It took Rheba a moment to figure out exactly what Satin was asking. "I—I don't know," she blurted, unable to think of a lie or keep silence.

"You don't know." Satin laughed sadly. "Sweet green gods, what a waste. I suppose you come from one of those dreary little dung balls that forbid more passion than it takes to make dreary little dung-ball preachers."

"No," said Kirtn, "she's just too young."

Satin looked from Rheba to Kirtn and back again. "Too young? No child fights for her man the way she just did." She made an abrupt gesture, silencing whatever objections either might make. "Never mind. Your delusions aren't important to me. Still, if she isn't enjoying you . . .?" Satin's smile transformed her from formidable to fascinating. She radiated sensual hunger the way a star radiated energy.

Kirtn could not help but feel the pull. He was Bre'n; sensuality was in his genes. And even at her most calculating, Satin was every molecule a woman. If he could cut a loop out of time and share it with her, he would. But he could not.

Satin's smile changed, becoming humorous rather than enticing. "Thank you," she said, her voice husky. "That's the nicest refusal I've ever had. If your hot woman-child frustrates you too much, remember me."

Rheba looked from one to the other, feeling an undefinable anger prickle along her akhenet lines. Satin reminded her of a lustrous spider in the center of a jeweled web.

"Don't be jealous, child," murmured Satin, looking at Rheba out of long dark eyes. "It's just that I'm tired of having nothing but insects to play with." She sighed and swept the ruined gems to the floor. "You did me a favor when you killed Jal. Now I'll do one for you. I saw a face in your control room, a young man with eyes like winter ice."

"Daemen?" said Kirtn.

Satin's face changed. "So he even uses the name,

does he? Most would hide it.'' Her eyes were very black now, as cold as the void between the stars. "When you leave the planet, make sure he's aboard. When you come out of *replacement,* space him."

Rheba was too shocked to say anything. Kirtn leaned forward until his eyes were on a level with Satin's. "Why?"

She made a curt, negative gesture. "I've named your devil, but I'll be damned if I'll describe it. And I mean that literally. Take my advice. Space him before it's too late."

"No," said Rheba flatly. "He's just a boy. He's done nothing to us."

Satin stood. "You have fifteen standard minutes to get off the planet. If you run, you'll just make it." Her expression softened. "May your gods go with you. You'll need them."

The gambler's voice was calm, but her mind screamed in Rheba's: *Space him!*

VI

"Two minutes!" said Rheba, peering over Kirtn's shoulder to see how close he was to finishing the installation of the new navtrix.

The run from the Black Whole had been short and furious. Kirtn was working over an opening in the control board that the *Devalon* had provided on command. The old navtrix was balanced precariously on his knee. The new one was in a glittering nest where the old one had been. There were no wires or other physical connections to be made—Equality science was primitive, not barbaric—but there was the necessity of precisely positioning the new navtrix within the old matrix.

"Got it," he said. "I hope. Light it up."

One minute.

Neither one spoke aloud, but both heard the echo of the clock running in Rheba's mind. She instructed the ship to energize the navtrix and held her breath. Long seconds passed. Nothing happened.

Kirtn muttered words that Rheba ignored. Akhenet lines rippled and glowed along her body. If the ship could not activate the navtrix, she would have to try. It was not a skill she had been taught on Deva, being too young to work with intricate energy constructs such as a navtrix. But if the ship failed, she would have to try.

Twenty seconds.

She sensed the curiosity of the others in the cabin, yet no one spoke. The urgency that Rheba and Kirtn radiated was sufficient explanation for the moment. A slim figure moved forward, straining to see what was happening. Rheba felt warmth and a slight pressure from another body. She had started to turn her head to see who was crowding her when the navtrix began to glow.

"Thank the Inmost Fire," she breathed. "That was a lovely bit of luck."

As though the word triggered something in her mind, she turned to look at the person who had been crowding her. Daemen. But there was no time to explore the ramifications of his presence, and perhaps no need—the Yhelle navtrix simply could have taken longer to energize than the Senyas variety it replaced.

"Hang on," she said curtly. "We've got to clear this planet *now.*"

Kirtn warned the rest of the passengers as Rheba pulled the pilot mesh around her. The *Devalon*'s outputs lit up with racing colors. The air quivered with instructions that only someone used to the Bre'n language could understand.

"Three!" yelled Rheba.

The passengers shifted, seeking purchase against the coming surge of energy. No one protested. They

were a tough lot, accustomed to worse than the ship
was going to deliver. When the *Devalon* leaped
upward, flattening them against each other and the
floor, there were no complaints.

Rheba took the first *replacement* almost immediately,
clearing Onan's gravity well just enough to ensure
that the ship and its passengers were not wrenched
apart. She did not want to argue with Satin over niceties of measurement—off-planet usually meant out
of the gravity well.

It was a short jump. At its end, Rheba looked
around to see if anyone was injured. People lay in
various piles around the room and spilled into the
tubeway, but no one seemed hurt. Daemen, she
noticed, had landed on top rather than on the bottom
of his pile. She signaled him to come to her.

"Does your planet go by any other name than Daemen on Equality maps?" she asked.

"No."

Rheba instructed the navtrix to display the coordinates of a planet called Daemen and held her breath,
wondering what he had done to Satin that she would
urge killing him the instant he was out of Onan's
gravity well.

The coordinates appeared in the color, sound and
number code of Senyas. Rheba sighed silently; she
had been afraid the new navtrix would force them
to use only Universal, thus rendering the ship vulnerable to takeover by anyone who could speak Universal.

"There it is," she said, satisfaction in her voice.
Then satisfaction changed to dismay as she read the
replacement code. The planet hung like a pendant on
a broken chain at the far side of the Equality's tenuous
sprawl. "Five *replacements* and three changeovers. You
live on the back side of nowhere," she muttered.

Then, realizing how she had sounded, she added, "Lovely place, I'm sure. It would have to be for anyone to stay there."

Daemen laughed. "It's a dismal place, but it's home. My home."

There was a possessive emphasis on the word *my* that made Rheba examine him more closely. He did not notice. His gray eyes were focused on Rainbow dangling from the small cargo net over the control board. As he watched the Zaarain construct, Daemen looked older, harder . . . even dangerous. Then he smiled, transforming his face, making her doubt that she had ever seen anything but the charming boy-man who stood before her.

With an uneasy feeling, she turned back to instruct the computer to connect with a planet called Daemen. She hesitated, then chose a far orbit around the planet. She wanted to take a discreet look at the Equality's most distant world.

After several moments the computer whistled sweetly, telling her that her program was accepted and accurate. All that she had to do was whistle the correct response and the *Devalon*'s ill-assorted passengers would be on their way.

She turned to look a final time at Daemen. He smiled, eagerness and anticipation plain on his young face. She could not help smiling in return.

"It will be a while," she said, "but you're going home." She whistled a complex trill.

The ship shivered faintly and its lights dimmed. The first *replacement* was a long one, well beyond the range of most Equality spaceships. In order to make the maneuver accurately, a high speed was necessary. Until *replacement* was completed, the ship would spare its passengers and crew only minimal energy.

Rheba's akhenet lines pulsed in the diminished light. She felt Daemen's speculative glance. Her lines were much more obvious since she had stripped to her brief scarlet ship clothes.

"I've never seen a race like yours," said Daemen. "You're beautiful," he added matter-of-factly. "I'll bet you brought a high price on Loo."

Rheba grimaced. "The Loo-chim preferred furries."

Daemen laughed, but the sound lacked humor. "The Loo-chim didn't like anything but themselves. Are you sure they're dead?"

"Yes."

The quality of her voice did not encourage further questions about Loo, the Loo-chim, or her part in destroying both.

"How long will it be until we reach Daemen?" he asked.

"About one Onan day."

Daemen looked around the crowded control room, plainly wondering what he was going to do for that day. Others were dealing with the same question. As Rheba watched, some passengers lay down while others pushed back to give them room. After a few hours the sleepers would trade with the ones who were awake. The longer Rheba watched, the more seductive the idea of sleep became. She had not had any decent sleep since she had become a slave. She looked around for Kirtn, wanting nothing more than to curl up against her Bre'n and let go of all conscious thought.

"He's with that fantastic snake," said Daemen, guessing whom she was looking for.

"Kirtn?"

"Is that his name? The big man, gold hair?"

"Yes." She paused, struck by a thought. Daemen was one of the few people since Deva who had not remarked on Kirtn's "fur," although the very short, very fine hair that covered him was more a texture than a pelt. Even so, it was enough to brand him an animal among the Equality planets and peoples she had met so far. "You didn't call him a furry."

Daemen looked surprised. "At home, people come in all colors and textures. Nobody thinks much about it."

"I think I'll like your planet."

Daemen's smile was like music. "I hope so, Rheba."

She looked at him again, realizing that he was not so young as he appeared. His own culture might even consider him a man. The way he was watching her said that he, at least, considered himself fully grown. "Why did you leave your home?" she asked. Then, quickly, "I'm sorry. I didn't mean to pry."

His smile returned, but it was not the same. Before he could say anything, Kirtn approached. Around his neck hung Fssa. Kirtn took down the fine-meshed net that held Rainbow and examined the crystal mass.

"It's bigger," said Rheba, leaning over to look at Rainbow.

"Fssa said Rainbow took the jewels, sort of crumbled over them, and then got all solid again," said Kirtn, turning Rainbow around as he spoke. There were no visible breaks or joinings. Rainbow looked as though it were simply a mass of crystals grown on the geologic whim of some planet. "Pretty, isn't it?"

"Even better than before," agreed Rheba.

Fssa made a flatulent noise. He had thought himself ugly until Rheba told him he was beautiful. Now he was slightly vain and more than a little jealous of any non-Fourth People that Rheba considered attractive.

"It's not bad," he conceded, "even if it *is* lopsided and some of its crystals are scratched."

Rheba smiled, but did not tease the Fssireeme. He was too easy to hurt. She noticed that metallic colors were running in random surges the length of his body. That usually only happened when he was uneasy, verging on fearful. "What's wrong, Fssa?"

The snake moved in a sinuous ripple. His blind opalescent "eyes" quested toward her hair. "Have you—did you—" Fssa made a strangled noise and tried again. "Ssimmi," he hissed, using the accents of his native language. "Does the navtrix know where Ssimmi is?"

She touched him lightly, letting energy course from her fingertip through his body. The Fssireeme shivered in delight. "I haven't asked yet," she said. "Go ahead."

Fssa whistled a complex trill. The *Devalon*'s computer responded, lighting the navtrix while the two energy constructs exchanged information. It took only an instant for the negative to chime.

"Maybe you garbled the translation," said Rheba. Then, at Fssa's indignant squawk, she added, "You're excited, Fssa. Maybe you just weren't as careful as you could have been. Or maybe the Equality knows Ssimmi by another name. Don't look so sad." She stroked the snake's darkened body, trying to call up a ripple of color. "Try again," she coaxed.

Fssa questioned the computer again. He used the Bre'n language, making the dry question resonate with melancholy and regret. Only a bare hint of hope echoed after the query.

The negative chimed again.

The snake darkened, then changed. He asked the

question again, using another language, another name for his home planet of Ssimmi.

The negative chimed.

More languages, more questions, more names. And the same answer.

"I just wanted to swim Ssimmi's seething sky/seas once before I die," whistled Fssa. But the Bre'n words said more, much more, telling of loss and longing, a winter seed calling to the heart of a vanished summer.

Rheba lifted the sad Fssireeme off Kirtn's shoulders and wound the snake into her hair. She gathered energy until her hair crackled and shimmered, comforting Fssa in the only way she could. "There are more planets than the Equality knows," she said, "and more navtrices. We'll find your home if we have to turn the galaxy inside out."

Fssa's head rested on top of her ear. He sighed a Fssireeme thank you and coiled more securely in her hair.

"Is it—he?she?—all right?" asked Daemen. He had not understood Fssa's Bre'n whistles, but the emotions had needed no translation.

"Just a little sad," said Kirtn in Universal, easing his fingers through Rheba's hair until he found the Fssireeme. He stroked the snake, knowing that Fssa appreciated touch as much as any legged being. "He hoped that the Equality navtrix would know where his home was."

"Maybe the Seurs can help him," said Daemen.

"Who or what are they?"

"The people who instruct my planet."

"Teachers?" asked Kirtn.

Daemen hesitated. "They are hereditary mentors. That's as close as I can come in Universal. They investigate all the histories of Daemen, then bring back their discoveries and instruct people in their proper use.''

"*All* the histories? What does that mean?" asked Rheba. "How can a planet have more than one history?"

"All planets do," said Daemen, surprised. "They've been settled and resettled, colonized and recolonized, conquered and freed at least as many times as there are Cycles. We count Seventeen Cycles in the Equality. And that doesn't begin to recognize events and dominions that were limited to one planet."

Rheba blinked, surprised by Daemen's sudden enthusiasm and . . . assurance. He was more man than boy now. He spoke in the accents of someone used to being heard. "Are you a Seur?"

"I'm *The* Seur, just as I'm *The* Daemen."

"What does that mean?" asked Kirtn, measuring Daemen's sudden power and remembering Satin's warning. "Are you some kind of king or emperor on Daemen?"

Daemen's face showed an amusement far beyond his apparent age. "That's one way of putting it. But it's not that simple. Cultures rarely are, you know. I can't just wave my hand and thousands of people kiss my toes." He sighed. "Do you know anything at all about my planet?"

The wistful tone made him back into a child again. Rheba leaned forward and touched his hand comfortingly, drawn as all akhenets were to vulnerability. "No, but we'd like to. Will you tell us?"

Daemen's fingertips caressed the back of Rheba's hand. Neither one of them noticed Kirtn's sudden stiffness. But Rheba did not object to the familiar touch, so Kirtn did not.

"We've been settled, and unsettled," he added

wryly, "more times than any other Equality planet. We're on a natural *replacement* route. Do you know about those? No, I can see you don't. It doesn't matter. Your ship has power to spare."

"How do you know?" said Kirtn roughly. He and Rheba had been careful to say very little about their ship. The dead Trader Jal's lust for the *Devalon* had been part of why they had been enslaved on Loo. They had no desire to arouse the greed of anyone else.

"Only five *replacements* to Daemen. Isn't that what you said?" he asked Rheba.

"Yes. And three changeovers."

Daemen dismissed the changeovers with a flick of one long finger. Even the most primitive ship could change direction and speed. "Daemen has some of the highest technology available to the Equality, thanks to the Seurs. Yet it took my family's ship eleven *replacements* to reach Onan."

"Eleven? Are you sure?" asked Kirtn, surprise clear in his voice. "You were very young, weren't you?"

"I was young, but I wasn't deaf and blind. It was my first time in space. I remember each changeover and *replacement* perfectly. It was a dream come true. It was the first time I really believed that I was the luckiest man alive." His face changed as he remembered the nightmare that had followed. "Eleven *replacements*. I'm sure."

Daemen looked into Rheba's cinnamon eyes, trying to see if she believed him. "Your ship represents a quantum leap in knowledge to me. I'm The Seur. I'm interested in technology that might help my people. That's why The Daemen—my mother—left home. She hadn't been very lucky at finding useful technology in the old places. And without such finds, my people will eventually die.''

Rheba and Kirtn looked at one another. Each knew the other was remembering Deva, where their own people had died. Finally, Rheba spoke. ''Are your people in immediate danger?''

''I don't know. I think so. The situation must have been desperate or the Seurs wouldn't have sent our planet's Luck into space looking for a solution.''

''Your planet's luck?'' asked Rheba, not understanding.

''My mother, The Daemen. She was our planet's Luck. We're bred for it. But there was some sort of problem with her. She never found anything useful after the first time—and even that was a minor find, a way of dyeing synthetic fibers red. Unfortunately, she didn't find a way of making synthetic fibers that would take that particular color.''

Rheba and Kirtn exchanged another look. It was Kirtn who turned back to question Daemen. ''So your mother went out into the Equality to find new technologies to help your people, is that it?''

Daemen smiled crookedly. ''Mostly, yes. The Seurs insisted she take her whole family with her. Probably thought she'd need all the Luck she could lift.'' The smile faded. ''It wasn't enough. We hadn't been on Onan a day before we were kidnapped and sent to Loo.''

''Trader Jal?'' asked Kirtn.

''Greasy man with blue hair, blue skin and a scar on one hand?''

''Yes.''

''That's the one. He kept complaining that we weren't worth the energy to transport us to Loo. Actually''—his lips twisted in a mocking smile—''he was right. Everyone died in the Pit but me, and I didn't bring much of a price." He paused. "You did kill him, didn't you?"

"Jal?" Kirtn touched Rheba's hair where Fssa lay hidden. "The Fssireeme killed him."

Daemen looked at Rheba's hair with new interest. "Poisonous?"

"No." Then, before he could ask more questions, Kirtn asked one of his own. "Who's ruling—instructing—the planet while you're gone?"

"The Seurs."

"Are they going to be glad to see you?" asked the Bre'n bluntly.

Surprise crossed Daemen's unlined face, making him look even younger. "Of course. The planet must be in a bad way by now. Its Luck has been gone for years."

"There are many kinds of luck," pointed out Kirtn. "Most kinds you're better off without."

"Are you saying that my mother was *Bad Luck?*" Daemen's face was flushed, furious. He spit out the last two words as though they were the most offensive epithet he knew.

Before Kirtn could reply, the ship chimed and warned of a coming *replacement*. There was a subdued rush for handholds and braces; at high speeds, *replacement* could be unpleasant. The ship shuddered once, sending its interior into blackness. Gradually the light and colors returned, but in the subdued halftones that indicated the ship was still in *replacement* mode.

Kirtn let go of the pilot mesh and turned to look for Daemen. No one was there. He remembered the angry young face and sighed. He had not meant to offend Daemen. He certainly had no desire to kill Daemen, as Satin had ordered.

On the other hand, Kirtn knew he would not be entirely comfortable while Daemen was on board. He told himself it was because of Satin's enigmatic warning—but he kept remembering Daemen's pale fingers stroking the back of Rheba's hand.

VII

Rheba awoke moaning and clutching her head. She lashed out reflexively, trying to reach the source of her pain. Her hand hit the hard muscles of Kirtn's chest. He woke, realized what was happening and held her tightly against his body.

"Fssa!" yelled Kirtn. *"Fssa!"*

There was no answer. Kirtn combed his fingers through Rheba's hair, knowing that he would not find the snake there but hoping anyhow. As he had feared, the Fssireeme was not there. He was off somewhere on the ship, talking to Rainbow, causing Rheba's pain.

She screamed, half asleep, knowing only that an animal was trapped in her brain and gnawing its way to freedom. She writhed and fought Kirtn while he tried to keep her from banging her head against the unyielding walls.

A slim form bent over the bunk and grabbed one

of Rheba's flailing hands. Kirtn looked up and saw Daemen. The young man's face was tight with fear.

"What is it?" asked Daemen, wrestling with Rheba's surprising strength. "Is she sick?"

"No. She's just—"

Rheba's body convulsed. Her akhenet lines flared as though she were under attack.

"Let go of her," said Kirtn, realizing the danger.

"She's hot! I didn't know anyone could be so hot and live!"

"*Let go!*" Kirtn's harsh tone said more than words.

Daemen leaped back just as Rheba burst into flames. Energy coursed dangerously, leaping out toward the crowded control room. Kirtn's strong hands pressed against the pulse in her neck. Just as the first searing tongues reached Daemen, Rheba groaned and went limp.

Kirtn held her, singing Bre'n apologies into her hair.

M/dere pushed forward, holding a black Fssireeme in her hard hands. Wordlessly, she tossed the limp snake onto the bunk. Kirtn did not need a translator to tell him she would just as soon have killed the odd being who had caused her J/taaleri so much pain. The Bre'n was in complete agreement. He glared at Fssa, who was mortified by what had happened.

"Say something," snarled Kirtn. "Tell me why I shouldn't tie you in little knots and stuff you into the converter."

"I thought . . . I thought I was out of her range," whispered Fssa miserably. "It was all right the other times I spoke to Rainbow." The Fssireeme was dead black, not even a hint of color along his sinuous length. "I don't know what happened."

"Where were you?"

"In the tool niche." Fssa did not add that the tool niche was precisely where Kirtn had told him to go to talk with Rainbow.

The Bre'n swore, then sighed. He stroked Rheba's hair. She was sleeping now, true sleep, not the unconsciousness he had forced on her moments ago. Her strength had shocked him then. It made him thoughtful now. She was years too young to be so powerful. Already she commanded greater fire than many mature dancers he had known.

He smiled ruefully to himself, remembering that it was the potential of devastating/renewing energies that had first drawn him to a sleeping Senyas baby called Rheba. She had fulfilled her promise—and more.

Fssa made a small noise. In a Fourth People it would have been called throat-clearing, but the Fssireeme had no throat to clear. "Rainbow is bigger since it absorbed those other crystals," said Fssa in Senyas. "It speaks much more clearly now, although its memories are still only fragments of a greater past."

"It speaks much *too* clearly now," Kirtn said grimly. "Rheba went into convulsions and nearly slagged the control room before I stopped her."

Silence spread outward from the Fssireeme. He became an even denser black. Kirtn sighed again. The snake was not at fault; he had not known that Rainbow's increased size would also increase its range and ability to cause Rheba pain.

"I just wanted to know if Rainbow had ever heard of Ssimmi," whispered Fssa. Though he spoke in Senyas, he added a whistle of Bre'n longing that made everyone within hearing ache with sympathy.

Kirtn's anger slid away. He knew what it was to lose a home. The cataract of fire that had destroyed his planet was also burned into his brain. Even in his dreams, Deva was dead. "Did you find your planet?"

Kirtn's gentle tone brought a glimmer of lightness back to the snake's body. "No," said Fssa sadly. "Rainbow had never heard of it under any of the names I know. But if we find more stones, maybe more of Rainbow's memory will return. Maybe then it will know Ssimmi."

"Maybe. But snake—"

"Yes?"

"Be sure you're out of Rheba's range when you ask. Be *very* sure."

Fssa's whistled agreement was full of apologies and promises. Before the last note died, the ship chimed and announced that the final *replacement* was imminent. The Fssireeme repeated the announcement, loudly, in several languages at once. There was a subdued scramble for secure positions.

The maneuver was brief and smooth, but it woke Rheba. She retained only a vague memory of pain. It was enough. She looked at Fssa with anger lighting the cinnamon depths of her eyes.

"He was asking about Ssimmi," said Kirtn quickly. "In the tool niche."

She absorbed the information in silence. Then, "Did he find his home?"

"No."

"Too bad. That would have made it worth the pain. Almost." She grimaced and rubbed her temples, trying to banish the echoes of agony. "Where are we?"

As though in answer, the ship chimed and announced that it would come out of *replacement* in three seconds. The ship quivered very slightly, chimed, and announced that it had taken up a far orbit around the planet Daemen.

Rheba pushed forward to the pilot mesh, but did not object when Kirtn pulled it over himself instead of her. The aftermath of Fssa's chat with Rainbow had affected her reflexes just enough to make communication with the computer a chore rather than a pleasure.

Kirtn quickly checked that there were neither active nor passive defenses in the area. Apparently the planet was either unarmed or so subtly armed that the *Devalon's* sensors were defeated. Judging from Daemen's remarks about the advanced technology of the ship, Kirtn decided that the planet was probably as harmless as it appeared from orbit. With a silent prayer to the Inmost Fire, he guided the ship into a close orbit.

The planet ballooned in the viewscreen, then shrank into seeming solidarity as the image was transformed into a hologram. Rheba and Kirtn watched in silence as the rust-colored world with the vanishingly thin atmosphere turned overhead in the control room.

As Daemen had said, the planet was a dismal place. Rock and not much else.

"Is it as dead as it looks?" asked Rheba finally.

Daemen answered over her shoulder, startling her. "That depends on what you're used to. It's not all overrun with plants like Loo or oceans like Onan. We have a lot of space to ourselves."

Kindly, Rheba did not point out that few other Fourth People in the galaxy would want to live in that space. She remembered some of the geological history she had been taught on Deva and looked thoughtfully at the world turning slowly overhead. "Didn't you ever have oceans or big lakes—something?'' she asked as the planet revealed a waterless southern hemisphere.

"No. Actually, the Seurs believe that Fourth People or any other kind of advanced life couldn't have evolved here. We think we were colonized during the Zaarain Cycle. They're the only ones who would have had a technology equal to tapping the planet's core for energy and water. When the planet was first colonized—and that was so long ago the records are preserved as fossils in sandstone—there were no other life forms above the level of lichen. There still aren't, except for us, and we depend entirely on installations left over from Cycles we know almost nothing about.''

"Why did anyone ever colonize this misbegotten rock?'' asked Rheba absently, thinking aloud.

"I told you. It's on a natural *replacement* route,'' said Daemen, his voice a bit defensive. However repellent the planet might be to a fire dancer, it was his *home.*

"I didn't mean it the way it sounded,'' said Rheba. "It's only that . . . there just isn't much to the planet.''

"It's more than you have,'' said Daemen tightly. Then, "I'm sorry. Please don't look like that.'' He smiled and touched her cheek. "Forgive me?''

Rheba smiled in spite of her anger. She could no more blame Daemen for defending his home than she could blame Fssa for searching for his.

"Are there any landing regulations?'' asked Kirtn brusquely, jostling Daemen as he rearranged the pilot mesh.

Daemen's hand dropped from Rheba's cheek. "I don't think so. We didn't have more ships after we left. Nobody ever comes here, either.'' His expression became both amused and hard. "Superstitious idiots! They believe their own myths.''

Kirtn, remembering Satin, said, "Oh? What myths?"

"They act as though Luck were contagious," muttered Daemen. "See that dark spot?" he asked, pointing over his head to the southern hemisphere.

"Here?" asked Kirtn, pointing to a blot not far from the south pole of the planet.

"Yes. That's Center Square. All of our cities are on a modified grid pattern that connects to other Squares. At least, they used to connect. There are some pretty big mountains to avoid," he added, explaining the absence of people in various parts of the southern hemisphere.

"What about here?" said Rheba, pointing to a similar network of lines and splotches in the northern hemisphere.

"Ruins," Daemen said curtly. "They were farthest from Center Square. When the master grid energy went eccentric, they died." He saw the look on her face and added, "It was a long time ago. At least two Cycles, from what the Seurs have been able to find. We don't go up there much. The farther you get from Square One, the less advanced the technology, as a rule."

"Someone might have survived," said Rheba, oddly moved by a disaster hundreds of thousands of years in the past.

"Someone did." Daemen made a dismissing motion. "They're savages now. That's a long way to go to study savages. We've got plenty closer to home." His slim finger pointed to a tawny patch of land over the south pole. "There, for instance. The energy grid went eccentric in the last Cycle. The Seurs patched what they could, but the mountains here are terrible.

Square One survived—at least, its food installation did. It still registers on our maps.''

Daemen stared at the spot for a long moment. ''Mother wanted to go there. It was the first colony. She believed it would have the most advanced technology there, buried, waiting to be found by The Luck. But the other Seurs talked her out of it. We went out into the galaxy instead.'' He made a wry face. ''The Daemen isn't coming home with his hands full of miracles. The Seurs will be disappointed.''

Rheba put her hand over Daemen's in silent sympathy. It would be hard on him to go home with nothing but his family's death to give to his people. Her hair stirred, curling across the young man's cheek.

Kirtn glanced away from the *Devalon's* outputs, saw Rheba's hair silky across Daemen's cheek, and asked coldly, ''Just how disappointed will they be?''

Daemen looked confused. ''They won't be hostile, if that's what you mean. They'll be glad enough just to get their Daemen back. Without me to guide their archaeological searches, they might just as well pick a dig on a random basis.''

''You're rather young to be so knowledgeable.'' Kirtn's voice was neutral, yet somehow challenging.

''What does age have to do with it? I'm *The* Daemen.''

The Bre'n gave a muscular shrug. ''Your culture, your problem. Ours is to get you home in one piece. Is there a spaceport beacon?''

''I don't know.''

Kirtn turned back to the outputs. Bre'n whistles and Senyas words filled the cabin. An output turned blue-gray with silver dots. A flat mechanical tone replaced the discourse between man and machine. Kirtn looked back at Daemen. ''You have a spaceport beacon. Primitive, but effective. We're locked on. If we stray, the tone will vary. You should be home in"— he glanced down at the outputs—"about seventeen minutes."

Although he said nothing more, his listeners had the distinct impression that Kirtn would have been happier if the figure had been in seconds.

Rheba looked closely at her Bre'n, wondering why he had taken such a dislike to the charming Daemen. She let go of Daemen's hand and touched Kirtn's shoulder, silently asking what was wrong. He ignored her. The only thing he wanted to say on the subject of Daemen was *goodbye.*

Kirtn raced the ship toward the planet at a speed that was only marginally safe. Though the *Devalon* was equipped to protest, it did not. The ship's Senyasi builders had also programmed it to recognize the energy patterns of Bre'n rage.

VIII

No one met them at the spaceport. A cold, fierce wind blew in a cloudless sky, making the *Devalon* hum like a too-tight wire. The ship quickly extruded stabilizers. The humming ceased, but not the feeling of unease that it had caused. Scraps of plastic chased clouds of grit across the scarred apron. None of the scars were new, and there were no other ships in sight.

Rheba looked at the hologram of the spaceport and shivered. She did not need the ship's outputs to tell her that Daemen's namesake was a cold, barren planet.

Daemen, as though seeing the city for the first time, looked as dismayed as Rheba. It was obvious that the reality outside did not match his memories.

"How long were you gone?" asked Rheba.

"Four years."

"Just four? But you said you were a child when you left."

Daemen turned, focusing his rain-colored eyes on her. "My years are longer than yours. In Loo terms, call it seventeen years."

Rheba shuddered. In Loo terms, that was an eternity. Slaves might have shorter lifespans, but it certainly did not seem that way to the slaves. She looked speculatively at Daemen again, wondering how such a vulnerable young man had survived so long on Loo.

"Ready?" asked Kirtn abruptly.

Rheba turned toward her Bre'n. "But there's no one out there. We can't just dump Daemen downside and leave!"

Kirtn's expression said that he could do just that with no difficulty at all. He was very tired of her longing looks at the handsome young enigma who was so important that a whole planet was named after him. "What do you suggest we do—start a baby-sitting service?"

Akhenet lines lit beneath Rheba's skin, giving her a sullen glow. "I *suggest,*" she said angrily, "that we either wait for some contact or give him an escort to whatever passes for the local palace." She turned her back on Kirtn and spoke gently to Daemen. "Which would be better, Daemen? Wait or go looking?"

Before Daemen could answer, Kirtn spoke. His words were clipped, his tone as cold as the wind dividing around the ship. "Looks like we don't have a choice. Company coming."

He whistled curt instructions to the computer. The hologram of the spaceport shifted, zooming in on one area. As the magnification increased, the figures walking up to the edge of the spaceport became clearer. They were a ragged lot, yet they walked with the assurance that came from power.

"Know them?" asked Kirtn.

Daemen bent forward to peer into the hologram, which had descended to chest height. The Bre'n noted sourly that Daemen chose to lean over Rheba's shoulder rather than take a half step aside to improve his view. A curt whistle shifted the hologram back up to the ceiling. Unfortunately, it did not shift Daemen's position.

"Seurs," Daemen said after a moment. "You can tell by the walk. They usually wear special clothes. Guess the synthesizer still goes eccentric from time to time."

Rheba looked at the approaching group. The only thing "special" about their clothes was the wretched fit and color. The last time she had seen something that repulsive was when the *Devalon's* food cycle had crossed outlets with the ship's sanitary arrangements during a rough *replacement*.

"Do you remember any of them?" asked Kirtn.

Daemen stared at the approaching men and women. He shifted and stared again. "They're thinner than I remember," he said dubiously. "One of them might be Seur Tric."

"Friend or foe?" snapped Kirtn.

Daemen turned to face the hostile Bre'n. "Why do you keep hinting that the Seurs don't want me back?"

Kirtn's gold eyes took on the sheen of hammered metal, but his voice was neutral. Even so, Rheba put her hand on Daemen's arm in a gesture that was meant as both warning and protection. Kirtn ignored her glance, but her hand on Daemen's arm rankled more than the young man's demanding tone.

"Correct me if I'm wrong—you're the leader of this planet?" asked Kirtn softly.

"Yes."

"But you've been gone, so the Seurs have been running things."

"That's their job," said Daemen shortly.

"Do they like it?"

Daemen looked surprised. "Of course!"

"Then what makes you think they'll just tamely hand over the power to you?"

"I'm *The Daemen.*"

"Is that another word for stupid?" asked Kirtn, disgust clear in his voice.

Before Daemen could answer, Fssa stuck his head out of Rheba's hair. "The only possible translation of 'Daemen' in any language is 'luck.'"

"Shut up, snake!"

Hastily, Fssa ducked back out of sight.

Rheba looked at Kirtn. The lines on her body still rippled with light, but now it indicated unease more than anger. Her Bre'n mentor was not acting rationally—or at least not very politely. It was unlike him to be so abrupt with a vulnerable young being like Daemen. With an unconscious, worried frown, she rubbed the akhenet lines on the back of her arms and turned away to study the hologram.

The group's clothes did not improve on further examination. If anything, the color combinations became more repulsive. Also—She leaned forward with a muffled exclamation. Some of them were wearing ropes of jewels, great clumps strung haphazardly from crudely formed plastic links. In all, the gems were almost as ugly as the clothes. There was one cheering sign, though. "They aren't armed," she said. "At least, not in any way I can see. What do the *Devalon*'s sensors say?"

Without comment, Kirtn turned away from his disgusted contemplation of Daemen's innocence. A whistled trill sent colors racing over the ship's outputs. The Bre'n watched a moment, then commented, "Not enough metal on them to make a baby's ring." He looked up at Daemen. "What kind of weapons do you use?"

"We don't. Well, not often. Whips," he said finally, reluctantly. "Mother wouldn't touch the plastic knives. If they don't shatter, they bend. She said they weren't worth the shit that went into making them."

Kirtn smiled, wishing it were the mother rather than the son who had been rescued from Loo. She sounded a lot more practical. But she had not survived. He looked at Daemen, speculation bright in his yellow Bre'n eyes. How had the insolent halfling outlived the rest of his family? Was he as treacherous as he was handsome?

"I don't see any whips," said Rheba. "As for knives . . . those clothes are so baggy they could be wearing a service for twelve and not make a wrinkle."

"Don't worry about knives," said Daemen, smiling reminiscently. "Mother was right. About all they're good for is drawing designs in warm pudding. Besides, once they see who I am, knives will be the last thing on their minds."

Kirtn disagreed silently and strenuously. If he were the Seurs, knives would be the *only* thing on his mind, unless better weapons were available.

The group stopped at the edge of the apron, looking up at the slim alien ship. They talked among themselves in low murmurs that the *Devalon*'s sensors easily picked up.

As the first syllable of the language sounded in the cabin, Fssa reappeared and went into a series of astonishing contortions. After trying a variety of shapes, he settled on his usual form plus a concave extension ringed by metallic blue frills. Using the extension, he sucked every bit of alien language out of the air, learning and extrapolating with fantastic speed.

Daemen, who had never seen Fssa as anything more than a snake, stared at the transformations in open awe. "What is he doing?"

"He's—" began Rheba.

"Stretching," interrupted Kirtn. When Rheba would have finished her explanation, he closed his hand firmly over her wrist and thought an emphatic negative.

Rheba flinched at the *no* ringing in her mind. She started to argue, thought better of it, and pointedly turned away from Kirtn. She was not, however, going to go against such a direct order from her mentor, even though she could not understand why he did not want Daemen to know the nature of the Fssireeme's genius as a translator.

She stared at the hologram as though the skinny, badly dressed natives were the most fascinating thing in the galaxy. Gems winked back at her, as gaudy and improbable as diamonds on dung beetles.

When he was sure that she would not disobey him, Kirtn released Rheba's wrist and watched Fssa. The snake turned his sensors toward Kirtn without moving the odd extension he had made. A Bre'n whistle issued from some undetermined place to the left of the dish. Kirtn listened until he was sure that the Fssireeme had learned the new language. Only then did he turn back to Daemen.

"What are they saying?" asked Kirtn blandly.

"Not much. They're excited by the ship, wondering who we are and why we're here, that sort of thing," said Daemen absently. He swayed forward, closer to the hologram—and Rheba—as he tried to identify individual Seurs.

"Fssa?" whistled Kirtn. "Is that what they're talking about?"

"Yes," answered the snake in Bre'n. "They're wondering if we might have some technology to trade."

"And they're hoping we'll trade technologies," added Daemen, still staring into the tube.

Kirtn gave the young man a hard look, but Daemen did not notice. "Still think they'll be happy to see you?" asked the Bre'n.

"They'd be happier if I were bringing them something," admitted Daemen.

Rheba looked around. "That shouldn't be too hard," she said. "We have lots of odds and ends that we don't use." Her glance fell on Rainbow. It was wrapped in its fine cargo mesh, hanging from a recessed hook over the control board. Rainbow dangled overhead whenever it was not in the tool locker, bending Fssa into improbable shapes. "Too bad you aren't a machine," said Rheba to the crystal mass. "I'd trade you for something useful."

Daemen stood on tiptoe, leaned, and unhooked the cargo net.

"What are you doing?" demanded Kirtn.

Surprised at his tone, Daemen took a step backward. "I'm sorry. I didn't know it was valuable to you."

Kirtn looked sourly at the crystals gleaming through the fine cargo net. Remembering Rheba's agony, he was not too sure that Rainbow *was* valuable to him. "Maybe it isn't. So what?"

Fssa made an anguished sound. His body darted protectively toward Rainbow, but it was out of reach.

Daemen looked at the snake nearly falling out of

Rheba's hair, then at the expressionless Bre'n. Daemen glanced at Rheba. She, too, looked as though
she were trying to decide if Rainbow was more trouble
than it was worth.

"Some of these crystals are very old, as old as any
my mother ever found," said Daemen simply. "But
the machine must be badly tuned, or it wouldn't give
you such a vicious headache every time it's activated."

"What are you talking about?" asked Rheba. "Rainbow isn't a machine."

"Of course it is. It's a Zaarain machine—or what's
left of one."

"Are you sure?" asked Kirtn, looking at Rainbow
with new interest.

"Look," said Daemen confidently, "your people
may build the best ship in the galaxy, but mine know
more about history than any six races put together.
That," he said, tapping a fingernail on one of Rainbow's scintillant surfaces, "is a Zaarain construct. A
machine."

Kirtn frowned. He knew that Zaarain constructs
were not necessarily machines. The Zaarains had con-
structed unusual life forms as well as incredible
machines. Nonetheless, Rainbow as machine made
more sense than Rainbow as living entity. Of course,
the lithic races of the First People were both improbable and very real.

"Rainbow is part of an installation core, I think.
Hard to tell," added Daemen, turning the net so that
he could see all sides of the crystal mass. "Not much
is left."

"Then how can you be sure?" asked Kirtn.

"The carvings," said Daemen in the patient tone of
a teacher talking to a very stupid student. "Etchings,
really. Or *viasynth,* if you want to be technical."

"Then it isn't . . . alive?" asked Rheba.

Daemen laughed. "It's a machine. How can it be alive?"

Fssa burst into rapid Bre'n speech, arguing in stanzas of desperate poetry that his friend was as alive as he himself was. Rainbow was fragmented, to be sure, but that did not change the fact of its viability.

Kirtn whistled a shrill imperative. Fssa subsided. He was very black as he wove himself back into Rheba's comforting hair.

"Assuming it's a machine," said Kirtn, "what good is it to you?"

"None, probably. But it's better than empty hands. I'll pay you for it as soon as I can. Although, if the synthesizer is snarky, it might be a while until I can make something useful for you."

Rheba hesitated, torn between Daemen's need and Fssa's affection for Rainbow. She turned toward Kirtn. "Daemen did, after all, steal most of the price of the navtrix. . . ."

Kirtn could have pointed out that without her, Daemen would have been stuck on Loo. But he did not. If Rainbow was a machine, it belonged to Rheba, for it had been Rheba who insisted on saving it from the depredations of slave children. If Rainbow was not a machine, it belonged to itself, and could not be given away or sold.

She looked from Rainbow dangling passively in the cargo net to Daemen. He looked both vulnerable and hopeful; despite his brave words about being welcomed back, it was obvious that he was worried about coming home empty-handed.

Fssa keened softly. It was hard for Rheba to think with the Fssireeme mourning beautifully against her neck. There were no words for his sadness, simply emotion transformed into music. She had not heard anything so sorrowful since Loo, where First People sang of eternal slavery.

Kirtn whistled gently, telling Fssa to be quiet. It was Rheba's decision. With a tiny wail the Fssireeme obeyed. She looked at Kirtn, wanting to ask his advice; but it was like looking at the face of a stranger. She saw as though for the first time his inhuman beauty, a perfection attained only by Bre'ns, strength and invulnerability. There was no help there, only a mentor waiting to see how well his protégée had learned. She looked toward Daemen, slim and vulnerable, needing her as her mentor did not.

And she could not decide.

Her akhenet lines surged raggedly. She closed her eyes and spoke a dancer litany in her mind. The currents of energy flickering through her steadied, then faded into normal modes, invisible beneath her skin. She looked at Rainbow, caught in a cargo net, swinging beneath Daemen's fingers. What had made her think she was choosing between two men? The only choice was whether Rainbow was machine or bizarre sentience, dead or living. That had nothing to do with Kirtn or Daemen.

The ship chimed once and said, "Downside connections are in place. The downside com channel is hot."

Rheba turned back to the hologram. The group outside had gathered around a slender, slanting pole. She assumed it was a communication device, and that it was now connected to the ship. Otherwise the *Devalon* would have referred to the com channel as cold, not hot. She hesitated, then faced Daemen and held out her hand. "I'm not sure Rainbow is mine to give away. Until I'm sure . . ."

With a wry, understanding smile, Daemen gave the cargo net and its enigmatic burden to Rheba. "I'm still The Daemen. Empty hands or not, I'm home. Thank you."

His words only made Rheba feel worse. She looked at the desolate spaceport and the grubby, painfully thin people waiting there, their jewels incongruous against their awful clothes.

"I don't know much about machines," she said suddenly, "but I'm from a culture your people have never heard of. If they're historians, that will be worth something to them, won't it? I'll go with you."

Daemen's delight was as obvious as Kirtn's displeasure. The young man grabbed her in a hug that was not brotherly. "I'd like that!"

"How long are you staying?" asked the Bre'n, his face a mask that should have warned her.

But she was too distracted by Daemen's hug to notice Kirtn. "We can't stay too long. The ship's overtaxed as it is with all the people aboard. A day, maybe two?" she asked, searching Daemen's gray eyes. "Will that be enough?"

Kirtn looked at Daemen's face and wondered how he had ever thought of him as anything but a man— a man who was as aroused by Rheba as the Bre'n was himself. Daemen might be as smooth and slender as a Senyas child, but any resemblance ended there. Unfortunately, that was more than enough to engage the akhenet protective instinct.

The drive to have and nurture children had been artificially enhanced in both Bre'n and Senyas akhenets until it was an obsession. It had been a necessary, if drastic, solution to the problem of producing more akhenets. Only very rarely did a Bre'n-Senyas couple produce offspring, yet the pairing of most Bre'n-Senyas akhenets was so complete, so exclusive, that the birth rate had fallen off to almost nothing. The artificial, obsessive focus on children was all that had saved the akhenet gifts in both races from extinction.

As Kirtn watched Rheba in Daemen's arms, he sourly concluded that akhenet exclusivity would not have been a problem with him and his fire dancer. Unless *he* was the one excluded. His eyes narrowed and anger uncurled along the same channels he used to reinforce Rheba's akhenet talents.

He felt the heat, knew the danger, and invoked Bre'n discipline to keep himself from sliding closer to the deadly berserker state known as *rez*. The transition of Senyas akhenet from child to adult was the most difficult—and dangerous—of times for a Bre'n-Senyas pair. The Senyas could not help sending out conflicting sexual signals; and every Bre'n was more passionate than patient. It was not uncommon for akhenet pairs to die, killed by a jealous Bre'n in *rez*. Such tragedies were a theme in many Bre'n poems and resonated in Bre'n songs.

But Rheba did not know those songs, for Deva had died before she could learn. Nor could Kirtn tell her, not now. It was her choice, Dancer's Choice. She must make it without coercion from him.

Grimly, he instructed the ship to activate the downside com channel. His amplified voice cut across the mutters of the group outside. Although Fssa could have acted as translator, Kirtn preferred to act as though he had no access to the native language.

"Hello, downsiders," he said in Universal. "We've got a present for you. Do we have your permission to leave ship?"

There was an excited outburst of sound, then the group subsided. A man stepped forward. His clothes were dreadful but he wore more jewels than anyone else. As he bent over the com pole, his necklace turned and flashed in the sun.

"Greetings," said the man. "I'm Seur Tric, and you are most welcome on our planet. Are you traders?"

The eagerness in Tric's voice made Kirtn smile thinly. "We're not traders, but we have something for you."

Tric's puzzlement showed clearly on the hologram. "A gift? That's not necessary. We have no port fees. We're scholars, not profiteers. Everyone is welcome here."

Kirtn stared at the hologram and wondered if Tric was as innocent as he sounded. Somehow, he doubted it. Power and innocence did not go together. "I'm glad everyone is welcome," said Kirtn dryly. He leaned over, grabbed Daemen, and put him in front of the ship's pickup. At a whistled command, the ship took Daemen's image and projected it outside. The result was lifelike—and startling. "Recognize him?"

Only Tric stood his ground without flinching. He squinted, peering myopically at the hologram of Daemen. "Jycc? Is it you?"

"Not Jycc. Not anymore. I'm The Daemen now."

A sound rose from the group. As one they stared at the image of the boy who was Jycc no longer. Tric raised trembling hands toward the hologram, then bowed his head. His breath came in a deep sob.

"Oh my Seurs," he said, hiding his face, "The Luck is with us again."

Kirtn looked between the group outside the ship and The Daemen within. The Bre'n would have felt a lot better if he knew whether the emotion shaking the Seurs was pleasure—or fear.

IX

Rheba pulled heavy clothes out of a concealed cupboard. She began to dress for the cold outside. Kirtn read the downside statistics on the computer outputs and reached for his own clothes cupboard. Even for a Bre'n, it was a bit chilly on Daemen. Rheba looked out from the hooded green wraparound she had chosen and saw that Kirtn also was dressed for downside weather.

"You don't have to go," she said.

"I'm going whether you like it or not."

She flinched as though he had slapped her. She had never heard such coldness in his voice before. She started to ask what was wrong, then decided not to. She knew better than to interrogate an angry Bre'n.

"Fssa." Kirtn's tone was such that even Daemen turned to stare. The Fssireeme quickly showed his head, sensors wheeling with color. "Tell M/dere to guard the ship. No one is to board or leave without my direct permission.''

Rapid, guttural sounds issued from the snake. M/dere looked from Kirtn to Rheba, but did not protest receiving orders from the Bre'n—particularly when the orders were eminently sensible tactics. She grunted assent and went to stand where the downside portal would open in the wall of the ship.

''Tell Rainbow to make himself into a necklace,'' said Kirtn, his tone still abrupt. ''And be quick about it, Fssireeme.''

Fssa assumed a bizarre shape. Rheba closed her mouth into a thin line, anticipating pain. She did not protest. Even though he was angry, she knew her Bre'n would not let her be hurt unless it was necessary.

The pain was very quick, gone almost before she had time to flinch. Fssa whistled soft apologies. She stroked his body reassuringly. With a last trill he disappeared into her long gold hair.

Kirtn reached into the cargo mesh and pulled out Rainbow. Instead of its usual sunburst shape, it had shifted to become a long necklace of stones held together by force fields only it understood. Kirtn examined the necklace, tugged gently, then with more force. The necklace remained intact. He slipped it over his head. If a gaudy string of jewels constituted status on this planet, he would go suitably attired.

''Snake.'' His voice was curt.

Fssa's head poked out of Rheba's hair over her ear. His sensors were iridescent as he sought out the Bre'n. ''Yes?''

''Translate, but don't let anyone except me hear you unless I tell you otherwise.''

He used the precise Senyas speech. There could

be no way for the Fssireeme to misunderstand: It
was Kirtn, not Rheba, who would give orders for this
expedition.

Rheba glanced quickly at her mentor but did not
object. Not yet. He had done nothing unreasonable.
She did not know why he distrusted Daemen and his
people, but she did know that her Bre'n was balanced
on the thin edge of rage. She would do nothing to
push him over and everything she could to draw him
back.

"Open," snapped Kirtn.

His flat command did not need to be repeated.
The ship opened promptly, allowing the thin, cold
air of Daemen to sweep through the control room.
Kirtn went first, an impressive figure of strength moving easily down the steep ramp, jewels winking in the
attenuated sunlight. Behind him came Rheba, her
akhenet lines pulsing uneasily, lighting her face until
it echoed the metallic gold of Kirtn's eyes. Last came
Daemen, no taller than Rheba, both of them diminished by Kirtn's bulk.

Daemen's gray eyes lit with delight as he saw Seur
Tric waiting at the bottom of the ramp. Daemen ran
past Rheba and Kirtn and threw his arms around the
older man.

The variety in appearance among Seurs was astonishing. One was quite tall, another had fur as long
as Rheba's hair, a third had tricolored strips running
diagonally across his body. Seur Tric, by comparison,
was modestly endowed. His skin was pink and he had
tufts of hair at cheek, chin and first knuckles.

"Uncle Tric," laughed Daemen, stepping back to
look at his mother's younger brother. If she had died
without bearing children, Tric would have been The
Luck. But she had had many children, one of whom

had survived to become The Daemen. "You're so thin! And your clothes! Who dropped a shoe in the synthesizer this time?"

Tric's face struggled between emotions that Kirtn could not name. Obviously Tric was happy to see the boy he had once known as Jycc. It was also obvious that being in the presence of The Daemen was not a happy thing. It could simply have been that Daemen's presence meant that Tric's sister was dead . . . or it could have meant something less comforting, something that echoed the fear in Satin's voice when she had said, *Space him!*

Kirtn looked away from the uneasy welcome. The other members of the group were murmuring among themselves and staring at Rainbow hanging across Kirtn's muscular chest. He had worn his cape open, the better to display the multicolored crystals.

The long-furred man leaned closer, staring at a peculiarly carved crystal. His hand moved as though to grab the necklace but stopped well short of actually touching Rainbow or the Bre'n.

Tric turned away from his nephew. "Are you the ones responsible for bringing The Luck back to Daemen?" asked the Seur in accented but understandable Universal.

Kirtn was not sure he liked the way the question was phrased, but answered anyway. "Daemen was a slave on Loo. So were we. There was a rebellion." His torso moved in a Bre'n shrug. "The Loo-chim died. We didn't. My dancer"—he indicated Rheba—"promised all slaves a ride home. Her promise is kept."

Before Kirtn could turn and stride back up the *Devalon's* ramp, the group of Seurs fragmented into a babble of sound. Fssa's artful translations could not

be kept secret if Kirtn made the Fssireeme shout up
the ramp to him.

With obvious reluctance, the Bre'n turned and
faced the Seurs again. When he saw that Rheba was
still at the bottom of the ramp, her hand on Daemen's
arm, the Bre'n gestured curtly for her to return to
the ship.

"There's no purpose in being rude," whistled
Rheba softly, resonances of confusion and regret
woven through the complex Bre'n words. "If nothing
else, we need clothes for the slaves."

"The ship will manufacture clothes," he answered
in curt Senyas.

"Only if we let it renew itself from downside con-
verters," answered Rheba in Senyas. "It ate a lot of
power getting here so quickly." She did not add that
it had been Kirtn's idea to tear across the galaxy. Had
she been the pilot, there would have been a slower,
more energy-sane passage.

She saw rage like a darker shade of gold pooling
in his eyes. Instinctively she ran up the ramp, touched
him, telling him of her concern—and drawing energy
out of him with a skill that shocked Kirtn. It was not
a cure for his turmoil. It was simply a temporary means
of keeping him from sliding any closer to *rez*.

He should have thanked her. He should have
hugged her and held her, reassuring her. He had
always done so in the past when the complexities of
his Bre'n nature frightened her.

But it was not the past. She was older now, a woman
in everything but understanding of her Bre'n . . . and
Daemen stood at the bottom of the ramp, slender
and beguiling, making Kirtn feel as clumsy as a stone.
He did not blame Rheba for being more attracted to
Daemen's smooth-skinned grace than she was to her

mentor's uncompromising strength. He did not blame her—but he did not like it, either.

He looked at her eyes. It was like looking into fire, searing him with possibilities. He looked at Daemen. And then he looked at neither of them.

"You must come to the installation," said Seur Tric, climbing partway up the ramp. It was not so much an invitation as a command.

"Yes," said Daemen enthusiastically, following Rheba's steps back up the ramp. He took her hand and smiled. "Please. I want to show you my world."

Even Kirtn felt the enchantment of Daemen's smile. And then the Bre'n felt cold. He wanted to grab Rheba, run inside and throw the *Devalon* into space. Yet it was her choice, always. Dancer's Choice.

Rheba looked up at Kirtn, silently asking if it would be all right to stay on the planet, but it was like looking at a stranger, a face made out of wood and hammered gold. Sudden anger flickered in her, echoed by akhenet lines. Anger, and something close to fear. It was cold on the ramp, and lonely. She turned back to Daemen, to the warmth promised in his smile. Without a word she let him lead her onto the space-port's cracked and pitted surface.

Kirtn did not move.

In spite of herself, Rheba listened for his footsteps. She told herself that she was so angry she did not care whether he came or went back to the ship. But she felt worse with every step. She did not know what was wrong with her Bre'n; Fssa's melancholy mewing in her ear did nothing to make her feel better.

Just as she was about to turn around and run back to Kirtn, she heard the snap of his cape in the wind. He was following, but very silently, more like a preda-tor than a friend.

She shivered and regretted the impulse that had led her down the ramp. Discreetly, she slowed her walk until Kirtn had to come alongside her or step on her heels. As he moved to go around her she put her hand on his arm. So great was her emotion that the touch joined them in minor mind dance. For a devastating instant she knew his consuming anger/hurt/fear—and he knew hers.

Kirtn jerked away, afraid that she would discover the jealousy that was driving him. But he could not bear the flash of her pain at his rejection. He called what shreds of discipline remained to him and stroked her seething hair, hoping that nothing more than a Bre'n's deep love for a Senyas dancer would be transmitted to her.

Relief and pleasure surged through her, setting fire to her hair and akhenet lines.

Daemen flinched as a strand of Rheba's hair crossed his face like molten wire. His startled cry told her what she had accidentally done. Across his pale cheek was a thin scarlet line.

"I'm sorry," she said, her voice contrite, her eyes warm with concern and the fire that coursed through her. "I didn't realize . . . I'm not used to being around people who burn easily."

It was to Daemen's credit that he did not draw back when she lifted her hand to trace beneath the scorch mark on his cheek. He turned his head until his lips brushed her palm. "That's all right," he said, his eyes dancing with light and laughter. "I'll just have to learn when to duck."

Rheba giggled and touched Daemen's lips with hair that no longer burned but sent sweet currents of energy surging through him. "I only burn when I'm not paying attention. Is that better?"

Daemen's smile was as incandescent as her eyes.

Kirtn grimly hoped that she would forget herself and burn the young charmer to ash and gone—but he was careful not to touch her as he thought it. Then he saw Seur Tric looking speculatively from Rheba to Daemen. The Daemenite frowned and looked away.

Yet Kirtn was sure that he had seen fear naked on the older man's face in the instant before his wan face turned toward the buildings that ringed the spaceport. Why would the thought of The Daemen paired with Rheba bring fear to Tric? Or was it simple xenophobia that moved the Seur?

As he passed the sagging fence that divided spaceport from city, Kirtn whistled softly to himself. The transceiver that doubled as a cape fastener carried his whistle back to the *Devalon*. "Any interference, Ilfn?"

"None," whispered his fastener in soft Senyas.

"Are the passengers restless?"

"Yes, but not to the point that they'll take on J/taal mercenaries. Besides, no one wants to chance being enslaved on another grubby planet."

Ilfn did not add that she thought it was foolish to the point of insanity that Kirtn and Rheba were on the planet alone. Nor did she need to. Her last sentences had been in Bre'n, a language that conducted emotions as inevitably as copper conducted electricity. She also did not need to say that she understood the jealousy that had goaded Kirtn into being so foolish. That, too, was conducted by her whistle.

"How is the ship handling the downside power conversions?" he asked.

"No problems yet. The spaceport must be better equipped than it looks."

"How long before we have the power to travel *and* take care of our passengers?"

"Several hours."

"Hours! I thought you said the spaceport is better equipped than it looks."

"It looks," whistled Ilfn crisply, "as if they're still banging rocks together to get fire."

Kirtn glanced around at the time-rounded, lumpy stone buildings and silently agreed. "Let me know as soon as we're thirty minutes from full power."

"Of course. And Kirtn?"

"Yes?"

"Your dancer is older than you think."

Kirtn's answer was harsh and off-key, loud enough to carry to Rheba. She looked away from Daemen to the intimidating lines of an angry Bre'n face. "Is something wrong on the ship?" she asked quickly.

"Nothing the J/taals can't handle."

"Is that why you made them stay on board?"

Kirtn had left the J/taals behind as a precaution. On a strange planet, it was smart to keep a force in reserve. But he was not going to say that to Rheba. She was so taken by Daemen's charm that she would not believe his people might pose a danger to her. "Someone had to protect Ilfn and Lheket," he said neutrally.

Rheba made a noncommittal sound. Ilfn needed about as much protection as a steel fern. She was Bre'n, and Bre'ns were *strong*. Lheket, however, was a child. Like Daemen. She looked covertly at The Luck walking alongside her. Not precisely a child, but certainly not a man, either. Somewhere between Lheket and Kirtn, neither child nor yet man. Like Lheket, Daemen still needed protection. She wondered why Kirtn could not see that, why he was not drawn to Daemen's vulnerability as she was.

Seur Tric stopped to confer with the four men who had come with them from the spaceport. For the first time, Kirtn realized that one, perhaps two men had been left behind. He swore silently at his carelessness. He had been so absorbed in jealousy that he had not noticed there were two less of the skeletal Seurs escorting them. He took a grim satisfaction in the knowledge that M/dere and her mercenaries would not be similarly blind.

"What happened to the rest of the group?" Kirtn asked Daemen.

The young man glanced around. "Is someone missing?"

"One man. Maybe more." Kirtn looked over his shoulder, but the corner of a building cut off his view of the spaceport. "Do you always leave guards on off-planet ships?"

"Guards?" Daemen laughed. "What could you guard with a plastic knife? If anyone dropped back, it was probably sheer fascination. Show a Seur a machine that works and you'll never get him away from it! I'm surprised Tric didn't demand a tour of every cupboard and relay on the *Devalon.*"

Daemen's explanation failed to reassure Kirtn. The last person who had been that fascinated by the *Devalon* was Trader Jal. That fascination had cost Rheba and Kirtn their freedom and Jal his life.

Kirtn murmured instructions into the transceiver. Behind him, out of sight, the *Devalon* closed into a seamless whole, impervious to any method of attack short of nuclear annihilation. The only connection the ship retained with downside was through his transceiver—and the downside power draw. He would not shut that off until an actual attack was mounted.

Then he told himself he was being foolish. The planet had no technology on it superior to the *Devalon's* armaments. The people he had seen on the streets were lethargic, obviously on the edge of starvation. He doubted if they had one good fight left in them. And even if they did, what could plastic knives do against lightguns?

Yet he could not help glancing back over his shoulder, unable to shake the feeling that he had overlooked something.

X

The Central Installation, called Centrins by the natives, was huge. It was created from a single multihued material that seemed to sway gracefully, like flowers blooming beneath a clear river. Neither cracks nor stains marred the flowing walls and arched ceilings where colors called to each other in voices undimmed by time.

And much time had passed, more time than any man should have to sense, much less to live among its colored shadows. Kirtn felt time like an indefinable weight on his shoulders, a thickness in the very air he breathed.

Rheba leaned against his arm, reflexively seeking the comfort he could give her. She, too, sensed time like an immense entity brooding over Centrins. She drew Kirtn's presence around her, warming herself against the distant intimations of eternity pouring by, a chilling concept to entities for whom a handful of centuries spelled the whole of life.

Yet Centrins itself looked just born, sleek with new-
ness. It glowed warmly, inviting human presence.

Even on closer inspection, the compound preserved its pristine appearance. The ground around
Centrins might look old, the stone walls thrown up
by later, more barbaric men might be worn to sand,
but Centrins itself was untouched.

"Stasis?" asked Rheba, using Senyas because she
could not bear to describe Centrins with emotional
Bre'n.

"Did you feel any energy shift when we entered
the compound?"

"No."

"Then it's not stasis," said Kirtn flatly. "Even the
Zaarain Cycle was stuck with the same physical laws
we are. Where energy exists, perfect stasis doesn't."

"Zaarain?" asked Rheba. Then, "Of course. It has
to be. No other Cycle had the ability to preserve its
artifacts so well."

"Too bad they weren't as good with cultures."

"People aren't as amenable as matter/energy equa-
tions."

He wondered if she was alluding to him. He stroked
her arm and was rewarded with a smile that made
him ache.

"At least this is as beautiful as I remembered it,"
said Daemen, drawing Rheba away from Kirtn. The
young man pointed to a museum that opened off the
great hall they had entered. "That was where I first
learned to recognize the Cycles by their artifacts. Seur
Tric"—he smiled at his uncle—"was my best
teacher."

Seur Tric's smile was small and fleeting, showing
cracked teeth of several colors. He hurried on down

the hall despite Daemen's obvious desire to poke through the Seur museum.

Kirtn lingered, staring at the cases and pedestals holding objects that cried out to be seen and understood. Rheba, too, looked into the room, curious about Cycles she had heard of only in myths. Then she turned abruptly and hurried after Tric. Kirtn did not need to touch her to know what she was thinking: Deva had no museums, no monuments, no students eager for her past.

With one last, long look around the room where time was labeled and enclosed, Kirtn followed the retreating figures of Daemen, Rheba and Tric. No one else was around. The men who had followed them from the spaceport had vanished soundlessly into Centrins' multicolored recesses. He looked again, then murmured into the transceiver.

"Any problems there?" he asked.

"None. The outputs showed a flux in energy a few minutes ago." Ilfn's voice was disembodied yet very clear. "We stopped drawing power through the downside connectors. Then we started up again. Must have been a surge in the downside power core, or whatever this primitive place uses for energy."

Malaise prickled like heat over Kirtn's body. "You're sure we're still drawing power?"

"Yes. Five hours to optimum capacity."

"Five? I thought—"

"So did I. But the ship cut back on its downside draw after the surge. Shall I override?"

"No. Not yet. The *Devalon* knows its needs better than I do. Anything else?"

"Lheket wants Rheba back," Ilfn said dryly. "He's in love with her electric hair."

Kirtn laughed shortly. Lheket was blind and a child,

but apparently not impervious to Rheba's charm. It was just as well. Lheket would be the father of her children as soon as he was old enough.

That, at least, was one liaison the Bre'n would support. Just as Rheba called Ilfn sister because she carried Kirtn's unborn children, he would call Lheket brother when Rheba was pregnant with a new race of Senyas. It was the way Bre'n and Senyas had survived in the past. It would be the way they survived in the future.

If they had a future . . . two Bre'ns, two Senyasi. So few. But there must be more who had survived Deva's death. There must be others scattered through the galaxy, seeking more of their own kind just as Rheba and Kirtn were. They had tracked the rumor of Lheket to the slave planet Loo. And then they had freed Lheket and his Bre'n. Where two had been found, there might be others. Not on Loo, but somewhere.

"Kirtn?"

Rheba's call startled Kirtn out of his thoughts.

"Anything wrong?" she whistled, the sound like pure color floating through the ancient hall.

"I was just thinking about the . . . others." He did not need to elaborate. His whistle carried enough sorrow and speculation for a long Senyas speech.

She left Daemen and ran back down the hall to her Bre'n. "We'll find them," she said fiercely. "First we'll take the slaves to their homes and then we'll be free to look again. Who knows? Maybe we'll even find some of our people on the way."

He rubbed his fingers through her crackling hair. "Maybe we will, little dancer. Maybe we will. But not here," he added sourly. "This place isn't exactly the crossroads of the universe."

"Rheba?" Daemen's concerned voice preceded him up the hall. "What's wrong?"

Tersely, she explained her planet's death and their quest for others of their own kind.

"I didn't know," said Daemen softly. "You must have thought it terrible when I complained of being the only survivor of my family. You've lost an entire world."

"I didn't lose everyone," she said, rubbing her palm over Kirtn's arm.

Daemen and Kirtn exchanged a long look, but Rheba did not notice.

A peculiar tenor bell rang throughout Centrins. From the end of the hall, Seur Tric called in rapid Daemenite.

"We're coming," answered Daemen. "Uncle's worried," he said, turning back to Rheba. "That's the dinner bell. The dining room serves food only to occupied chairs. If we're not there, we don't eat until the next time the room feels like making a meal."

She blinked, not sure she had heard correctly. When she looked at Kirtn, he shrugged. Neither one of them understood, but Tric's impatience was apparent. They hurried down the hall to catch up with him. As they did, a tenor bell again rang sweetly through the building.

"Uh oh," said Daemen, breaking into a run. "If we don't hurry, I'll miss my first home meal in years."

The four of them raced down the hall, skidding at a final sharp turn. The location of the dining room was obvious. Seurs and their families were jammed into a wide doorway, struggling for passage. No one noticed the strangers, because everyone wore costumes of wildly varying cut and color. The people were as varied as their costumes. Combinations of skin, fur, height and color were not repeated. The only thing Daemenites seemed to have in common was an almost skeletal thinness.

Once in the room, everyone raced for a seat. If there was order or precedence, it was not apparent. Hunger was, however.

"Make sure your chair is lit," yelled Daemen over the hubbub. "The dark ones don't work."

Kirtn made a sound of disgust. He had seen cherfs use better manners at the trough. "Up!" he said to Rheba. He swung her into his arms, above the worst of the jostling. When his sheer strength was not enough to clear a path, her discreet jolts of electricity were.

The tenor bell sang again. Whatever dignity might have remained was trampled in a rush for seating. Kirtn slid Rheba into a chair, sat next to her, and watched the final scramble with blank astonishment. A disheveled Seur Tric popped out of the crowd and threw himself into a chair across from Kirtn.

Daemen was right behind, laughing with delight. He was the only Daemenite who seemed amused by the frantic race to food. But then, he was the only Daemenite who had flesh on his bones.

"That's what I hated most about Loo," said Daemen as he vaulted into a chair next to Rheba. "The meals were so *boring*. On Daemen, we know how to get the juices flowing before we sit down to eat."

The tenor bell sang a fourth time. All empty chairs went dark. There were groans and curses from people who had not found a chair. Some threw themselves at chairs even though they knew their reflexes were not capable of outrunning the machine's sensors. A rude, fruity sound issued from the chairs that had been occupied too late.

"What was that?" said Rheba, peering around.

"The cook," said Daemen.

"The cook?" she repeated.

"It's laughing at the people who missed dinner."

"It? Is the cook a machine?"

"Of course." He smiled and touched her chin with the tip of his finger. "Didn't you have cooks on Deva?"

"Machines don't laugh at people," she said impatiently.

"Maybe they didn't on Deva. They do here." He ran his hands over the seamless tabletop. "What's for dinner, uncle?"

Seur Tric looked unhappy. "I don't know. We may not even get any food."

"Oh no!" groaned Daemen. "Don't tell me the cook is eccentric too?"

"Sometimes," conceded Tric grimly. "Last week, it called us to table twice. All it did was—"

Brrraaaacck! The sound came from Tric's chair.

With a pained look, Tric shut up.

Kirtn whistled softly. "Can you sense any energy, dancer?"

Rheba's hair stirred and slid strand over strand with a silky whisper. Her eyes changed, currents of gold turning in amber depths. Her answering whistle was vague, almost dreamy. "Yes. Everywhere. The whole room, the building, all of Centrins. Currents flowing . . . but not smoothly, not everywhere. Gaps and darkness, sudden cold."

A cataract of energy slammed into her.

Reflexively she threw away the energy before it could burn her to ash. The ceiling flared whitely. Every chair in the room lit like flash strips in a darkened ship.

The tenor bell screamed.

The room burst into confused cries as Seurs leaped out of their chairs. Only Kirtn had noticed the akhenet lines coalesce beneath Rheba's skin until she burned more hotly than any natural fire. Now her eyes were blank, veined with the same incandescence as her hands. He drained energy out of her with a touch, calling her back from her contemplation of the core's compelling currents.

She blinked. Slowly her eyes focused on him. "What happened?"

"I was hoping you could tell me. Are you all right?"

She sighed and stretched. "Yes. Just tired, as though you'd been teaching me a particularly hard lesson."

Kirtn remembered the pouring energies. "Did that machine—or whoever is running it!—attack you?"

She covered a yawn beneath a hand that was slowly fading back to its normal tan color. "I don't think so. Probably I just tripped a feeder or scrambled some commands."

"It could have killed you," said Kirtn flatly.

"Maybe. It was just a light touch, though. It has a lot more energy in reserve." She stilled her lashing hair with a shake of her head. "It wasn't as bad as the Equality Rangers' lightguns."

The tables in front of them changed. Dinner appeared, as colorful as the walls. Unfortunately, it smelled more like fertilizer than food. After a moment, though, the odor changed to something more appetizing.

With a silent sigh of relief, Rheba picked up a pointed instrument that had appeared with the food. She stabbed a morsel and chewed tentatively. She was not worried about being poisoned. Fourth People might find each other's food unappetizing—even vile—but if it would not kill a Daemenite, it would not kill a Senyas or Bre'n.

Kirtn watched her for a moment, then picked up his eating tool with less enthusiasm than she had shown. Bre'ns were notoriously discriminating about flavors. He took a tentative bite. The food was not as bad as he had expected. It was merely bad rather than dreadful.

Around Kirtn rose satisfied murmurs and lip smackings. The Daemenites fell upon their food as though it were the last meal they ever expected to eat. Even Seur Tric's sour expression lightened. He ate rapidly, belched immodestly, and continued stabbing bright food as fast as he could manipulate his eating tool.

Tric looked up, saw Kirtn watching, and waved his arm expansively. "Eat! It's not often the cook is in a good mood, especially not lately."

Kirtn looked toward Daemen. The Luck was eating as fast as he could get food into his mouth. He, too, belched often and loudly. Kirtn concealed his distaste. The slave compounds of Loo probably had not taught the boy much about good food.

Rheba leaned over and whispered a Senyas phrase in Kirtn's ear. "Burp."

"What?"

"Burp," she repeated. "Fssa says that we should burp. Apparently it's some kind of communication."

Kirtn muttered something clinical in Senyas. Rheba frowned. He swore and gulped air until he gave up a mighty belch. Nearby Daemenites looked over approvingly. Kirtn stabbed more food and chewed unhappily. Among Bre'ns, belching was not only bad manners, it was a sign of bad food. Among Senyasi it was worse. Senyasi only burped as a prelude to vomiting. He hoped no one would notice Rheba's silence.

She squirmed uncomfortably, muttering to herself. Kirtn guessed that she was arguing with Fssa, explaining to him why she could not be polite and burp. The argument became heated. When she offered to throw up to prove her point, Fssa subsided.

Then, apparently from Rheba's mouth, came an epic belch.

As one, the Daemenites stopped eating. They banged their eating instruments approvingly against the tables. Both Daemen and Tric looked as gratified as parents whose offspring has just done something particularly clever. Kirtn strangled his laughter and hoped that no one had noticed Rheba's hair blowing out with the force of Fssa's gassy cry.

Serenely, as though nothing unusual had happened, Rheba continued eating.

The rest of the meal was a long silence punctuated by burps. When tabletops and fingertips had been licked clean, the Daemenites relaxed and began congratulating each other on the quality of the meal. A few people called out to Seur Tric, asking him if some traveling Seurs had returned with new knowledge that he had used to reprogram the cook. Tric muttered and made a vague gesture with his hands, consigning questions and cooks to the Last Square.

But the questioners were not to be so lightly put off. A group of people gathered around Seur Tric. They began to question him, then realized that the people with him were strangers. Oddly, Tric did not mention Daemen. Nor did anyone recognize him. All eyes were focused on Kirtn's necklace. Apparently each and every ancient crystal worn by Seurs was known in detail to the rest of the Seurs. Rainbow was not.

The longer they looked at the magnificent string of crystals, the more certain the Seurs became that Rainbow must have been responsible for the recent feast. Somehow the crystals must have been powerful enough to affect the core even at a distance. There was no other explanation possible.

Kirtn's disclaimers were first taken for modesty. When it became obvious that he was adamant, Seur voices shifted into hostility.

After a particularly irate exchange between Seur Tric and his fellow Seurs, Daemen stopped translating. Fssa, however, continued to whisper discreetly in Rheba's ear. She, in turn, whistled softly to Kirtn. After a few odd looks from the Seurs, she was ignored in favor of hot argument with Tric.

"Apparently," summarized Rheba, "the crystals are some kind of keys to the Zaarain machinery. Not all of them work, and the ones that do aren't dependable. None of them has worked lately on the cook. Apparently their skinny state isn't normal for a Daemenite. The cook has been all but starving them. But after I skirted the core currents, something clicked. The Seurs are raving about the dinner."

"Tonight's dinner?" Kirtn whistled incredulously. "Even a hungry cherf would have sneered. If that was the best the cook could do, they should dump it and go back to charring shinbones over a campfire."

"Think what they must have been eating before tonight."

Kirtn's stomach rolled queasily. "I'd rather not."

"They feel the same way. In fact—" She stopped

whistling abruptly as Fssa poured a rapid stream of words into her ear. "Ice and ashes!" she hissed.

"What's wrong?"

"They want Rainbow," she said tightly, "and they're not taking no for an answer."

XI

Kirtn looked at the faces crowding around the table. Attention was centered on Rainbow hanging from his neck. The sight of his powerful body gave a few Daemenites pause, but only for a moment. Their need for crystal keys overcame whatever common sense or scruples the Seurs might have had.

Beside Kirtn, Rheba's hair stirred, shimmering with hidden life. He sensed the currents of energy flowing around his fire dancer as she gathered herself for whatever might happen. Fssa keened softly, Fssireeme warning of a coming energy storm.

"Gently," whistled the Bre'n. "Perhaps Daemen can get us out of this."

She said nothing; nor did her hair stop shimmering. She leaned over the table and spoke quietly with Daemen, pretending she did not know what was happening—and grateful that her mentor had kept Fssa's gift hidden. It looked as though they would need an edge in dealing with Daemen's people.

"What's wrong, Daemen?" she asked in Universal. Daemen's face was drawn and his eyes were dark with worry. "Rainbow. The Seurs want it."

"Tell them that Rainbow isn't mine to give or keep."

"They wouldn't understand that," he said impatiently. "It's only a Zaarain construct, not a person."

"Then tell them that Rainbow is *mine.*" Her hair crackled, warning of fire-dancer anger.

"I did," he said tightly. "But things are different here. Zaarain constructs can only belong to a Seur. Technically, you're violating our laws."

"You could have told us that before we left the ship," snapped Kirtn, leaning forward until his slanted gold eyes were on a level with Daemen's.

"I didn't remember," said Daemen miserably. "I was so excited about being home again that I wasn't thinking of anything else."

The Bre'n curbed his anger. He could hardly blame Daemen for being excited. "But you're *The* Daemen," Kirtn said reasonably. "You're the king or whatever the local equivalent is, aren't you?"

"Yes."

"There's a 'but' hidden somewhere," said Kirtn, disgust clear in his voice. "What is it?"

"I'm The Luck," said Daemen reluctantly. "There's no doubt of that. It's my heritage."

"Go on," snapped the Bre'n.

"But . . ." Daemen stopped, obviously unwilling to continue. A look at Kirtn's fierce expression helped to loosen Daemen's tongue. He spoke rapidly, as though eager to have it over with. "But until the Seurs know what *kind* of luck I am, I don't have any real power. That's why the Seurs are ignoring me. If it turns out wrong they don't want to be anywhere near me."

"What do you mean?" asked Rheba.

The Bre'n whistled a sour note. He was afraid he knew exactly what Daemen meant. "Good or bad," said Kirtn in succinct Universal. "As in luck."

Daemen winced but did not argue.

Rheba simply stared at Daemen, trying to understand the ramifications of what he had said. "Do you mean that you won't be a ruler until the Seurs decide whether you're good or bad luck?" she said finally, incredulous.

His handsome young face was drawn into tight planes that made him look years older. "Please," he said in urgent Universal. "Don't say the other kind of luck again. If the Seurs hear you, they'll think you're cursing them. Then we'll *all* be in the soup."

"In the soup?" she asked, more puzzled than ever.

"A barbarian expression," he explained impatiently. "They feed their criminals to the zoolipt. When you're in the soup you're in the worst kind of trouble."

Kirtn saw Seur Tric's dark-eyed appraisal and remembered that Daemen's uncle understood at least enough Universal to follow their conversation. He nudged Rheba's leg under the table.

She glanced at him, startled by the distinct image of a Bre'n hand over her mouth that had formed in her mind when he touched her.

Seur Tric stood up abruptly, silencing the rest of the group. He surveyed everyone with narrowed eyes. "Today The Luck came back and already we're at each other's throats."

"You also got your first decent feed in months," pointed out Daemen, puzzled.

"Proving nothing," shot back his uncle.

"That's right," snapped Daemen. "Nothing has been proved. Not good and not *other*."

Uncle and nephew glared at one another. Kirtn had a distinct, cold feeling that The Luck's return was not a matter for celebration as far as the Seurs were concerned. He wondered for the first time if Daemen's mother had left the planet willingly or been exiled.

What was it Daemen had said about his mother going out into the galaxy in search of new technologies because the old ones were falling apart? Was it that simple, or had the superstitious Daemenites shipped off their ruling family in a bloodless attempt to change their luck?

Malaise blew over the Bre'n like a cold wind. The people who brought back the son of a deposed ruler were not likely to be greeted with enthusiasm.

Grimly, Kirtn measured the distance to the exit. Far, but not too far. The Daemenites carried no visible weapons except for an occasional whip. Between Bre'n strength and Senyas fire, escape should be relatively easy. Certainly easier than it had been the first time on Onan, when Equality Rangers' lightguns had blazed after them every step of the way to the spaceport.

"Fire dancer." He spoke in Senyas, his tone that of a mentor. "We're leaving."

"What about Daemen?"

"He's home." Dryly. "His fondest wish come true. What more could we do to him?"

She winced at the irony in his tone. "Can I at least offer to take him with us? I can't just leave him."

Kirtn's eyes flattened and changed, cold as only a Bre'n's could be. "Tric understands Universal. If you talk to Daemen, we'll lose the edge of surprise."

She said nothing, merely looked stubborn as only a Senyas could be.

"All right," snapped Kirtn. "Wait until I've instructed the ship. Then you can stay here and talk to the pretty smoothie until your teeth fall out!"

Surprise, anger and hurt warred inside Rheba. Only the danger of their situation kept her from a shocking display of emotion.

He ignored her. Whistling softly into his transceiver, he explained their position.

There was no response.

He whistled again, very sharply.

Nothing.

"What's wrong?" demanded Rheba, forgetting her anger.

"The transceiver is dead. I can't raise the ship."

Her hand shot out and closed over the elaborate clasp that was a disguised transceiver. Gold lines rippled across her hand as she probed. "It's working, but there's no power from the ship. The *Devalon* is in max defense mode. Nothing goes in and nothing goes out."

"Defending against what?" he demanded. "Whips and plastic knives?"

But even as he spoke, he manipulated the clasp so that it switched to emergency send/get mode. If Ilfn had had enough warning to leave a message capsule outside the ship, the transceiver's squeal would call it up.

Rheba's fingertip hovered near the clasp, waiting until he was finished.

"Ready," he said tersely.

Her hand burned gold as energy poured into the transceiver, replacing the ship's energy that had ceased the moment it went into max defense mode.

The transceiver came alive. The send/get mode squealed—and struck a message.

Ilfn's whistle sounded in a compressed, lyric summary of the situation. Something had gone wrong with the downside connectors. There was enough power to keep the ship's vital functions and defense going, but no more. The*Devalon* had analyzed the situation and concluded the ship was under attack. It had given a five-second warning, recorded Ilfn's message, and shut down.

"We've got to go back," said Rheba, glancing around the room with eyes that were more gold than cinnamon, danger and fire growing in their depths.

"What good would that do? We don't have enough power to take off."

"Ice and ashes!" swore Rheba. Then, "If I were inside, maybe I could hash the downside connectors until we had enough power."

"Assuming you could get energy where the *Devalon* couldn't—and that's quite an assumption, fire dancer—if we breach the ship's security to get inside, we might leave it defenseless. Until we know more about the nature of the attack, we'd better tiptoe."

She did not disagree, but impatience flared in every akhenet line.

Daemen, who had listened to their whistles and curt Senyas words without understanding either, leaped into the silence. "If you wouldn't mind just *loaning* Rainbow to me, maybe I can solve this problem."

Seur Tric broke in with a demanding burst of Daemen's native language. The young man turned and answered impatiently. Hidden in Rheba's hair, Fssa translated.

"What do you mean those crystals aren't mine?"

asked Daemen, glaring at his uncle. "They came to the planet with *me.* You have no right to those crystals, nor to impede me in any way. Be very careful, uncle. *I am The Luck!*"

Tric's face changed, anger and fear overwhelming whatever affection he might have had for his nephew. "You are your mother's son in arrogance, at least. She couldn't find a single Luck-forsaken thing to improve our lot, yet how she screamed when we refused to let her go among First Square's savages in search of the fabled First Installation. We saved her life by giving her the last ship we had, but was she grateful? No! She raised you to be as Luck-forsaken a whelp as she was!" He made a strangled sound. "Why in the name of Luck didn't you die? We were better off without your mother. We would have been better off without you. Better to have no Luck at all than to have *Bad* Luck!"

For a moment, Daemen was too shocked to speak. Then, slowly, as though to be sure that there was no possibility of misunderstanding, he asked, "Did you exile my mother?"

"And all her Luckless family," agreed Tric grimly. "If she died out there, we didn't want any of her children living here to inherit The Luck. We wanted to be free of you."

Daemen's eyes paled until they looked more like ice than rain. "A lot of good it did you," he spat, looking around the group of listening Seurs. "Centrins is worse off than when mother left, isn't it? *Isn't it?*" he yelled, standing up and staring at each Seur until the Seur looked away, unable to stare down The Luck. "You should be blessing your luck that I'm back. Now maybe you'll get something better than garbage to eat every night!"

"Or something worse," muttered Tric.

"What could be worse?"

"I'm afraid we'll find out."

"Afraid," sneered Daemen. "No wonder you got rid of Mother. She wasn't afraid of anything."

"I know," sighed Tric, "I know. As long as other people did the suffering, she wasn't afraid at all."

Kirtn grabbed Daemen just as he lunged at his uncle. The Luck struggled uselessly in Kirtn's hard grip.

"If killing him would help," Kirtn said conversationally, "I'd do it myself. Would it?"

"What?"

"Help."

Daemen sagged in Kirtn's grasp. "No. It would just make things worse. But he's wrong about my mother," said the young man fiercely. "He never saw her in the Loo slave Pit. She fought for her children until she—she—"

Kirtn stroked Daemen's black hair in silent sympathy. The Loo slave compounds had been worse than any hell dreamed of by distant philosophers. That the child Daemen had survived at all was a miracle that made Kirtn believe that Daemen had every right to be called The Luck.

"What should we do now? They're your people," added Kirtn at the young man's startled look. "You must know them better than I do."

Daemen frowned, then leaned closer to Kirtn, as though depending on his strength to stand. "Run for your ship," he whispered. "If only half of what the slaves told me about Rheba is true, the Seurs don't have anything that will stop her."

"They've got something that stopped our ship,"

said the Bre'n dryly. "We don't even have the power
to lift off."

"*Bad Luck!*" swore Daemen. "I forgot about the
core drain."

"The what?"

"The core drain. It's part of the spaceport. It can
give energy to ships—"

"Or take it away," finished Kirtn.

"Yes." Daemen looked miserable. "I remember we
had trouble making it work when we took off. Mother
laughed because she thought her Luck was working
to keep her on Daemen. She was furious when Tric
figured out how to reverse the core to make it give
energy instead of take it away. I guess . . ." He swallowed several times and then whispered, "I guess her
Luck wasn't always good."

It was a difficult admission for Daemen. It did not
make Kirtn feel very good, either. If luck was inherit-
able, and it was beginning to look as though at least
bad luck was, then anyone who was close to Daemen
would be caught in the backlash. The Bre'n had a
sudden, queasy feeling that was exactly what Satin had
meant when she had told Kirtn to kill The Daemen.

On the other hand, Daemen had survived Loo. His
luck could not be all bad. The Loos, however, had
paid a high price for his survival. Not that the Loos
were innocent bystanders—they profoundly deserved
being burned to ash and gone—but it was not a
comforting thing to think of. What was good luck for
Daemen might be sudden death for anyone nearby.

Rheba's hand wrapped around Kirtn's arm as
though she knew exactly where his thoughts had led
him. "It's just superstition," she said in Senyas that
dripped contempt. "Besides, even if it *is* true, Daemen has brought nothing but good luck to us."

Pointedly, Kirtn looked at the hostile faces circling him.

"He'll get us out of it," she said confidently.

But she was still touching Kirtn. He sensed her desperate question in his mind: *Won't he?*

"Let me try my idea," said Daemen.

As one, Kirtn and Rheba focused on The Luck. "It had better be good," said Kirtn flatly. He took off Rainbow and hung the beautiful crystals around Daemen's neck.

The Seurs muttered restlessly but did not interfere. Tric's mouth thinned into a grim line. With a curt gesture he turned to face the Seurs.

"We sent The Luck out into the galaxy to find technology. In its new incarnation, The Luck has returned. Now we will test the strength and kind of Luck that came back to us."

The Seurs muttered again, but again there was no real objection. Testing The Luck was one of the oldest rituals they knew, and one of the most sacred.

Tric read their agreement in their silence. He gestured imperiously at the exit, then strode out without waiting to see who followed. The Seurs shifted restlessly, then moved in a body after their leader.

Rheba and Kirtn looked at each other. They would never have a better chance to escape, but what good would it do if the *Devalon* was grounded?

"Come on," said Daemen, guessing their thoughts. He took Rheba's hand. "You can always run if the test goes bad."

Even Kirtn could not argue with Daemen's pragmatism. "Where are we going?"

"Centrins' core," said Daemen, leading them out of the room. "We'll try Rainbow's key crystals there and see what happens."

"But if Rainbow really is a machine, or quasi-machine," Kirtn amended hastily when Fssa hissed hot disagreement, "you might unbalance all of Centrins."

"Yes," serenely, "that's where The Luck comes in."

Kirtn stared at Daemen's retreating back. Daemenites were either the most courageous or most stupid people in the Yhelle Equality.

Installation control was a small room, hardly big enough for the twenty people who crowded into it. The Seurs squeezed aside just enough to permit Daemen, Rheba and Kirtn to stand next to Tric. Kirtn did not like turning his back on the Seurs but did not see a way to avoid it.

Tric made a curt gesture, demanding silence. He took a finger-sized crystal from the chain around his neck, inserted the crystal into a hole in the wall, and waited.

The wall slid soundlessly aside, revealing a fabulous conglomeration of crystals. They looked as though they had grown there spontaneously, with neither pattern nor intelligence to guide them. Light slid over carved surfaces as quickly as thought, uniting the crystals in a lambent energy field.

Rainbow flared in multicolored glory, reflecting the light of the larger Zaarain construct.

Seur Tric turned and regarded his nephew sourly. "You know your duty."

The Luck took Rainbow from his neck and stood for long seconds with crystals hanging scintillant from his fingers. Without warning, he tossed Rainbow toward the machine.

The chain of crystals hung in the air for a moment, probed by energies only Rheba could sense. She screamed, clutching her head. Rainbow spun frantically, throwing off painful shards of light. Rheba screamed again and again, mindless with agony. She crumpled and began to fall.

Rainbow dropped into the machine.

All light vanished.

It was like being hurled into midnight. Kirtn grabbed for Rheba, felt a sharp pain and blacked out. He was unconscious before he hit the floor.

XII

Kirtn awoke with his head in his fire dancer's lap and a Fssireeme keening softly into his ear. Rheba was stroking his face, calling his name in a low voice, but it was her fear for his life that called his mind out of the drugged darkness into which the Seurs had sent him.

He tried to sit up. Rainbow swung and moved against his chest in subdued crystal chimes. The world spun horribly. For an endless time he was afraid he was going to be sick, then currents of dancer energy soothed his outraged nerves.

Fssa whistled gentle greetings and wove himself invisibly back into Rheba's hair.

"Don't sit up yet," said Rheba, kissing Kirtn's cheek, her relief like wine in his mind. "Whatever they gave you passes quickly, if you just lie still."

He stifled a curse but took her advice about lying still. "Is this the local equivalent of jail?"

It was Daemen, not Rheba, who answered. "Seurs don't believe in jails."

This time the Bre'n cursed aloud. "The only people I've known who didn't believe in jails didn't need to. They killed their criminals."

"Oh no," said Daemen. "We're not barbarians."

"Neither were they," said Kirtn sourly. "Just pragmatists." The room lurched and rolled slightly.

Despite Rheba's urgings, Kirtn sat up partway. "What—?" He looked around wildly. There were windows everywhere. The floor was transparent. Lounges of a peculiar sunset color were strewn the length of the long room. An incredibly bleak landscape poured by on all sides. Spectacular ruins came and went in the space of seconds. In between ruins was nothing but rock and blue-black sky glittering with a billion stars. "What in all the names of Fire is going on?" asked Kirtn.

"We are," said Rheba tiredly. "Going, that is. To First Square, Square One, or whatever in ashes the natives call it."

Daemen winced at the malice in her voice when she said "natives." Obviously he did not wish to be lumped with them.

Kirtn smiled and began to feel better immediately. Perhaps Daemen's charm was losing its appeal for Rheba. On the other hand, exile was a high price to pay for her awakening.

Kirtn sat up completely, bracing himself on the clear, curved wall. The room continued to move but it no longer disturbed him. Movers, after all, were built to move. "All right, Daemen." He sighed. "Tell us about it."

The young man's eyes met Kirtn's, then slid away, then returned. "I don't know where to begin."

"Everywhere," said Kirtn, gesturing to the red and gold rocks pouring by on each side, to the blue-black sky, much darker than it had been over the city. "We have lots of time, don't we?"

"Ahh . . . yes, I'm afraid so. A lifetime, unless I get very lucky. But I will, you know. I am The Luck."

"Tell me something I don't know," Kirtn said sarcastically.

Rheba touched her Bre'n, silently pleading with him to be gentle with Daemen. She sensed a lightning stroke of anger at her defense of the young man, then Kirtn's mind closed to her. Hurt, she withdrew her touch, only to have him take her hand and put it back on his arm.

Daemen watched, withdrawing more into himself with each second that passed. "Every Daemen has to test his or her Luck," he said at last. "Normally we do that by going to the Zaarain ruins—or any of the technologically advanced ruins—and looking for artifacts that will improve our lives." His full lips twisted, showing pain as his voice did not. His laugh was too old for his unlined face. "I understand so much more now. Too late. Mother was right, and wrong, *by The Luck she was wrong!*"

Kirtn and Rheba waited, knowing it was very difficult for Daemen to speak.

"Mother always believed that her Luck was good, even when it got us thrown off Daemen, lost all our money on Onan, and sent us to the slave pits of Loo. She kept on believing that it would work out for the best, that somewhere on Loo was the answer to our planet's needs and she was the chosen Luck, the one who would bring a renaissance back to her people."

A subdued, flatulent sound wafted out of Rheba's hair, Fssireeme commentary on the willful stupidity of some Fourth People. Rheba whistled a curt admonishment to the snake, who subsided instantly. Daemen did not notice, too deeply caught in his past to hear anything of his present.

"Naturally," continued Daemen, "I believed, too. I was her son. I couldn't even think that her luck might be . . . *bad*. I'm still not sure it was."

Rheba's hair stirred with Fssa's incredulous comment, but it went no farther than her ears. Kirtn agreed with the Fssireeme but saw no point in saying so. It would just make Rheba more eager in the handsome Daemenite's defense.

"Anyway," said Daemen, "when I saw Rainbow I remembered what Mother believed. I thought that she was right, except that I would be The Daemen to bring home the renaissance."

Kirtn waited while silence and the bleak landscape filled the moving room. When he could wait no longer, he leaned toward the younger man. Rainbow swung out from Kirtn's chest, catching light and dividing it into shards of pure color. Daemen looked, shuddered, and closed his eyes.

"What happened?" asked Kirtn, his gold eyes catching and holding Daemen like twin force fields.

Daemen tried to smile, and failed. "I . . ." His voice died. He cleared his throat and tried again. "How much do you remember?"

"You chucked Rainbow into the machine. There was an explosion of light. Rheba screamed and kept on screaming. Before I could help her, somebody knocked me out."

Daemen's eyes slid away from contact, then returned with a steadiness that Kirtn could not help but admire. There were few beings who could meet an angry Bre'n's glance.

"The lights went out," said Daemen simply.

"I know," snapped Kirtn, then realized that Daemen was not referring to the fact that the Bre'n had been drugged into unconsciousness. "No, I don't know. Tell me."

"Rainbow did something to Centrins' core. It stopped working. That's all I know. They knocked me out, too."

"Fssa." Kirtn's voice was controlled, but the Fssireeme appeared instantly. "What did you sense?"

The question was in Senyas, very precise. The answer was the same. "The machine communicated with Rainbow, causing Rheba's pain. I couldn't follow more than a thousandth of the exchange." Admiration and frustration tinged the Fssireeme's voice. "Such compression—incredible!"

Kirtn's lips twisted into a silent snarl. "No doubt. But what in ice and ashes did they *say* to each other?"

"I don't know. But after the lights went out, when the three of you were unconscious, Rainbow and the machine parted company. Or, at least, most of the machine parted company with all of Rainbow."

"I don't understand," snapped Kirtn, "and Senyas is a *very* precise language."

"Rainbow is bigger now."

Kirtn grabbed the long chain of crystal around his neck. He examined the colorful quasi-life carefully, then gave up the attempt. Rainbow could, and did, rearrange itself according to whim or need. What had started as a double handful of crystals could become a crown, a necklace, or a random conglomeration of facets. "You're sure? It feels about the same."

"Its energy pattern is quite different. Besides, Rainbow is like me in some ways. Its force fields can make it weigh more or less, depending on need, so weight isn't a very reliable index of Rainbow's mass at any given moment.''

Kirtn frowned, but did not question Fssa further. If the Fssireeme said that Rainbow's energy pattern had changed, then it had changed. Period. "Then . . . Rainbow stole part of Centrins' core?''

Fssa sighed very humanly and rested his chin on Rheba's shoulder. "I don't know,'' he whistled, switching to the greater emotional complexities of Bre'n. "Is it stealing when you take something that was once part of you?''

"Do you mean that Rainbow was once part of Centrins' core?'' demanded Rheba before Kirtn could speak.

"Perhaps, but most probably not. The Zaarains grew many machines,'' explained Fssa. "The core of most of them was identical. The machine and Rainbow shared certain similarities. And you know how *fanatic* Rainbow is about recovering lost parts of itself. I think it saw some usable crystals, snapped them up . . . and the lights went out.''

Kirtn groaned. Daemen looked from Fssireeme to fire dancer and back to Bre'n. The Luck did not understand either of the languages they spoke, but knew that the subject was Rainbow.

"What's he saying?'' demanded Daemen finally.

Kirtn and Rheba exchanged a glance, wondering how much to tell Daemen. Quickly, before she could, the Bre'n spoke. "He doesn't know much more than we do.''

Daemen looked skeptical, but said nothing.

"Did you wake up first?'' asked Kirtn.

"Yes. Either they gave both of you a bigger dose, or you're more susceptible to the drug.'' Daemen looked apologetically at the Bre'n. "How do you feel now?"

"I'll survive."

Daemen sighed. It was apparent that Kirtn's hostility toward him had not abated. "Rheba woke up after the mover reached full speed."

Kirtn looked out of the window-walls and said nothing. The landscape was whipping by at a speed that blurred all but distant rock formations. "Where are we going?" asked the Bre'n, turning back to Daemen.

Daemen hesitated, obviously reluctant. "Square One," he said.

"Wasn't that where your mother wanted to go, but the Seurs wouldn't let her?" asked Rheba.

"Yes."

"Why not?"

There was a long silence while Daemen searched for the right words.

"Why not?" repeated Rheba.

"People don't come back from Square One," said Daemen finally.

"Why?" asked Kirtn and Rheba together.

"We don't know. Maybe it's the mover," he added with obvious reluctance.

"The mover," prodded Kirtn. "What about the mover?" he asked, looking around at the bullet-shaped, transparent room hurtling along an invisible track toward an unseen destination.

"I don't think ..." began Daemen. His voice sighed away. "I'm not sure that the mover goes all the way to Square One. There's a break in the power somewhere beneath the mountains."

Kirtn's slanted eyes seemed to grow within his gold mask. "A break." He shrugged. "So we'll walk the rest of the way."

"Part of the way . . . but not very far," said Daemen softly.

"Why not?"

"There's no air."

"What?" said Rheba and Kirtn together.

As one, they turned and looked out the windows where remnants of unnamed Installations were divided by sterile tracts of stone. It was Kirtn who realized first what the blue-black sky meant.

"It's not night!" His glance went to the quadrant of the mover that was opaque, shielding its occupants from the distant sun's radiations. "The sky is dark because there isn't any atmosphere."

"Yes," said Daemen, his voice miserable. "Only the Installations have air. Oh, there's some atmosphere out there, but not enough for anything bigger than bacteria."

"But—but," stammered Rheba, stunned by a planet almost as desolate as a burned-out world, "how do you grow food?"

"Grow?" Daemen looked puzzled. "The Installations give us all the food we need." Then, remembering Seur Tric's complaints, he added, "Most of the time, anyway. Didn't machines feed you on your world?"

"No," said Rheba with a shudder. The idea of being so wholly at the mercy of inanimate matter disturbed her.

Kirtn simply looked shocked, then thoughtful. His eyes measured the landscape with new awareness. Planets like this were common, much more common than the warm, moist worlds where life was easily sustained. If the Zaarains had found Daemen useful because of its location on a natural *replacement* route, they would have colonized it. Their technology was more than adequate to the task. But either the Zaara-ins did not remake the planet in their own image, or the machines that remade it had fallen into disrepair. In either case, the result was the same.

"Even the air you breathe is manufactured and held in place by machines and forces your people can't name, much less duplicate or service," murmured Kirtn, his tone both shocked and wondering.

"Of course," said Daemen matter-of-factly. "It's been that way for hundreds of thousands of years. It will be that way as long as our Luck holds."

"As long as your luck holds . . ." Rheba said no more, but her horror was as clear as the akhenet lines pulsing over her arms.

"That's why the Seurs shipped out your family," said Kirtn slowly, his voice neutral. "The planet couldn't afford anything but the best of Luck any-more. Your machines are getting too old."

Daemen made a gesture of sorrow and resignation. He had aged since the moment the lights had gone out in Centrins. He no longer believed reflexively in the quality of his own Luck, much less his mother's. "I could," he whispered, thinking aloud, "even be . . . *other*."

Kirtn and Rheba both wanted to disagree, vehe-mently, but could not.

"I'm surprised the Seurs didn't just kill you," said the Bre'n finally.

The Luck's laughter was both sad and angry. "That would be the worst thing they could do. If they murder me, whatever *other* Luck I carried with me would stay loose in Center Square until the end of time."

"Why didn't they let us take you off planet?" asked Rheba.

"Seur Tric wanted to," said Daemen. "But the

others said that I'd come back again, carrying even worse Luck with me. Then the lights came back on in Centrins. Not as bright and not as many, but better than darkness.

"That's when the Seurs decided that I might do better going back to Square One as my mother wanted to." He hesitated, then continued. "If my Luck is good, I'll make it there and back. And if it isn't, my Luck won't be hanging around their Installation. I mean, it wouldn't be as though they murdered me," he said defensively, not looking at the sterile vistas sweeping by on all sides. "Square One exists. Its Installation registers on ours. They're not sending me to certain death."

Neither Kirtn nor Rheba knew what to say.

Fssa's sad sigh filled the transparent room. If being stranded in that desolation was not certain death, the Fssireeme did not know what it was. He might possibly survive, but his Fourth People friends would surely die.

Mountains swept down on them from the distance, mountains whose peaks blotted out half the stars.

Rheba and Kirtn watched in horrified fascination, waiting for a rending crash as the mover's irresistible force met the immovable mountain mass. Then their stomachs quivered as the bottom dropped out of the world. Stars and mountain peaks vanished as the mover plunged into an opening in the earth. The world shifted again, telling them that the mover had resumed a course parallel to but beneath the planet's surface.

Silence and darkness stretched unbearably. Despite their knowledge that the mover was making fantastic speed beneath the mountain mass, each person felt

as though the mover had stalled in the endless center
of midnight.

"Where's the break?" asked Kirtn finally, his voice
casual.

"At the edge of Square One," Daemen said tightly.
"We're not there yet. We're still moving."

"How can you tell?" asked Rheba.

"We still have air. When the mover stops, it dis-
solves, and so does the air."

As though in response to Daemen's words, the
mover vanished. With it vanished warmth and the
odd lounges that had supported the passengers.

Between one breath and the next, they were
dumped onto the tunnel's cold stone floor.

XIII

Kirtn held his breath reflexively, trying to hoard all of the precious air he could even though he knew it was futile. At the same instant, Rheba burst into flame, shaping energy into a shield that would hold in the dissolved mover's air. It was a reflex as strong and futile as Kirtn's. Her fire guttered and died out. There was no energy source to draw on other than the human bodies around her. That would bring death as surely as asphyxiation.

She clung to her Bre'n and waited to die.

There was a long time of silence. Then The Luck began to laugh softly, triumphantly. "It seems I'm not *other* after all!"

Cautiously, Kirtn took a deep breath, then another. With a whoop of joy he swung Rheba in a circle. "There's air, fire dancer. Breathe it!" he commanded.

Fssa's glad trill echoed in the confined spaces of the tunnel. Rheba breathed. The air was thin but sweet, and not so cold as she had expected. Nonetheless, she shivered after the warmth of the mover. Immediately, Kirtn shrugged out of his cape and fastened it around her. She did not protest. Bre'ns were much better equipped to withstand cold than Senyasi.

There was air, there was some warmth, but the only light came from cracked, yellowing discs beneath their feet on the tunnel floor. The light did not reach an arm's length into the tunnel.

"Fssa," said Kirtn. "What's ahead of us?"

Darkness presented no barrier to the Fssireeme's opalescent sensors. He directed a soundless stream of energy down the tunnel, reading what was ahead by the returning patterns. "The tunnel breaks up into a rubble barrier. There are openings, but they are far too small for Fourth People. They're even too small for a Fssireeme."

Silence grew in the wake of Fssa's summary. Then, "How solid is the barrier?" asked Kirtn.

"It's permeable to air," said the snake. "Otherwise you would have suffocated and I'd be uncomfortable."

"It is cemented, or just a jumble of rock?" asked Rheba. "Was it built or did it just happen?"

Fssa's sensors pointed back down the tunnel. Rheba could almost sense the energy he used, but it was like the next instant of time, always just beyond her grasp. The snake turned toward them and reported in crisp Senyas.

"A jumble, probably the result of a cave-in. Accident, not intent. The air you are breathing comes from the far side, as does the warmth. I therefore postulate the existence of an Installation. However . . ." Fssa's sensors darkened. He was not pleased with the rest of what he had to tell them.

"An Installation," whistled Rheba in lilting Bre'n. Though she said no more, the emotional language told of relief.

Kirtn, seeing the snake's sensors almost dim to invisibility, waited.

Fssa made a subdued sound, protesting that he had to puncture Rheba's happiness. When he spoke, it was in Senyas. "I suspect that you are thinking of moving the rubble, thereby gaining passage to the Installation beyond."

The snake's prim speech made Kirtn grateful for the darkness. He did not want Rheba to see his expression. Whenever the Fssireeme retreated into scholarly sentences, there was trouble ahead. "Yes," Kirtn said, "we're going to go through the rubble."

The snake sighed and his sensors winked out. "I fear not, my friend," he whistled. Then he reverted to Senyas. "The rubble is loose, yes, but some of the rocks are quite large. To move them would require heavy machinery or a command of force fields such as the Fourth People have not seen since the Zaarain Cycle."

"Or a determined Bre'n," said Kirtn.

Fssa said nothing.

Kirtn turned to go down the tunnel. He had walked no more than a few steps in the blackness before he tripped over a piece of rubble. Instantly, Rheba made a ball of light to guide him. He wanted to object to the drain on her strength, but did not. He needed the light even more than she needed his cape.

After a first, startled sound, Daemen accepted the light that Rheba had created. He was fascinated by it. He peered at the blue-white ball from all sides, enchanted to discover that it was as cool as the darkness it lit.

Rheba set a tiny ball of light on his nose, dazzling him. His eyes glowed with admiration and reflected fire-dancer light. She smiled, then she took back the energy before Kirtn noticed. He would object to her wasting her strength, and he would be right.

The barrier was not far away. The random stones that had turned beneath Kirtn's feet became hand-sized chunks of rock carpeting the tunnel floor. The rubble became thicker, deeper, raising the floor level so much that first Kirtn, then Rheba and Daemen had to bend over to avoid the ceiling. Amid the slate-colored stones was an occasional ivory shine. Kirtn looked, then increased his speed subtly.

"What was that?" asked Daemen, hanging back.

"Bone."

"But we don't have any animals to die in the tunnel. Oh . . . the Seurs. The Seurs who didn't come back."

"A fair assumption," said Kirtn neutrally, not wanting to think of how those people had died, because thinking about it would do no good.

Daemen had more chance than he wanted to examine bones. The farther Kirtn led them over the rubble, the more often they found silent skeletal huddles. There were a few tatters of clothing, but no more. The Seurs had died as anonymously as any men ever had.

Not surprisingly, most of the bones were piled around the barrier itself. The desperate Seurs had clawed futilely at the cold stone. They had succeeded in creating a space in which to stand and work. And then they died.

"Can you give me more light without tiring yourself too much?"

Rheba laughed shortly. "I suspect that death is very tiresome, mentor."

Kirtn's laugh was softer than hers had been. He touched her cheek. Her hair floated up, curling around his wrist. "I suspect it is, fire dancer. But I don't want to tire you. I just want to reconnoiter. When I start digging, I'll need your light even more."

Fssa made a small noise, a Fssireeme bid for conversation.

Reluctantly, Kirtn shifted his attention. "What is it, snake?"

"I'd like to probe the barrier. I might be able to tell you where to dig."

"Go ahead," said Kirtn, waving his hand toward the rocks piled across their path.

"It might hurt Rheba. Some of the energy configurations I want to try are similar to those I use with Rainbow. I can't hold down the volume if I hope to penetrate all that rock. Even as tightly as I can control direction, there will be scattering and backlash."

"I'll survive," she said curtly, but knew that her tension was transmitted by the hand touching Kirtn's chest.

"Be as gentle as possible," said the Bre'n to Fssa, "or I'll hammer your flexible ass into the tunnel floor."

Fssa's sensors darkened. His friends knew that only Fssireeme pride—not flesh—was vulnerable to harm. Silently, the snake wished that it were the other way around. Pride healed so much more slowly than flesh.

Kirtn stroked the Fssireeme's sinuous body. "I didn't mean that the way it sounded. Not quite."

Fssa hissed and stroked his chin over Kirtn's hand. "Would you put me about halfway up the barrier?"

"You'll get too cold," said Rheba quickly, remembering a Loo cell where the Fssireeme had nearly died. Fssa could take—and enjoy—appalling heat.

Cold, however, made him shut down to a state the Fssireemes knew as "dreaming." A few degrees below that state was death. "It's almost as cold as that dungeon was."

Fssa brightened until traceries of silver raced his length. "I'll be all right," he said, his voice almost shy. "We lasted for quite a while in that dungeon. I'll only be out of your hair for a few minutes. But thank you."

Reluctantly, Rheba handed Fssa over to Kirtn. As always, she was amazed that he weighed so little in her hair and so much in her hands. He had told her once that he took her dancer energy and twisted it around him so that he would weigh less. When she asked how that was possible, he had sighed and told her she did not have the words to understand.

Kirtn lifted Fssa to the barrier and held him until he changed shape enough to hang on to the rock. Kirtn watched him struggle, tried not to laugh, then suggested, "Wouldn't it be easier if I just held you up?"

"Of course it would," snapped the snake, slithering from one cold crevice to the next, "but the energies I'll use might turn your brains to batter. Assuming that you have any brains to—" Fssa's muttering stopped abruptly as he changed shape again, swallowing up the mouth he customarily used to communicate with his friends.

Kirtn drew Rheba back from the barrier. He nearly stepped on Daemen, who had been waiting with diminishing patience while they spoke in languages he could not understand.

"What's the snake doing?" asked Daemen.

"Back up," was Rheba's only answer. She sent the

light ahead of them, for Fssa certainly did not need it for his work.

They stood slightly bent over to avoid the ceiling, and waited. Rheba was in front of Kirtn. Lines coursed uneasily over her body. He put his hands on her shoulders and pulled her against him, comforting and supporting her. Reflexively they slid into the special rapport of an akhenet pair. Light began to glow around them, fed by her lines until they became so dense that her hands and cheeks were gold.

When the first pain struck her, she built a cage of fire around herself and her Bre'n, unconsciously trying to shield both of them. Fire shimmered up and down her arms, transparent fire that could burn unprotected flesh to the bone. But not Kirtn's flesh—never his. He pulled their bodies closer together, glorying in the barely leashed energies that the two of them could call.

Each time Fssa slid into a shape of communication painful to her, fire leaped up, disrupting the painful backlash from Fssireeme energy constructs. Fssa did not notice, for Rheba's shield interfered only with backlash energies, not with the tight probes he sent into the barrier in front of him.

While Daemen watched at a safe distance from both akhenets and snake, the Fssireeme changed shapes endlessly, illuminated by dancer light conjured out of otherwise very human flesh. Behind Rheba loomed Kirtn, eyes molten gold, fixed on dangers and joys that the Luck could barely suspect, much less comprehend.

Fortunately—or perhaps, inevitably, considering his heritage—Daemen felt no pain from the backlash of Fssireeme energy constructs.

At length, Fssa changed back into his snake mode

and whistled plaintively to be rescued from the cold rocks. His sensors picked out Bre'n and Senyas united inside a protective shield of energies. Intrigued, he changed shape rapidly, probing the shield as he had probed the barrier. But more delicately, much more delicately. Fourth People's flesh was much more fragile than stone.

Before he had time to try more than a few shapes, Kirtn realized that Fssa was no longer probing the barrier. The Bre'n touched his Rheba's neck lightly, calling her out of her dance. Fire shifted, then was sucked back into her akhenet lines. She looked toward the barrier, where Fssa's sensors made tiny pools of opalescent light.

"Are you finished?" she asked.

Fssa whistled agreement.

"Good," she muttered as they went back to the barrier. "But it wasn't nearly as painful as I'd expected," she admitted, scooping up the snake and weaving him into her hair.

"Thanks to your talent," whistled Fssa, "and Kirtn's. Together you bend energy into fascinating new shapes." He preened slightly and his sensors brightened. "You don't have the range of a Fssireeme, of course, but what you create . . . ah, *that* is extraordinary."

"What," said Daemen in forceful Universal, "are you babbling and whistling about?"

Rheba realized that they had rarely spoken Universal since they had awakened on the mover. With few exceptions in the last hours, Daemen had been left alone among strangers who did not even have the courtesy to speak his language.

"I'm sorry," she said, touching Daemen's cheek with a hand that was more gold than brown. "We're not used to speaking Universal when we talk to each other." She turned to Fssa and murmured in Senyas, "Translate for him if we forget to speak Universal."

"Translate some of it," amended Kirtn.

"How much?"

"Pretend he's Seur Tric."

Rheba looked at Kirtn, surprised by his continuing suspicions of Daemen.

"We only have Daemen's word that he was drugged when we were," pointed out Kirtn. "Neither one of us saw it happen."

"What possible benefit could he get from spying on us?" she countered.

"I don't know. But that doesn't mean there isn't one," said Kirtn with a sideways glance at the handsome, smooth-skinned Daemen.

Fssa's sensors swirled as he looked from one of them to the other. Then, without comment, he began lecturing in Universal on the strengths and weaknesses of the barrier. "The rocks are crystalline, quite heavy, and not easily broken. The barrier itself is nearly three times as thick as Kirtn is tall."

Daemen measured Kirtn's height and made a gesture of despair. The Bre'n was nearly half again as tall as Daemen. "No wonder they died," muttered the Luck.

Kirtn said nothing, but his glance was enough to galvanize the snake.

"The rocks are piled loosely," Fssa added quickly, "which is both help and danger. I think there is a way through that will avoid the heaviest stones."

"You think?" snapped the Bre'n.

"I won't know until I see whether the rubble shifts when you dig into it," said Fssa apologetically.

"Shifts!" cried Rheba, looking from the pile of

rock of her Bre'n. "But you would be crushed if all
that rock—" She stopped, seeing her own reflection
in his eyes. He had discovered that danger long before
she had, and accepted it.

"Fssa will monitor the rocks," Kirtn said. He did
not add that Fssa could not guarantee to sense movement in time for Kirtn to escape.

"Can you do that?" she demanded, pulling the
snake out of her hair so that she could watch his
sensors as he answered.

"Yes," he said. But his sensors darkened.

"You're lying."

"I hope not," whispered the snake.

Kirtn snarled soundlessly. The Fssireeme had a million mouths but he could not lie to Rheba out of any
one of them. The Bre'n turned toward Daemen. "You
can help Rheba move the smaller rocks out of the
way. And when I tell you to get back, make sure she
goes with you!"

Fssa slid out of her hair and dangled from her
neck. Kirtn draped the snake around his own neck
and turned to face the barrier. Rheba sent light ahead
of him, a light that was much brighter than it had
been.

Kirtn examined the barrier in the new light. Some
of the rocks were bigger than he was, others were
obviously in precarious balance with their surroundings. The rockfall reeked of weight and danger, and
bones of dead Seurs gleamed whitely at its base.

"All right, snake," said the Bre'n. "Where do we
begin?"

XIV

"On the left," said the snake softly. "The rockfall is thinner on that side."

Kirtn strode up to the dark pile of stones that went from ceiling to floor. "Here?"

Fssa hissed agreement.

Kirtn began digging with his bare hands. The rocks were cold and sharp. He worked steadily, stacking stones to one side for Rheba and Daemen to haul away.

Almost immediately he encountered the rock that had defeated earlier Seurs. Jagged, two-thirds his height and half as wide, the boulder lay securely wedged beneath a thin blanket of smaller rocks. Kirtn studied the position and mass of the boulder. Light followed him, brightening in answer to his needs.

"You're sure that's the best route?" asked Rheba dubiously, peering underneath his arm as he pushed against the enormous rock.

The boulder did not budge. "Fssa said it was the best," grunted Kirtn. "He didn't say it would be easy."

Kirtn leaned against the slab of stone. Muscles bunched from neck to heels, bulging beneath the few clothes he wore. Rainbow swung out from his neck and rattled against the slab. A trickle of grit fell down one side of the boulder. He grunted and heaved harder. The slab gave fractionally. He sighed. "Any advice, snake?"

"The rockfall is more stable on the right side of the tunnel. But if you dig around the left of the boulder, the rocks you encounter will be smaller."

Wordlessly, Kirtn put Rainbow around Rheba's neck and began removing stones from the left side of the boulder. He soon discovered that "smaller" did not mean small. He rocked, dragged, shifted and lifted stones that weighed as much as he did. The rocks that were too big for Daemen and Rheba to handle he carried out of the way himself.

Daemen looked from the barrier to the tireless Bre'n. He was doing the work of ten Daemenites. His unusual suede skin-fur was dark with sweat and his breath came in deep gasps, but his pace never slowed.

Rheba saw beyond Kirtn's strength. She saw that the rocks he handled were marked by blood. She redoubled her own pace, trying to save him any unnecessary effort. If she could have lifted the bigger boulders for him she would have, but she could not.

Kirtn flexed his back and shoulders, trying to shake off the fatigue that was gathering on him like invisible weights. With a deep breath, he knelt and attacked the slab of rock that he had dug around. The boulder had to be moved if they were to get through the barrier.

His bloody fingers found no purchase on the huge

stone. There was no way to lever it aside. He swore and wished aloud for a pry bar.

"How long a bar?" asked Fssa.

"All lengths," snapped Kirtn. If he was going to wish futilely, he might as well wish big.

"I am all lengths," said the Fssireeme simply.

Kirtn swore like the Bre'n poet he had once been. He pulled Fssa off his shoulders. The snake became a bar as long as Kirtn's arm and one third as thick. The Bre'n stared, amazed. "Are you sure this won't hurt you?"

Laughter hissed out of the bar. "I'm Fssireeme."

Kirtn used Fssa tentatively at first, then with greater confidence. He pried around the edges of the slab. The slab quivered slightly.

"Longer," he grunted, shifting his grip.

The lever became longer but not thinner. Fssa simply increased the space between his densely packed molecules to achieve a greater length with no sacrifice of strength.

The slab grated against the tunnel floor. A shower of small rocks fell over Kirtn. He ignored them. "Can you bend around the rock and still give me enough length?"

Fssa changed again. Kirtn took a deep breath and heaved against the bar with a force that made the slab shudder.

"Get back!" he called hoarsely over his shoulder.

Daemen and Rheba backed away. They could not take their eyes off the straining figure of the Bre'n. In the eerie light of the tunnel he looked like a creature out of myth, taking the weight of eternity on his own shoulders so that lesser beings would not be crushed.

Kirtn's hands slipped, oiled by sweat and blood. He swore and shifted his grip.

Fssa changed subtly, roughening his exterior. Kirtn felt the new texture as pain across his bloody palms, but he welcomed it. He strained against the bar. The slab shifted minutely. He pushed again and again and again.

The slab tottered but would not fall.

"Make yourself wider at my end if you can," panted Kirtn.

The part of the lever he had held changed until it was as broad as both his hands held together.

"Good," grunted Kirtn, wiping his slippery hands on his thighs.

He reversed his position, turning his back on the bar. With bent knees he braced himself between the bar and the side of the tunnel. He breathed deeply several times . . . and then he straightened his legs.

The boulder shivered, grated horribly and fell forward into the tunnel. Somehow Kirtn spun out of the way in time to avoid being crushed.

"Fssa!" cried Kirtn, looking frantically in the rubble for his friend.

A thin whistle answered. The Fssireeme slithered out from the shadow of the slab. Bre'n blood and pulverized rock coated his body, concealing his normal metallic brightness beneath a grubby patchwork of gray and black.

Kirtn snatched Fssa out of the rubble. "You're beautiful, snake."

Fssa glowed in shy delight. It was the one compliment he could never hear often enough, for he had spent eons believing himself to be repulsive in the eyes of the Fourth People.

"Are you all right?" asked Rheba, hurrying forward.

"Yesss." The answer was as much a satisfied hiss as a word. "But Kirtn almost bent me that last time." Twin sensors changed colors with dizzying speed. "Your flesh isn't like mine, Bre'n, but you're strong just the same."

"Strong!" Daemen laughed shortly. "He's more than strong, he's—" The Luck made a baffled gesture, finding no words to describe Kirtn's strength.

Kirtn flexed muscles that knotted and quivered painfully. He felt about as strong as a gutted cherf. With a suppressed curse, he turned back to the barrier.

"Wait," said Fssa. "Put me in the opening."

Before Kirtn could respond, Rheba took the Fssireeme. She scrambled over the slab until she could place him in the opening created when the huge boulder had toppled into the tunnel. Then she retreated, not wanting to be near while Fssa probed the altered dynamics of the rockfall.

She created two more balls of light and examined Kirtn. Her lines pulsed in protest at what she saw, but she said nothing. The bruises and scrapes she had expected. His hands, however, made her ache. Even as she watched, blood ran silently down his fingers and dripped onto the stone tunnel floor.

He jerked his hands away from the light, but she was faster. Her fingers closed around his wrists. Energy crackled. Instantly, his hands were numb.

"I can't work that way," he said.

"I know."

Without looking at him, she summoned fire in her fingertip and burned off strips of her green cape. She wrapped his injuries carefully, ignoring Daemen, ignoring Fssa, ignoring everything but her Bre'n's battered hands. When she was finished, only his fingertips were free.

"Rheba," gently, "I still can't work. My hands are numb."

"As soon as Fssa's finished," she snapped. "Or are you in a hurry to hurt again?"

Kirtn brought her hand up to his cheek. She avoided his eyes, but her anger was transmitted in images of fire. He kissed her hand, silently thanking her, unruffled by her anger. He knew that her emotion came from her inability to prevent further pain to him. He did not point out the illogic of her reaction; were their roles reversed, his response would have been even less rational.

"It's not as safe as it was," called Fssa from the tunnel, "but it's as safe as it will ever be."

Kirtn looked at Rheba and waited. Reluctantly, she touched his wrists again, drawing away the energy that had blocked messages of pain. Other than a slight narrowing of his eyes he showed no reaction.

"Doesn't he feel pain?" asked Daemen wonderingly.

Her hair hissed and seethed. "Yes!"

Daemen hesitated, then seemed to decide that even the Luck should not press an angry fire dancer. In silence, he followed her back to the barrier.

Beyond the slab, none of the rocks were much larger than Kirtn's chest. He worked steadily, sending rocks back over his shoulder as fast as Rheba and Daemen could carry them away. Fssa alternated between being a lever and listening for the first hint of shifting stones.

A shower of rocks tumbled from the ceiling of the narrow tunnel Kirtn was digging. Fssa snapped out, becoming a hard sheet stretching across the tunnel above Kirtn's head. After deflecting the worst of the rockfall, the Fssireeme changed into a shape that allowed him to probe the stability of the rocks that surrounded them on three sides. Kirtn waited, staring at the bloody shreds that were all that remained of his bandages.

"It isn't safe," said Fssa finally.

"Tell me something I don't know," snapped Kirtn, his exhaustion showing in his ragged voice. "At least it would be a quick way to die," he muttered, grabbing a rock and heaving it over his shoulder for Daemen and Rheba to carry away. "Dehydration isn't."

Fssa said nothing from any of his possible mouths. His silence, as much as the languid way he resumed his customary shape, told Kirtn that something was wrong with the Fssireeme.

"Did you hurt yourself in the rockfall?" asked Kirtn, picking up the snake.

"No . . ." There was a long pause. Then, "Rocks can't hurt a Fssireeme."

Kirtn realized that Fssa was cold in his hands, colder even than the rocks. He remembered that the more Fssa stretched out, the more heat he needed to maintain himself. He had been moving over chill stone, probing for instabilities, listening for the first tremors of a rockfall and finally thinning himself into a sheet to protect Kirtn from falling stones. Fssireemes were tough creatures, but they had their limits—especially where cold was concerned.

"Take some of my heat," Kirtn said, looking at his arms, where sweat and rock dust coated his fine copper fur. "I've got plenty to spare."

"No." The answer was flat.

"This is no time to be coy!"

"*No.*" This time the answer was an anguished Bre'n whistle, carrying with it all of Fssa's shame at his heritage as a parasite who lived off warmer creatures' body heat.

Kirtn was too tired to think of an argument to equal Fssa's shame. Rheba was more practical. She sent minor lightning coursing through the tunnel until incandescence ran like water over the Fssireeme.

Kirtn threw a protesting glance toward Rheba. In the cold tunnel, she simply did not have energy to spare. She stared back at him, cinnamon eyes burning. "Without Fssa, you would have been knocked silly by those rocks. Without you, we'd die."

"Next time," said the Bre'n to Fssa, "use me."

Daemen simply stared. "I thought I'd seen every kind of weird creature on Loo," he said, looking at the Fssireeme glowing softly in Kirtn's bloody hands, "but that snake is the other side of incredible. Can't it make its own heat as we do?"

"No," said Rheba, her voice tired.

"Then how does it survive?"

"There's work to do," cut in Kirtn, knowing that Fssa would be mortified by any discussion of his peculiar physiology. "Save your breath for lifting rocks."

"Do you always make heat for the snake?" continued Daemen, looking at Rheba. "If you make heat, why don't you warm the tunnel? It's cold enough in here to make a stone shiver."

"She can't make heat from nothing," snapped Kirtn. "When there's no external source of energy, she has to use her own body. If you're cold, work more and talk less."

Daemen was too busy trying to figure out his companions' peculiar biologies to be insulted. He smiled at Rheba, a smile that could warm the coldest of

Deva's hells. "If *you* need energy, I'd be delighted to share mine."

Kirtn snarled soundlessly and attacked the remaining barrier. Rocks skidded down the tunnel, narrowly missing The Luck. Fssa whistled a protest—not at the barrage, but at Kirtn's reckless disregard for the barrier's stability.

Kirtn ignored the snake's warning and continued moving rocks at a dangerous pace. Fssa protested again, then realized what any Senyas would have known: An angry Bre'n listens to nothing but his own rage unfolding. The Fssireeme wasted no more time carping. He braced part of himself on the tunnel floor and probed the rockfall with a burst of energy that made Rheba stagger and grab her temples.

She turned in startled protest just as the front part of the tunnel shifted. Kirtn whistled shrilly. The Bre'n warning needed no translation. Daemen grabbed Rheba and yanked her out of Kirtn's burrow before she could protest.

"Kirtn!" she screamed, looking over her shoulder where rocks shifted and slid coldly over one another.

"You can't go back!" said Daemen, struggling to hold her. "The rest of the tunnel could go any second!"

She looked at him with eyes that were blind with fire. He released her a split second before she would have burned his hands to the bone. She turned and dove into what remained of the tunnel. Her frantic whistle cut through the random sounds of settling rocks.

Fssa answered with an odd whistle, so thin that it almost could not bear the weight of Bre'n complexity.

"Is Kirtn—are you—?" Her whistles were ragged, breathless. Kirtn groaned. She heard rocks shifting.

Fssa whistled again, the sound still flat. She moved rocks frantically. The tunnel had only partially collapsed. Within minutes, she had cleared enough debris to reach Kirtn.

"Kirtn?" she whistled, peering through the dust. She coughed and whistled again. Even when she stepped up the power of her light, she could not penetrate the darkness enough to see her Bre'n. She felt around with her fingers, searching for the warmth and resilience of Kirtn's flesh. What she found was a smooth, cold sheet between herself and whatever lay at the end of the tunnel. "Fssa?"

A strained whistle answered, sound without meaning. She realized that she was touching the Fssireeme . . . and that he was *cold*. When she tried to give him fire, her lines only flickered. Like her friends, she was near the end of her strength. She would have taken Daemen's energy if she could, but only a Bre'n could establish the necessary rapport.

Deliberately she slowed her breathing, murmuring akhenet litanies until her heart stopped pounding messages of fear through her body. She built a shell of tranquillity around herself. Wrapped in its shelter, wholly focused, she called on her Inmost Fire.

The call was an emergency measure taught to all dancers, a state almost like Bre'n *rez*. It was so dangerous to the dancer that it was rarely used.

Fire beat in her veins like another kind of blood. Her body turned on itself, consuming reserves of fat and flesh. Energy poured into the Fssireeme. With a soundless cry he soaked up life itself.

Beneath him, shielded by Fssireeme flesh, Kirtn groaned and woke to darkness and pain. For a moment he did not know where he was. When he remembered, he groaned again. He felt around himself, expecting to find the dimensions of his tomb. What he found was Fssireeme, a canopy of incredible flesh between himself and the rockfall.

And then he sensed energy flowing, fire-dancer energy, Rheba pouring herself into Fssa so that her Bre'n would not be buried alive.

"Kirtn?" Fssa's whistle was odd, but understandable.

"I'm here, snake," said Kirtn. "Which way is out?"

"Dig in front of your head. It isn't far," he added.

Kirtn burrowed like a cherf, taking debris from ahead and shoving it back along either side until he could force his body forward. Fssa stretched with him, a protective membrane. Kirtn bunched his shoulders, using his hands as clubs to batter out of the rockfall.

Light came in like an explosion. A triumphant whistle carried back into the tunnel. He pulled himself out into Daemen's thin daylight, but it seemed as thick as cream after the tunnel's midnight.

"Can Rheba—get through?" he asked, panting.

"She's very weak," whistled Fssa, ashamed that he had caused it.

Kirtn threw himself back into the burrow. When he found Rheba, he hauled her unceremoniously into the open. He buried his hands in her lifeless hair, forcing rapport as only a Bre'n could. Skillfully, he gave her some of his own energy. After a moment she sighed and awakened.

Daemen emerged from the burrow covered in grit. He laughed and stretched as though to hold the sun in his hands. "The Seurs were wrong!" he said exultantly. *"I am Good Luck incarnate!"*

The burrow collapsed with a grinding sound as Fssa slithered into the light. "I hope so," he said sourly. "We're too tired to fight."

"Fight?" asked Daemen, confused.

With a sinking feeling, Kirtn turned and looked over his shoulder.

Ten Daemenites stood nearby, watching with predatory intensity. They were armed with knives and slingshots powerful enough to smash bone.

Kirtn glared at Daemen and wished he had spaced the unlucky cherf when he had the chance.

XV

Daemen turned toward the ten people and spoke rapidly. Fssa translated, but manipulated his voice so that only Kirtn could hear.

"I'm The Daemen," he said, walking confidently toward the waiting people. "Are you Square One Seurs?"

The people muttered among themselves, but their lowered voices could not elude a Fssireeme's sensitive hearing. Rheba scooped up the snake and stood very close to Kirtn. Fssa vanished into her hair. His voice remained behind, seeming to form out of the very air between her and the Bre'n.

". . . Luck? . . . told me that trouble was coming," said a woman with startling red hair and skin as black as the tunnel had been.

"You can't trust the Voice. Sometimes it . . ." retorted a man with luxuriant silver fur on his arms and face, and eyes of a startling pink.

"Have you considered the possibility of . . ." cut

in a woman whose skin alternated between brown and gold.

Fssa made a frustrated noise. His hearing was *too* good. It picked up overlapping sounds, making little sense of the group's muttering. Their dialect was different from Centrins' speech. It was not different enough to require learning the language all over, but enough to make translating group babble impossible.

Kirtn and Rheba listened without appearing to. Daemen made no attempt to hide his curiosity. He seemed a bit piqued that they had not responded to The Luck's presence with more appreciation.

"Are you Seurs?" he demanded.

"We're Scavengers," said the red-haired woman proudly.

"That's close enough," answered Daemen, smiling. "Are you the leader, First Scavenger, or whatever you call it?"

"Super Scavenger," said the woman. "No . . . not yet." She looked at Kirtn and Rheba possessively. "But when I return with those two, Ghun will be back on scout." She squinted at Daemen. "The Luck, eh? That should be worth a few extra points."

Daemen took a moment to digest the implications of the woman's odd words. "Is Ghun the Super Scavenger?" he asked hesitantly.

"Only until I get back with the three of you," the woman said, nodding her head emphatically. "Then I'll be Super Scavenger. Unless—" She leaned forward and looked anxiously along the cliff face where the tunnel had emerged. "You Seurs have any more of those holes?"

"No. That's the only mover that still works."

The word "mover" was obviously unfamiliar to the woman. She squinted at Daemen, then moved her shoulders as though to shake off doubts. "Then no other scouts are going to come back with more Treats?"

"Treats?" Daemen's tone was as perplexed as his expression.

"Treats," agreed the woman. Then she realized that Daemen did not know what she was talking about. "They must do things different on the other end of that hole. Around here, strange things are called Treats. The Scavenger who brings in the best Treats is the Super Scavenger until the next Hunt. But we haven't seen anything like those two. Ever. So I should be Super Scavenger for a long time."

"Ahh . . . excuse me," said Daemen. He turned toward Rheba and Kirtn and switched to Universal. "Apparently they play some kind of elaborate game here. Scavenger Hunt. Whoever brings in the strangest thing becomes the Super Scavenger until the next Hunt."

Kirtn and Rheba made encouraging noises.

"We," continued Daemen, "are very strange. Therefore, we'll be the winning Treats."

Kirtn did not like the idea of being anyone's Treat. "What happens to the Treats after the Hunt?"

Daemen hesitated. "Excuse me." He turned back to the red-haired woman. "What do you do with your Treats?"

She stared at him, unable to believe that even a stranger could be so ignorant. "We give them to God, of course."

"You give them to God. Of course." A glazed look came to Daemen's eyes. Then, loudly, "What in the name of *other* does that mean?"

The people around the red-haired woman grabbed their weapons. She made a cutting gesture with her hand. They let go of their whips and slingshots, but fondled their knives with disturbing intensity.

"Don't shout, boy," she said calmly. "Makes them nervous. If they get too nervous, they'll forget that a dead Treat isn't much better than a stone, far as God's concerned."

"Your God likes Treats alive?"

"You're learning," she said, patting his arm. "An unwilling Treat is fewer points. A lot fewer."

"Fewer points," said Daemen helplessly.

Kirtn looked at Rheba and shrugged. If Daemen was going to handle the questioning, they would be a long time learning anything useful. For a graduate of Loo's slave Pit, The Luck was remarkably innocent. "Fssa, translate without showing yourself."

The Fssireeme hissed and changed shape within Rheba's hair. As Kirtn spoke, the snake translated so quickly that it was like speaking and understanding the language yourself. Fssa even duplicated the voice of whoever was speaking at the time.

"Can this Treat slide a few words in?" asked Kirtn.

Daemen stared at the Bre'n who seemed to be speaking flawless Daemenite. With a hurt look, he turned to Rheba. She smiled reassuringly.

The red-haired scout leader waited. Every time she looked at the big Bre'n with the odd copper skin-fur, she smiled possessively. A very big Treat indeed.

"What does your God do with Treats?" asked Kirtn reasonably.

"It loves them. All zoolipts love Treats."

Kirtn was tempted to ask *how* a zoolipt—whatever that was—loved its Treats, but he was afraid the woman would have an answer for that, too. "Does being . . . loved . . . by a God-zoolipt hurt?"

"Not if you're willing."

"The same could be said of rape," Rheba observed acidly.

Fssa refrained from translating her comment. He had learned on Loo that a translator had better be a diplomat, too.

"What happens after this love feast?" asked Kirtn, straining to keep his voice down.

"Good eats for everyone," said the woman enthusiastically. "Fat times and fancy flavors."

"For everyone? Even the Treats?"

"*Willing* Treats," corrected the woman.

"What happens to the *willing* Treats after the feast?"

"Same as everyone else. We eat, drink and fall in a shaval pile. We keep doing that until God gets bored. Then we have another Hunt."

"Bored? Your God gets bored?"

The woman took on a long-suffering look. "You said a truth, Treat."

Kirtn looked at Daemen.

"I don't know any more about these barbarians than you do," said The Luck in Universal. "Not about their personal habits, anyway. Once we get inside their Installation, I'll find some new technology, then go back to the tunnel and make a mover. Once the Seurs see what I have, they'll be glad to take us back. Then these creatures can eat themselves into a coma for all I care."

"Right," said Kirtn in sarcastic Universal. "You just stroll into the Installation, technology drops into your hands and we're home free."

"Right," said Daemen.

"You're a stupid, arrogant—"

"Kirtn!" said Rheba, horrified.

The Bre'n shrugged. Calling Daemen names would not help. On the other hand, it would feel good.

"I'm not stupid," began Daemen hotly, "and I'm not arrogant either! I'm The Luck!"

"Bad luck," snapped Kirtn.

Daemen stared, too shocked to be angry. "But we survived! For thousands of years Seurs have tried to reach Square One. We walked over their bones—*and we survived.* Do you call that bad?"

Kirtn looked at his exhausted fire dancer and his own bloody hands. He sighed. "No, that's not bad. And this," he continued, staring at the group of Daemenites, "isn't good. I don't know about here, but where I came from we *ate* treats."

Daemen's laugh was as beguiling as a Bre'n whistle. "Don't worry. Good Luck is with you. Whatever happens can't be bad."

"What are you yammering about?" demanded the woman, obviously tired of listening to noises she did not understand.

Kirtn smiled lopsidedly at her. "He was just reminding me that he's Good Luck."

"Good for him," she answered, unimpressed.

"And for his companions—I hope," muttered the Bre'n. He drew a breath so deep it made his ribs ache. He sighed again. "We're willing Treats. Now what?"

The Daemenites looked at the Bre'n, then at each other. They broke into cheers and mutual congratulations.

Daemen listened to the excited babble. He smiled triumphantly at Kirtn. "See? There's nothing to be afraid of. Apparently willing Treats are very rare, and therefore very prized. They'll take good care of us."

"Maybe the unwilling Treats knew something we
on't," retorted Kirtn.

For a moment Daemen looked uncertain, then his
ith in his own Luck reasserted itself. "We survived,"
e said, as though that answered all questions.

And, the Bre'n silently admitted to himself, maybe
did.

The Daemenites stopped congratulating them-
elves long enough to surround the three Treats. The
ed-haired woman grinned at them. "Call me Super
cuvee. Everyone else will in a few days."

Rheba's hair fluffed out as Fssa made a flatulent
oise. The snake, however, had the good sense to
nake it seem that the sound issued from a Daemenite.

Scuvee whirled and glared, but had only protesta-
ons of innocence from her followers. With a final
old look around, she led the party away from the
liff face.

They followed a dim trail through an area of gray-
lue rocks and drifts of gold that could have been
lust. Rheba and Kirtn looked around, memorizing
heir route. Out of the corner of her eye, she spotted
quick dart of movement.

"What's that?" she asked.

Instantly, every Daemenite was alert. Then Scuvee
aughed. "Just a runner. They're only worth a few
oints. Not much of a Treat," she added. "A flyer,
low, is pretty good. Lots of points. A real trick to
atch them, too."

The silver-furred man looked at the point where the
unner had disappeared. "You sure we don't need it?"

"With the Treats we already have?" she retorted,
aughing. "We'll be three days just adding up their
oints!"

"Yeah," agreed the man slowly, but he still looked

at the gold drift that had swallowed up the runner
"Seems a waste. There's been more than one Hun
when we'd have been glad to take even a dead runne
back."

"Skinny times are over," Scuvee said, smacking the
man on his shoulder with her fist. "Fat times and
fancy flavors!"

"Fat times and fancy flavors!" roared the rest o
the Scavengers. Apparently the phrase was a loca
shibboleth.

"Kirtn," murmured Rheba in Senyas. "They have
animals here. Centrins only had rocks."

"And Seurs." Kirtn looked around. "Wonder why
animals survived here and not there?"

A gold drift curved across the trail. As Kirtn walked
through it, a haunting fragrance filled his nostrils
He bent over and grabbed a handful of the dust. I
was cool and silky to the touch, clinging to his skin
in golden clouds of fragrance. He had an impulse to
lie down and wallow in the drift, covering himself
with its incredible, sensual fragrance.

"Smell this," he said, holding out a handful of
good dust to her.

She inhaled and made a sound of pleasure.
Akhenet lines pulsed as she responded to fragrance
It was almost aphrodisiac in its intensity. She looked
up at Kirtn, eyes lambent with promises.

Scuvee watched, grinning. "Well, you may be different, but you're still human. The last time we really
pleased God, it gave us shaval," she said, gesturing
toward the golden drifts that curled across low spots
in the land. Her grin increased. "I can hardly wait
to see what we get *this* time. Should be enough to
make a rock shout."

"Your God gave you this?" asked Rheba, smiling

dreamily. "That would be enough to make me take up religion."

Daemen dipped his finger in the dust, sniffed cautiously, then looked thoughtful. "How did you make this?"

"Can't you hear?" snapped Scuvee. "God gave it to us."

"How did you get your zoolipt—your God or whatever you call it—to make this for you?"

Scuvee looked at Daemen. Slowly her face settled into the lines of one who is being patient with a particularly backward child. "As I said, boy. We fed it a really good Treat."

"What was it?" asked Kirtn, curious.

Scuvee sighed. "Wish I knew. It was so long ago even God forgot."

"If I could find out how to make this," said Daemen in excited Universal, "the Seurs would have to call me Luck." He turned back to Scuvee and spoke Daemenite. "Does your God live with you?"

"Where else would it live?"

"Oh, over the mountain, across the sea, in the sky," said Daemen, remembering just a few of the religions he had encountered on Loo. "On another planet, maybe."

"What good would it be to have a God that lived somewhere else?" asked Scuvee, perplexed.

"Does your God live in the Installation?" Daemen asked hurriedly, not wanting to argue religious niceties with a woman who did not even know the value of Luck.

"What's the Installation?"

"The building that's all colors and never needs repairs."

"Oh, you mean God's House. Sure, where else would God live?"

Daemen threw a despairing look in the direction
of his friends. Kirtn almost felt sorry for him. Scuvee
had a death grip on reality that would not be weak
ened by nuances of any kind.

"Are outsiders allowed to . . . ah . . . worship in
God's House?" asked Kirtn, guessing the point of
Daemen's interrogation. Any technology to be found
would be found in the Installation. If the Installation
was sacred, getting into it could be difficult.

"Outsiders? Worship?" Scuvee looked from Kirtn
to Daemen and back. "You don't make any more
sense than he does. What do you mean, *worship*?"

Kirtn tried to think of words she would understand.
Fssa spoke for him, in tones that resonated with con
tempt. "Can we get inside God's House?"

Scuvee's face cleared. "Why sure, Treat. Glad to
hear you're so eager. You really told a truth when
you said you were willing." She patted Kirtn's chest
approvingly. "Such a *big* Treat, too. I can't wait for
the shaval pile."

Rheba's hair stirred, crackling with the beginning
of anger. "Then you won't mind if we go in God's
House?" she snapped.

"Mind? Listen, pretty Treat, you can go in God's
House anytime you like, anytime at all. In fact"—she
leaned forward, smiling—"I'll knife anyone who tries
to keep you out." She looked around her group tri
umphantly. "Willing Treats!" she crowed.

"Fat times and fancy flavors!" they shouted back.

The Daemenites turned eagerly back to the trail.
Kirtn and Rheba moved with less alacrity. They were
beginning to feel like a meal looking for a place to
be eaten. And they were afraid that God's House was
the place.

XVI

Super Scuvee kept them apart from the other
Square One inhabitants. It was not difficult. Like Cen-
rins, Square One had rank upon rank of uninhabited
buildings erected in the Cycles that followed the origi-
nal builders, the Zaarain. Scuvee and her group lived
n one of the least ramshackle houses. Its windows
were intact and its floors did not slant randomly. Its
loors, however, required muscle to open and close.

Despite Scuvee's assurances that her Treats could
get into God's House at any time, Rheba, Kirtn and
The Luck had only seen the Installation from a dis-
ance.

"I told you," said Scuvee, her voice rising, "you
have to wait until the Hunt is over."

Kirtn shifted restlessly. "Yes, you told us. But you
haven't told us when this damned Hunt ends. We've
been here five hours and all you've done is tell us to
wait!"

She sighed. "Treat, I'm glad you're so eager. But

I don't get points for stupidity. If Ghun doesn't *se*
me put you in God's House, I won't get points. And
Ghun can't see you if he isn't here. So until Ghun
gets back, you don't go into God's House. Got that
Treat, or do you want me to chew it for you again?'

Kirtn managed not to snarl. "When will Ghun be
back?"

Scuvee all but pulled at her bright-red hair. "I *told*
you, when the Hunt is over!"

"But when will the Hunt be over?" put in Rheba
quickly, reading anger in Kirtn's tense body.

"Pretty Treat," said Scuvee, "I already told you.
The Hunt will be over when Ghun gets back."

"Don't worry," soothed Daemen, taking Rheba's
hand. "Everything is all right. Remember, I'm The
Luck. Good Luck," he added quickly over Kirtn's
muttering. "Look at the food Scuvee gave us. Wasn't it
better than anything we had on Loo or in Centrins?"

"It was?" said Scuvee, shock in every line of her
face. "Little Treat, your zoolipt must be real bored."

"What do you mean?"

Scuvee's voice dripped patience. "Our food is rot-
ten. That's why we called a Hunt. Now, if you think
the swill we've been eating is good, it means that the
food you ate at the other end of that hole was hun-
dred-proof shit. Right?"

"Right," said Daemen, pleased that she understood. It was not always easy to get through to Square
One barbarians.

"The only way you could eat worse food than here,"
continued Scuvee relentlessly, "is if your zoolipt is
even more bored than ours. Don't you ever feed it?"

"Feed what?" asked Daemen.

Scuvee made a frustrated sound. "Your *zoolipt!*" she
shouted.

"Centrins doesn't have a zoolipt. We just have machines."

"Don't be more stupid than stone," she said, her face getting as wild as her hair. "You have a fancy colored building, right?"

"Right."

"You put garbage in one end and food comes out the other, right?"

"Well, that's an oversimplification. What actually happens is—"

"*Right, Little Treat?*" shouted Scuvee.

"Ahh, right."

"What do you think makes garbage into food?"

"A machine . . . right?"

"*Wrong!*" Scuvee gulped air. "It's the God in the machine that makes food. The machinery just shovels in garbage. But if all you ever feed it is garbage, all you get is garbage. Garbage in, garbage out. Right? Right," she continued relentlessly. "A bored God is unhappy. If it gets too bored, it starts making things."

Daemen moved as though to protest. Kirtn's big hand clamped down on the younger man's shoulder. "Let her talk," whispered the Bre'n. "She's finally saying something interesting."

Scuvee did not hear what Kirtn said. She was too involved in her own words to have attention for anyone else. "If you're lucky," she continued, "a bored God just makes bad food. We spend a lot of time running to the shit pits, giving back as bad as we got. The cramps are rough and it ruins a lot of clothes, but that's not as bad as the headbenders."

"Headbenders?" said Rheba.

"Right. You never can tell when it'll hit. You eat and then the world gets all runny around the edges and colors start yammering at you and then the devils

come screaming and clawing. It's bad, real bad, and
it stays that way until God gets bored with *that,* too.'

"Then what happens?" asked Kirtn, liking what he
was hearing less and less.

"We shovel in our dead and go on a Hunt. If we're
lucky, the runners have changed a little since the last
time, or the flyers. The more they've changed, the
bigger Treat they are."

"Changed?" murmured Kirtn.

"Right. A few legs more or less. Fur shorter or
gone. They have to eat what God makes, too. If you
eat godfood, you change."

"Do people change, too?" asked Rheba, struggling
with an unreasoning fear. *A few legs more or less.*

"Sure. But God learned to be careful with us. If
we change too much we'll all die and then God will be
more bored than ever. That's why it made crawlers—
crawlers can change a lot and not die. Where do you
think the diggers and flyers came from? Crawlers,
that's where."

Kirtn remembered the startling variation in pheno-
type among the Seurs. It was even more pronounced
at Square One. Apparently there was a mutagen in
the food.

"Their machine must be out of phase," said Daemen in Universal.

"What?" asked Rheba, still envisioning the nightmare Scuvee's words had conjured.

"Their Installation isn't tuned. It's a miracle
they've survived this long."

"God is on their side," Kirtn said sarcastically.

"I'm serious," Daemen snapped.

"So am I. Look around, Luck. Scuvee's people are
a lot healthier than the Seurs were."

"Nonsense!"

"Kirtn's right," said Rheba. "The Seurs were gaunt. There weren't many children. You were much stronger and taller by a head than most men. Loo's slave rations weren't much, but they were better than what the Seurs eat."

"Centrins doesn't make us sick or feed us mind-benders," Daemen said hotly.

"No. It just starves you and then teases you by announcing dinners that aren't served."

"It's a *machine,* not a person. It's out of tune, not *bored.*"

"That's your dogma," said Kirtn. "Scuvee's is different."

Daemen looked stubborn. "All civilized Installations are the same."

"Starving?" suggested the Bre'n. "You may not like it but Scuvee's dogma works," continued Kirtn, his voice soft, implacable. "What do the Seurs say to that?"

Daemen still looked stubborn, but there was also uneasiness in his expression. "The Seurs say that people who recycle whole corpses are disgusting barbarians. How can you eat food that once was your uncle?"

"Isn't that what they sent you here to find out?"

Scuvee cut in impatiently. "Yammer in words I can understand or I'll beat you bloody before grace even starts."

Only part of her words made sense, but it was a compelling part. "Daemen's people don't feed corpses to their god," said Kirtn succinctly. "He's surprised you do."

Scuvee snorted. "Corpses and criminals and every other damn thing we can lift. Too bad rocks don't work—enough of them for twenty Gods."

Daemen shuddered. "How can you eat?"

"Hunger, Little Treat. Works every time."

From the front of the house came the sounds of people shouting. A short, thick man swept into the room, followed by Scuvee's angry group. The man stopped and stared at Kirtn.

"Then it's true," said the man, shaking his head until his long black hair tumbled down to touch his powerful wrists.

Rheba stared. The man had eight fingers and a very long thumb on each hand. She looked at her own four-fingered hand and wondered how much godfood she could eat before she changed.

The man walked around them like a slave master inspecting newly arrived chattel. Whatever he saw did not please him. "No ropes?" he snapped.

"They're willing Treats, Ghun," said Scuvee smugly.

"I'm still Super Scavenger," he said harshly. "The Hunt isn't over yet."

"You're back. You can't go out again. You know the rules as well as I do, *Super*." The woman's voice was whiplike.

"My group isn't back yet. I came in early."

The red-haired woman smiled nastily. "At sunset we say grace and send in the Treats. I'll be Super before the second moon rises." She laughed. "I'll be Super until I die, Ghun. No one ever brought in Treats like these."

"No Treats last more than a meal. After the next Hunt, I'll be Super again."

"Willing Treats, Ghun. They'll last forever—longer than either one of us, that's for sure."

Ghun looked shrewdly at the faces of the Treats. "You don't know what she's talking about, do you?"

Kirtn, knowing an enemy when he saw one, did not answer.

Daemen did. "What do you mean?"

"You look a little young to die." Ghun cocked his head, searching the Treats for any sign of understanding. Kirtn and Rheba controlled their expressions. Daemen did not. Ghun leaned toward the Luck. "Didn't she tell you?"

"Tell me what?" said Daemen.

"She's going to feed you to God."

"So what?"

"So you're going to die."

"That's not true!" shouted the red-haired woman. "You're just trying to make them unwilling so I'll get fewer points!"

Ghun's smile made Kirtn more uneasy than a snarl would have. Daemen did not notice. He was still caught by the assured tone in which Ghun had pronounced their death sentences.

"It isn't true, Little Treat," Scuvee said persuasively. "He's just trying to scare you. Willing Treats are loved by the God. Nothing bad can happen when God loves you."

"How willing will they be when they choke on God and drown?" asked Ghun smoothly.

"Pucker your hole!" said Scuvee, turning on Ghun with hands that wanted to strangle his assurance and him with it.

Ghun smiled thinly. "Didn't you tell them, Scuvee? Didn't you tell them how they'll be scourged and driven into God's House? Didn't you tell them—"

Scuvee's knife tip hovered a finger's length from Ghun's mouth. Her strong hand was twisted into his hair, holding his head immobile. "If you don't pucker up," she said, "I'll feed your tongue to God."

Ghun puckered up.

"I found these Treats, and I found them willing. The whole town knows it. If they go all unwilling on me, that would be a crime, wouldn't it?"

Ghun swallowed and looked as if he were eating bile.

"Wouldn't it?" pressed Scuvee, drawing a bead of blood out of his thin lower lip.

"Uggg—yes!"

"Right. And you know what we do to criminals, don't you?" Her knife moved slightly, flicking blood out of his upper lip. "What happens?"

"They're fed to God," said Ghun, his lips barely moving.

"Right. Now, if you're through lying to my *willing* Treats, we'll just forget you ever opened your hole. Unless maybe you have a yen to visit God?" she asked softly.

Ghun made a strangled sound that Scuvee took as capitulation.

She released him so suddenly he stumbled. He threw a malevolent look over his shoulder as he hurried out.

Kirtn and Rheba looked at each other.

Daemen smiled at nothing in particular. "It's all right. I'm The Luck."

Daemen's litany did not comfort them. Kirtn touched Rheba and sensed the exhaustion beneath her fear. The meal and a few hours of anxious captivity had not helped to restore her strength—or his. They could probably fight their way back to the tunnel, but then what? Without a high-tech present for the Seurs, Daemen and his friends would be sent on another one-way trip by the Seurs. This time, Kirtn suspected the Seurs would overcome their scruples about killing The Luck.

With a growing coldness in his bones, the Bre'n realized that there was nothing to do but to wait until feeding time at God's House. Once inside the Installation, perhaps Daemen would find something useful. If not, they could always feed Rainbow to the machine and hope that the lights went out as fast as they had at Centrins.

What would Square One's barbarians do if the Treats proved to be indigestible?

Scuvee looked at her Treats. Their expressions were not reassuring. She smiled and clapped her hands. "Won't be long now, Treats," she said with forced lightness. "Don't look so worried. The shaval pile will take your minds off God's stomach. You eat a handful of that gold stuff and you won't care about one damn thing. Besides, willing Treats are loved by God. Believe me," she said earnestly. "As long as I've been alive, God never hurt a willing Treat."

The Treats said nothing.

Scuvee smiled encouragingly. "You won't even have to be graced," she said. "You're bloody enough already. Except," she added, looking critically at Daemen, "for Little Treat, here. Might have to break a bit more of his skin. Oh, nothing hurtful," she reassured them. "Just enough to let God know we care."

The Treats looked even less comfortable.

"Well!" Scuvee said enthusiastically. "No point waiting around. By the time we get to God's House, sunset will be all over the place."

Scuvee gestured to her group. They surrounded the Treats. Despite the barbarians' friendly smiles, there was no doubt that a reluctant Treat would be dragged to God's House.

Kirtn saw akhenet lines flicker over Rheba's arms.
"Not yet," he whistled, his tone urging patience as
much as his words. "We came here to get into the
Installation. Now we're going to do just that."

Rheba heard the irony as well as the wisdom in his
whistle. She smiled lopsidedly and took her mentor's
hand. With her other hand she reached out to Daemen. His answering smile was all the more charming
for its shyness.

Hand in hand in hand, the three of them followed
Scuvee across the barren rock toward God's multicolored House.

As they walked, Square One's population gathered. The carmine sky dyed all people the same shade,
disguising their variations under one thick color. The
natives stared, murmuring with delight and specula-
tions about the nature and source of the strange
Treats.

They approached God's House from the side. The
path hardly looked as though it led to anything more
sacred than a garbage dump. On either side, and
sometimes across the path itself, was debris that
ranged from worn shoes to malodorous lumps.

Rheba made a sound of disgust and scraped the
sole of her shoe across a protruding rock. "If this is
what they usually feed God, no wonder it rebels,"
she muttered.

"It's a simple recycler," said Daemen. "Just a
machine, not a God."

"I'm not ready to be recycled," she snapped.

"Don't worry," he soothed. "Nothing bad can happen. You heard Scuvee—in her whole lifetime the
recycler never hurt a willing Treat."

"I'd feel better if I knew that in her whole lifetime
the machine had been *fed* a willing Treat."

Kirtn sighed. He had hoped Rheba would not spot that flaw in Scuvee's argument.

Daemen looked startled, then he smiled. "It's a machine," he said softly, stroking the back of her hand. "Machines don't hurt people."

God's House rose ahead of them, massive, multicolored, opaque. With a sound like distant thunder, a door opened in the building's side. Daemen walked forward, willing if not especially eager to penetrate the Installation's mechanical mysteries. Kirtn and Rheba followed more slowly, but they did follow. The alternative was the knives that had suddenly appeared in their captor's hands.

Daemen looked over his shoulder. His smile was uncanny, beautiful. "Don't be frightened," he said. "I'm The Luck."

"Good for you," muttered Kirtn, "but not necessarily for *us*."

The door closed behind them, throwing the world into darkness.

XVII

Rheba created a sphere of blue-white light. It burned unevenly for a moment, investing the building with flickering shadows. She concentrated until the light steadied and shadows only moved when people did.

Kirtn squeezed her hand, feeling the peculiar warmth that came from her akhenet lines. She was not only tired, she was also afraid. The building stank of garbage and less appetizing organic matter.

"God's House," Rheba said with contempt in her voice. "Cherfs live in cleaner burrows."

Daemen turned back to her. In the akhenet light, his eyes were white, as uncanny as his smile.

Kirtn saw again the younger man's grace, his unusual beauty. The Bre'n looked away, not blaming his fire dancer for the smile she gave Daemen, but not liking it either.

"They put us in on the garbage conveyor," said Daemen, laughing.

Kirtn gave a derisive whistle. Being the centerpiece of a garbage dump was not one of his life ambitions. "Where's the core or whatever they used to control this place?"

Daemen closed his eyes, obviously trying to remember the floor plan of Centrins. "I think . . . yes, there should be a smaller branch of this room. Like a wide, short hall going off to the left somewhere up ahead. At the end of that there should be an access panel."

Rheba remembered the glittering mound of Zaarain crystals that had somehow controlled Centrins. She remembered the explosion of light when Rainbow had been flung onto the mound, and the darkness that had come without warning. She fingered the chain of crystals that she wore beneath Kirtn's cape and wondered if Rainbow would find more of itself here . . . and who would pay the price if it did.

"Lead the way," Kirtn said shortly. If anyone was going to stumble into the stomach of a hungry God, he hoped it would be the all too handsome Luck.

The room shrank on all sides as Daemen walked confidently forward. Rheba sent small light spheres to various points, trying to guess the room's dimensions.

"It's a flat-bottomed funnel," said Kirtn. "We're going into the narrow gullet."

"Do you have to put it like that?" she asked plaintively.

He stroked her hair, giving comfort with touch as he could not with words. He was becoming more and more uneasy with each forward step.

Ghun's words echoed in the Installation's silences, as though all the people who had been fed to the recycler whispered from darkened corners. The poet in Kirtn sensed eternity and the death of dreams, a death as final as Deva spinning ash-colored against the clean silver of countless stars. He tasted the irony of surviving the extinction of his people only to die in the shell of a building that had been old before his people were even born.

And he laughed, regretting only that he had never known his fire dancer's love.

Rheba leaned against him, pulling his difficult laughter around her, sensing his emotions like another kind of blood beating in her veins. Her bright, patterned hand rubbed down his arm. Her hair stirred with the pleasure his textures always gave her. Slowly her lines stopped flickering. With a sigh, she relaxed, letting go of discordant energies she had not even realized she had held, letting go for him as well.

Fssa hissed quiet satisfaction, reveling in the sweeping energies his friends created when they touched.

"Here it is!" called Daemen from up ahead.

Rheba sensed Kirtn's flash of irritation as clearly as though it were her own. "You're so hard on him," she whistled. "But you're so patient with other children, like Lheket."

"Daemen isn't a child. Lheket is."

"Hurry!" called Daemen, excitement making his voice uneven. Rheba laughed quietly. "Of course he is—listen to him."

"Keep rubbing up against him," whistled Kirtn roughly, "and you'll find he's man enough underneath all that charm."

Kirtn's whistle evoked a coarse sexuality that shocked her. "That's not fair," she said hotly. "Next to you, he's not a man at all!"

Kirtn stopped and looked down at her for a long moment. Then he smiled. "I'd like to lose all my arguments like that." He hugged her as though it were the last time, which he was afraid might be true.

The cape fell away as her arms came up around his neck. A network of light shimmered out from her as she responded to all the unspoken emotions seething in him. She smiled as she saw herself reflected in his golden eyes. "Share enzymes?" she suggested, half laughing, half serious, knowing only that she did not want to leave his arms.

It took all of his Bre'n discipline to stop at a single kiss. The fire she called was so sweet, burning away everything until only she was left and he was holding her and they were wrapped in blinding veils of light.

When he finally released her he saw Daemen nearby, his eyes bright with reflected fire.

"I found the access panel," said Daemen wistfully, as though realizing he might have lost something else. "Can I borrow Rainbow again?"

"Why?" said Rheba, but she reached for Rainbow even as she spoke. "It didn't work too well the last time."

Daemen made an odd gesture that could have signi-fied despair. "I don't have any other key to trigger the Installation. Either Rainbow loosens up some crys-tals for me, or I have to bash the core until I get some. I don't want to do that. The barbarians aren't much, but they're people. Without the Installation, they'll die. But without new technology, my own peo-ple will die." He made the gesture again. "It's all a matter of Luck. My Luck."

Kirtn looked at the young man and for the first time felt compassion. Whether Daemen deserved it or not, he carried the future of his people in his slim hands. The akhenets had carried that weight once . . . and ultimately they had lost, burned by a fire greater than they could call or control. The bitterness of that defeat was part of him now, and of Rheba. It was not a thing he would wish on anyone.

"Good luck," said the Bre'n softly. And meant it.

Rheba handed Rainbow to The Luck. As he turned to go back to the access panel, she took his arm. "Wait. Fssa, could you tell Rainbow what we want? Maybe that way it could do something . . .?"

Her tone was more wistful than sure. Kirtn started to veto the idea, then decided if she was willing to endure the communication he should not object.

"What do you mean?" said Daemen, looking from Rheba to the rope of colored crystals dangling from his fingers. "Rainbow is a machine—you can't *talk* with it no matter how many languages you know."

She pulled Fssa from her hair and held him out to The Luck. When he hesitated, she said, "He doesn't bite. He doesn't even have any teeth." She smiled encouragingly and did not add that Fssa no more needed teeth than a lightgun did. She knew that the Fssireeme made Daemen uneasy enough without telling him what an accomplished predator the snake could be. "Take him."

"What about you?" said Daemen, accepting the snake reluctantly.

"I'm getting as far away from him as I can," said Rheba fervently.

"Are you going back?" asked Daemen, sounding very lonely.

"No," said Kirtn. "The funnel would just send all Fssa's energies back over us. "Is there another room where we could wait?"

"Just beyond the access panel there's a hall. There should be a big room off to the right."

"What's in it?" asked Rheba nervously, not wanting to blunder into God's alimentary canal.

"It would be the hospital at Centrins. I don't know what it is here."

"Just as long as it isn't the dining room," said Kirtn dryly. "I think we'd be smart to stay away from anything that has to do with food while we're in here."

Daemen laughed. "Don't worry—it's the recycler we have to avoid, and that's on the left side of the hall."

They followed Daemen to the access panel. He set Fssa on the floor and piled Rainbow nearby. Rheba left a little light with Daemen and sent a much larger light ahead of Kirtn. Despite the Luck's reassurances, she had no intention of walking blindly out of God's stinking garbage pit and into an endless gullet.

The room was bigger than she had expected. Kirtn hesitated, not wanting to ask her for more light. The sphere brightened but not enough to overpower the shadows.

"I'm sorry." She sighed, realizing the extent of her tiredness. A child could have lit the room without noticing the energy it cost. For a moment she considered trying to tap the core power, then rejected it. Zaarain energies were both complex and painful. Even Deva's master dancers had avoided them.

Kirtn touched her reassuringly. "That's more than enough light. See? There isn't any garbage to stumble over here."

"I suppose the machine would keep the hospital clean as long as it could," she said, peering into the dense shadows at the far end of the room. She inhaled deeply, glad to breathe air that was not thick with the stench of decay. "What's that?"

He took a few steps forward, staring toward the

darkness. Vague turquoise lights glimmered back at him, shifting with a fluid grace that was fascinating. "I'm not sure."

The sphere of light moved farther into the room, lighting a different section. The turquoise dance beckoned as charmingly as The Luck's smile.

"A pool!" she whistled, delight sliding through each note.

Kirtn shared her joy but was more cautious. He had not forgotten that God's House might hold less than divine surprises.

She stepped forward eagerly, anticipating the feeling of warm water supporting her exhausted body.

"Rheba."

"But—" She sighed and slowed down. He was right.

"I like to swim even more than you do," he said quietly. "Remember the acid pond on Loo."

She stopped. She sniffed the air carefully, wondering if his more acute sense of smell had picked up the oily, biting odor of acid. She inhaled again. All she could smell was air that was both fresh and blessedly moist. Outside, the planet's air was not only thinner than she was used to, it was much more dry.

"It smells like water," said Kirtn.

Rheba did not answer. She grabbed her head and tried not to moan aloud. Fssa was talking with Rainbow.

Kirtn realized what had happened, even though he felt only mild discomfort. He picked her up and hurried farther into the room. Distance was the only medicine he could give her.

The sphere of light flickered madly, then went out, leaving only her racing akhenet lines to light the room. He swore with a poet's rage, wishing Fssa were within reach. He tried to give her his own energy to withstand the pain, only to discover that even his Bre'n strength had reached an end.

He carried her as far as the edge of the pool, then held her, trying to shield her with his body even though he knew it was impossible. Below his feet the pool shifted and slid, blue on blue, stirred by invisible currents. Streamers of turquoise wound throughout, leaving midnight shadows far below. If there was a bottom, he could not see it. He stared down, wondering what miraculous therapies the Zaarains had performed in the pool's depths.

And then the floor began to move.

Kirtn's reflexes saved him and Rheba from being shunted into the pool. As he leaped backward he spun and fled for the door.

The floor moved faster.

Rheba screamed and twisted in his arms, calling out for Fssa to stop. But the Fssireeme could not hear and she could not bear the pain any longer. She clawed wildly at Kirtn, not knowing what she did.

The floor hummed musically beneath Kirtn's running feet. He hung on to Rheba and forced his exhausted body to run faster, not to stumble despite her body twisting in his arms.

Stop it, fire dancer!

His need reached her as no words could. She went limp, biting her lips until blood blurred the akhenet patterns on her face.

The floor flew beneath his feet, but he was a man on a treadmill making progress only in his mind. She saw the pool looming over his shoulder, saw the turquoise glide of currents and blue depths.

Kirtn!

Her scream was as silent as his had been, a minor

mind dance that was born out of need and the close-
ness of their flesh. He reached deep into himself and
answered with a burst of speed that made the pool
fall away from her horrified glance.

But he was only flesh and bone, no match for an
immortal Zaarain machine. With a despairing cry he
felt the floor fall away, throwing them into the turquoise stomach of God.

The Bre'n's last thought was a smoking curse that
The Luck, inevitably, had avoided falling into the
soup.

XVIII

After the first shock of being thrown in passed, Kirtn realized that his worst fears were not true—the pool was nothing like acid. The liquid was both warm and cool, thicker than water but not at all sticky. It was wonderfully invigorating, like being in the center of an akhenet healing circle while minds danced in each cell of his body.

Buoyed by the liquid, he had to swim very little to keep Rheba and himself afloat. She lay loosely against him, only half conscious. If she still felt the agony of alien communication, it did not show on her face. Her hair spread out in the water, sinuous with invisible currents of energy.

If this was being "in the soup," Kirtn thoroughly approved. He was not reckless, however. He made sure that neither he nor Rheba accidentally drank any of the fluid.

And then he felt his clothes dissolve.

He watched in horrified fascination as his cape

thinned around Rheba's shoulders, revealing her glowing akhenet lines.

Rheba murmured sleepily. Her eyes opened, clear cinnamon with fires banked, at peace. Then she remembered where she was. With a startled cry she awoke fully. Her lines of power flared into incandescence, lighting the pool until it was like floating in the golden eye of God.

"What happened?"

"We're in the soup," whistled Kirtn smugly. There was an undertone of uncertainty in his whistle, however. He had not forgotten their clothes; the same thing could happen to their bodies. But he doubted it. Floating in the supportive warmth of the pool with his fire dancer alive in his arms, he found it hard to worry about anything. "How do you feel?"

"Good," she said simply. "I haven't felt this . . . *whole* . . . in a long time. Not since Deva."

He smiled as her hair flowed sinuously over his shoulder and curled around his neck. The energy that came from that touch was as smooth and controlled as any he had ever felt from master dancers on Deva.

"I wonder why the natives fight this?" She sighed, moving only enough to stay afloat.

"We haven't tried to get out yet," said Kirtn, but there was no force to his objection. If Square One's God wanted to kill them with kindness, so be it. There certainly were worse ways to die—he had seen them.

Rheba laughed, sensing his comfort because she was touching him. She concentrated on sending him a picture of a Bre'n floating smugly on a turquoise cloud. He smiled and wound his hand into her hair, noting absently that each strand was silky and . . . dry. Whatever the soup was made of, it had unusual properties for a fluid.

Her cheek rubbed over the palm of his hand. He sensed her surprise and the reason for it at the same instant she did.

"It's healed!" she said, grabbing his hand and looking at it from all sides. She took his other hand and touched it wonderingly. "Completely healed."

A sphere of light blazed forth and hovered overhead, making the room lighter than any day. She examined her Bre'n critically, swimming around him, trying to find the multitude of bruises, gashes and scrapes that the rockfall had left on him. His copper fur was sleek and bright, unmarred by so much as a scab or a smudge of dirt.

Kirtn reached out lazily, drawing her to him with the full strength of a Bre'n. "You're healed, too. Look at that light you made. Or are you drawing on the Installation's core?"

She moved her head in a slow negative, still fascinated by his strength, a fluid ease that echoed the power implicit in the currents coiling beneath their feet. "Although," she whistled, "I feel strong enough to take on a Zaarain core now."

"Don't," he said quickly. "Not unless we have to. No use in pushing our luck—or is it Daemen's?" He sighed. "I suppose we should go back and see how he's doing."

"Wait. Fssa isn't through yet."

"He isn't? Does it still hurt?"

"Sort of," she whistled, "but it's all far away, as though it were happening to someone else."

"I could get fond of this soup," he said approvingly. But even as he spoke he was measuring the height of the pool's rim, looking for a way out. The better he felt, the less willing he was to be the captive of even a benign God. "More light."

He had used a mentor's tone. She responded with a reflexive outpouring that nearly blinded him.

"Control," he said crisply, as though giving lessons back on Deva. "Outline the rim of the pool."

A line of light snaked around the lip of the pool, defining it. There was no place where the rim dipped down enough for him to grab it and pull himself out.

"Arm's length below water level," he said.

A second line of light bloomed. He swam along the side. There were no steps, no ramps, no irregularities in the seamless pool wall. Getting in had been easy. Getting out would be a trick.

Currents curled beneath him. Fluid humped up, lifting him until the lip was within reach. In a single motion he pulled himself out of the pool.

Getting out was as easy as wanting to.

A globe of light followed him as he walked back to where Rheba swam in the center of her own incandescence. "Come to the side," he called.

"I'm trying to." Her whistle was sharp, telling of the fear that was growing in her. "It won't let me!"

Kirtn's powerful dive brought him to her side in an instant. Currents swirled around her, holding her back from the side with exactly as much energy as she expended trying to advance. Her lines were so hot that steam began to curl up from the fluid.

"Don't fight it," he said.

She stopped trying to swim toward the side. Immediately the currents stopped trying to hold her back. She looked at him, her expression both perplexed and frightened. "Why won't it let me go?"

"I don't know. It practically threw me out." He swam behind her. "Let me do the swimming for both of us."

She relaxed against his grip, floating up behind

him as he stroked for the side. After a few moments he saw that he was not making any progress. He reversed direction. The current died as quickly as it had been born.

He experimented, swimming in all directions with Rheba. It became obvious that he could tow her anywhere in the pool, except to the side. Whenever he got within reach of the rim, currents swirled up and pushed him back to the center of the pool. If he let go of her, however, the liquid was very cooperative. He could swim where he pleased and get out as easily as he had the first time.

"Are you tired?" he asked, using Senyas, because he did not want to reveal any more of his fear than he had to.

"No. I think I could fall asleep and the damn stuff would keep me face up." Her tone was more frustrated than afraid, now. She felt better when he was in the soup with her. "I suppose I could just vaporize the little beastie."

Kirtn pulled himself out of the pool, the better to measure its size. It was big. "That wouldn't work unless you tapped the Installation core. And there's a good chance that some kind of defense mechanism is programmed into the recycler."

"*Self*-defense," she said firmly. "This soup is *alive.*"

He hesitated, then accepted her verdict. She had a much finer discrimination among energy patterns than he did. If she said it did not feel like a machine, then it was not a machine.

She took his hesitation as a question, however. "Mentor," she said in clipped Senyas, "when you first hit the soup, what did you feel?"

"Surprise, then pleasure. Intense pleasure," he added, remembering.

"But you should have been scared right out of your copper fur."

He realized she was right.

"What you felt," she continued, "was the *zoolipt's* pleasure. We were very nice Treats."

"I thought this was the hospital, not the recycler."

"To the Zaarains, the functions might have been the same thing. Or they became the same thing here, in Square One."

"That would explain the clean room," said Kirtn. "The zoolipt ate all the organic goodies."

"Right," said Rheba, sounding just like Scuvee. "Somewhere down there beneath my naked feet must be connectors leading out of the Installation to feeding stations."

"Wonder what the zoolipt is planning for dinner."

"I hope fire dancer isn't on the menu," she said, looking longingly at the lip that the soup would not let her reach. "Why did it let you go?"

"Maybe it doesn't like furries."

She made a flatulent noise and turned her back on him. "Kirtn, *get me out.*"

He did the only thing he could. He dove in and surfaced beside her. "It healed us when it could more easily have killed us," he said reasonably. "It's keeping Fssa from driving you crazy talking to Rainbow."

She held his hand and watched him with wide eyes.

"You sensed its pleasure," he added, wrapping a stray curl of her gold hair around his finger. "Do you sense any malevolence?"

She closed her eyes and drifted against him, concentrating on the intricate energy patterns that made up the zoolipt. She sensed its power, the sweeping currents that moved restlessly in its depths. She felt again its pleasure as it lapped around their alien chemistries. No matter how hard she concentrated, she could feel nothing else except her own fear and the distant pain that was a Fssireeme talking to a Zaarain construct.

"Nothing." She sighed. "But I'm not a mind dancer or even an empathic engineer."

He pulled her close, not knowing what else to do. They floated passively on the breast of the zoolipt. It responded to their unspoken needs, supporting their bodies like an invisible, infinitely comfortable bed.

"It's gone," she said, after a moment.

"What's gone?"

"The pain. Fssa must be finished." Then, fervently, "I want *out.*"

A current swirled her out of Kirtn's arms and deposited her on the lip of the pool. The zoolipt withdrew from her without leaving so much as a drop of itself behind.

He stared, then swam toward the side with powerful strokes. Fluid bunched up underneath him like a wave and flipped him neatly into the air. He landed on his feet beside her, looking as surprised as she did.

As one, they turned and stared at the glimmering turquoise zoolipt.

"I think," said Rheba slowly, "that it's like the *Devalon's* womb. It only lets you out when you're healed. As long as I felt pain, I was a patient. As soon as Fssa shut up, I was a human being again and could come and go as I pleased."

Despite her confident words, she backed away as she spoke. If her theory was wrong, she did not want to find out by ending up in the soup again. As an afterthought, she even took back all but a small sphere of her light. She did not want to irritate an organism that spent most of its time in darkness.

Daemen's voice came from the hallway beyond the room. "Kirtn! Rheba! Where are you?"

"In here," yelled Kirtn.

"But that's the recycler! I told you"—Daemen ran into the room breathlessly—"to turn right, not left!"

"We did," Kirtn said dryly.

"Oh." Daemen looked at his feet, obviously embarrassed. "I never could tell the two apart. . . ." He looked up again, then away, embarrassed for a different reason. "What happened to your clothes?"

Rheba remembered they were naked and smothered a giggle.

"The zoolipt ate them," said Kirtn blandly.

Daemen threw a frightened look around, for the first time noticing the pool where tone on tone of blue turned restlessly. "Oh!" He backed up nearly all the way to the hall. "That's *much* bigger than our zoolipt. And it's the wrong color. I'm not sure it's a recycler at all!"

"It recycled our clothes fast enough," pointed out Rheba, trying not to smile.

Daemen looked up, realized that neither Kirtn nor Rheba was embarrassed, and smiled at her in a way that made the Bre'n want to flatten him.

"You certainly look good—ah, healthy," amended Daemen, as he walked back to them. He stroked her skin as his raincolored eyes looked at her with obvious pleasure. "Beautiful. I mean, even the scrapes are gone."

Kirtn knew exactly what he meant.

"The zoolipt healed us," she said, feeling suddenly awkward beneath Daemen's admiring glance. She remembered Kirtn's insistence that The Luck was not a child. "Look at Kirtn's hands."

Reluctantly, Daemen turned away from the fire dancer's fascinating body where intricate curling patterns pulsed with light. He looked at Kirtn's powerful hands and then up at the Bre'n's metallic gold eyes. Kirtn smiled. Daemen backed away from Rheba.

"Where's Fssa?" she asked.

Daemen rummaged around beneath the frayed cape he wore. "Said he was cold," he explained, unwrapping the Fssireeme from around his waist and handing him to Rheba.

Kirtn sighed. Just when he was ready to strangle the little smoothie, Daemen proved he was not a cherf after all. The Bre'n knew that Daemen did not want to handle the Fssireeme at all, much less keep the snake warm by wearing him like a girdle. If The Luck would just keep his hands off Rheba, Kirtn might even come to like him.

Fssa was quite dark and noticeably cool to Rheba's touch. Immediately she gathered energy and held it in her hair. When it whipped and shot sparks, she wove the Fssireeme into place. Her hair calmed as the snake drew off excess energy into himself.

Within moments, Fssa was rippling with metallic colors, as bright as the dancer's hair he was woven into. He whistled a complicated Bre'n trill. Rheba and Kirtn listened, then turned toward The Luck. Rheba looked concerned. The Bre'n looked like a predator.

"What's he saying?" asked Daemen nervously.

"Not much." Rheba's voice was quick, her words rushed. "Rainbow is happy. It collected a few more crystals—two swaps and seven outright thefts, from what Fssa says." She hesitated, remembering Daemen's obvious fear of the zoolipt's blue depths. "The zoolipt is ecstatic. We're the first new taste it's had in Cycles. Fssa said it was very bored with garbage, sewage, and dead bodies."

Daemen's hands made small movements. Even talking about the zoolipt's gastronomic needs made him nervous.

"Fssa also said that the barbarians are waiting outside."

"For us?"

"For food. They didn't expect us to come out. At least, not as ourselves. The few live people who are thrown in die of fright."

"Sensible," muttered The Luck, looking nervously at the zoolipt's too-active blue surface.

"However," continued Rheba, "there are legends of willing Treats."

Daemen looked up, sensing that she was finally coming to the point.

"Do you know how the barbarians recognize willing Treats when they come out of God's House?" she asked gently.

"They're alive," snapped Daemen.

"That's part of it," she agreed. "The rest of it is that they're naked, clean, and in perfect health."

Daemen looked at the two of them and then at his own grubby, scuffed self. "Oh no . . ."

"Oh *yes!*" said Kirtn triumphantly.

Without warning, he snatched The Luck and heaved him into the soup. Daemen's indignant squawk ended in a huge splash.

"That was mean," observed Rheba.

Kirtn's only answer was a whistle that rippled with satisfaction.

XIX

."Do you suppose he'll be in long?" asked Rheba.

Kirtn stretched hugely, flexing muscles that were no longer strained and sore. "Doubt it. He was hardly scratched. Lucky cherf. Gets everyone else to do his work for him."

"What do you mean?"

He smiled and ruffled her electric hair. "His technology just fell into his hands, but he doesn't even know it."

"I think the zoolipt fed you something it didn't feed me. You're still floating."

He laughed and blew into her hair. It rose around him like fine gold smoke, shimmering with life. He had never seen her so vivid. "What do the Seurs need more than anything else?"

She sent up a tendril of hair to tickle his sensitive ears. "Decent food," she said, grimacing at the memory of her one Seur meal. "Reliable wouldn't hurt, either."

He peeled away the maddening hair and wound it around his finger. "Right," he said, echoing Scuvee. "And what does the zoolipt want?"

"Treats," she said promptly. Then, "Of course! But how do you get the Seurs to the zoolipt? I don't think they would mix well with Scuvee's folks."

"That's The Luck's problem."

They looked at the pool. Daemen was floating helplessly, a bemused look on his face. He obviously could not swim. It did not matter. The zoolipt supported him as surely as solid ground, and far more comfortably.

"Still has his clothes," noted Kirtn.

"I hope he's all right," said Rheba. "He was pretty scared."

The Bre'n made a flatulent noise that stirred Fssa's admiration. The snake hissed blissfully, reveling in Rheba's lively hair. He was all but invisible, matching his surface color exactly with the shimmering mass around him. He formed a pair of sensors and directed them at the pool.

"Daemen is fine," whistled Fssa. "He's laughing, not choking."

"I hope he doesn't drink any," she said anxiously.

"With his luck," muttered the Bre'n, "it would give him eternal life."

"There go his clothes."

"Shouldn't be long now," said Kirtn.

The zoolipt swirled in shades of blue around Daemen, then swelled into a wave.

"Here he comes." Kirtn measured the wave's direction and speed, moved three steps to the left, and caught Daemen before his feet touched the ground. "There," he said, setting The Luck upright. "That wasn't so bad, was it?"

Daemen gave the Bre'n a reproachful look. "You could have warned me."

"That's right," said Kirtn. "I could have."

The Luck hesitated. "I wouldn't have believed you anyway, I suppose."

Kirtn put his hand on The Luck's shoulder, liking him in spite of himself. "Let's pick up Rainbow and get back to the Seurs."

Daemen's smile faded. "I can't go back. I don't have anything. Fssa said that Rainbow won't work for me." He peered into Rheba's seething hair, looking for the Fssireeme. "Does he always tell the truth?"

Fssa's head darted out, sensors wheeling. He was so outraged that he formed two mouths, screaming his innocence out of one and his trustworthiness out of the other.

Rheba looked skeptical. Fssa considered Rainbow a friend and fellow sentient being. Daemen considered Rainbow a machine, and a badly tuned one at that.

"Quiet!" yelled Kirtn.

The Bre'n's bellow made Fssa wilt. One mouth vanished entirely. The other one shrank until it was almost too small to see. He blushed in dark shades of gray.

"Rainbow is irrelevant," said the Bre'n mildly.

Fssa's relieved sigh was very human.

"What do you mean?" Daemen said, his voice harsh with disappointment and irritation.

"You were just head over heels in the most advanced technology this planet has seen since the Zaarains," said Kirtn dryly. "What do you need with a collection of reluctant crystals?"

"We already have a recycler."

"Like that?"

Daemen turned and stared at the zoolipt. Turquoise lights winked back at him. "No, but . . ."

Kirtn waited.

Fssa spoke, his voice subdued but hopeful. "Square One's zoolipt is unique. When this Installation went discordant, the hospital zoolipt adapted. It spread through the connectors and merged with the recycler zoolipt. That was a long time ago. It sent some of itself through the other connectors to other Installations. That's all that saved your people when the grid went eccentric. A machine would have broken down. The zoolipt . . . evolved."

Daemen kept staring at the zoolipt, amazement and disbelief on his face. "Are you saying that pool is *alive?*"

"Yes," said Rheba before Fssa could answer. "I sensed it."

Daemen switched his look of disbelief to her. "I didn't know you were a *liwwen,*" he said flatly.

"Mind dancer," said Fssa, automatically translating the Daemenite word into a concept familiar to Rheba.

"I'm not. But a fire dancer is sensitive to patterns of energy. The zoolipt's pattern isn't that of a machine. It's alive."

Daemen looked back at the pool stretching away into the darkness. "All of it?" he said weakly.

Rheba blinked. "I hadn't thought of that."

Her hair shifted, then spread into a disciplined fan as she sampled the various energies that permeated the pool. Kirtn moved to position behind her, hands resting lightly where her neck joined her shoulders. His presence greatly enhanced both the power and precision of her search.

Daemen watched, fascinated by the play of energy through her akhenet lines. He was also more than a little fascinated by the supple body beneath the lines. His thoughts triggered the inevitable physiological response. He looked away, wishing the zoolipt had not eaten his clothes.

When Rheba was finished, she sighed and opened eyes that were as bright as her akhenet lines. Kirtn glanced over at Daemen, wondering how The Luck had reacted to seeing a healthy fire dancer at work. It did not take a mind dancer to know what The Luck was thinking. Not for the first time, Kirtn wryly decided that men had invented clothes as much to conceal their desires as to protect their genitals.

"I think just the currents are alive," said Rheba.

"What good does that do us?" said Daemen, his back to her as he stared at the zoolipt.

"It's a lot easier to take back a scoop of zoolipt than the whole pond," she said impatiently.

"I left my scoop at Centrins." Daemen's voice was more than a little sarcastic. "Besides, what good would it do?"

Rheba looked at him, puzzled.

Kirtn's lips struggled not to smile.

Fssa spoke in the tones of a patient mother. "Zoolipts are intelligent. Intelligent beings need variety. If they don't get it, they invent it. Bored zoolipts play tricks," continued the snake in round, patient tones. "If they get too bored, they go mad. Mad zoolipts eventually kill their people. I think the Centrins zoolipt is going mad."

Daemen looked around. The impact of the Fssire-eme's words drove all desire from The Luck. "What?"

"Your zoolipt is crazy," summed up the snake. "It's starving your people to death because that's more amusing than feeding them pap. It likes to see the Seurs run around and jump tables to be fed. Either it doesn't understand that it's killing the Seurs or it doesn't care anymore. It's been feeding Seurs for eons, you know," added Fssa almost apologetically. "And all it gets in return is garbage. It knows every molecule by name. The only variety it has is when something living falls into the soup. All those wonderful enzymes to play with. . . .

"At least, that's what Rainbow said about this zoolipt, and this zoolipt and yours were the same a very long time ago. Square One's zoolipt is part of a hospital zoolipt, remember. It was designed to make Fourth People healthy. If you put in some of this zoolipt with your zoolipt, the combination could be the salvation of Centrins."

The Luck stared at the Fssireeme and then at the fire dancer. "I think," said Daemen slowly, "that my Luck just ran out. I'm finally as crazy as that snake. The Seurs will never believe me."

Kirtn laughed shortly. "It doesn't matter what they believe." He leaned forward, forcing Daemen to look at him. "Don't tell the Seurs that Square One's zoolipt is alive and that Centrins' zoolipt is crazy. Just take some of this zoolipt home, pour it into the Centrins recycler and wait for 'fat times and fancy flavors' to pour out the feeding stations. After one good meal the Seurs will believe anything you tell them."

"Will it work?" asked Daemen dubiously.

"Do you have a better idea?" snapped Kirtn.

Daemen sighed. "How will we carry it?"

Rheba muttered and shook her head. Fssa dropped into her hands. "We just happen to have a container. Do your trick, snake."

With a disgruntled sound, Fssa swelled to three times his normal size. A network of metallic gray and blue glowed sullenly over his length, saying more clearly than words what he thought of the situation.

"Will that be enough?" said Daemen.

"You want any more," said Fssa, echoing oddly, "swallow it yourself!"

Rheba walked over to the pool. Currents of turquoise and blue lapped at the edges. Other currents curled just out of reach, thick and thin, more colors of blue than she could name. She looked back. "All the currents are different. Which one would be the best?"

Kirtn looked blank for a moment. Then he smiled. He took Fssa in one hand and Daemen in the other. "It's his problem. Let him solve it."

He threw snake and naked Luck into the pool.

A hearty splash was followed by hot Daemenite phrases. Very quickly, the zoolipt returned man and snake to their normal environment. Fssa bulged like a long, water-filled balloon. Kirtn snickered, further offending the Fssireeme's distended dignity.

"Are you *quite* through?" said Daemen icily to the Bre'n. "I'm tired of being tossed into the soup by an overgrown furry!"

"Anytime you can lift me, you can throw me in," offered Kirtn.

"I'll take Fssa," said Rheba, stepping between the two as she lifted the snake out of Daemen's hands. "If you made compartments," she whispered to the Fssireeme, "you wouldn't slosh so much."

Fssa's answer sounded more like a belch than anything else. He was too big to fit in his usual nest in her hair, and too heavy for her to carry easily. Kirtn saw the problem, took the snake and, apologizing, tied the Fssireeme in a loose knot around his neck.

Silently, the three walked back to the access panel.

It was closed. Rainbow was mounded in front of it, each facet shining as though it had been polished by a master jeweler.

"It's bigger," said Rheba unhappily. The bigger Rainbow got, the greater its range and the worse her headaches. "It must have swiped the core's biggest crystals." She picked up the Zaarain construct. It slid facet over facet until it was a double-strand necklace. "Here," she said, handing it over to Daemen. "You wear the damn thing. Maybe the Seurs will be impressed."

Rainbow made a wonderfully barbaric display. Shards of colored light splintered in the depths of crystals created by men and methods that were remembered only in myths.

Silently, The Luck pulled Rainbow over his head. He led Rheba and Kirtn to the front door of the Installation.

The three of them made a striking display as they stepped out of God's House and into the planet's brief twilight. The Luck's rare beauty was reflected in Rainbow's thousand facets. Kirtn wore only his suede-textured skin and a sullen Fssireeme knotted around his powerful neck. Between Luck and Bre'n stood Rheba, dressed in a blazing network of akhenet lines.

A nearby Scavenger took one look at the Treats, spun around and ran off yelling for Scuvee. She was not far away. Like most of the Scavengers, she was gathered around a feeding station, waiting for God's verdict on the Treats it had been fed.

Scuvee looked at the three people who had emerged from God's House. Then she looked at Daemen. "You must be The Luck, all right. Nobody else has walked out of there for as long as Scavengers can remember." She threw back her head and laughed triumphantly. "Fine eats and fancy flavors for sure. Then the shaval pile," she added, her glance sliding back to Kirtn.

Fssa's translation was slurred, but understandable. Rheba grimaced. "Some other time, maybe. We have to get The Luck back to his people."

Scuvee's smile vanished, leaving a hard expression behind. "Don't think so, Pretty Treat. Not until God gets bored with your taste."

Kirtn looked at the crowd that was gathering around them. The Scavengers wore expressions of awe, greed and anticipation. They watched the Treats with the eyes of a miser counting credits.

"How long will it take for God to get bored?" asked Daemen.

Scuvee spread her hands. "Not long. Two lives. Maybe three."

"Lives?" said Daemen weakly.

"Right. Don't worry, though. Legend says that when God likes your taste, it makes you immortal." She smiled, showing uneven teeth. "You've got all the time there is, Little Treat. And we've got ourselves the best eats ever."

The Scavengers folded possessively around their Treats.

XX

Sounds of muted and not-so-muted merriment fil-
tered into the house where the Treats were being
held. Scuvee's guards stood outside the door, grum-
bling about having to work while others played in a
shaval pile. They were not too disgruntled, however.
Their stomachs were stretched tightly over a dinner
that would be legend among the Scavengers.

God had truly enjoyed its Treats.

"Don't they ever sleep?" said Rheba, turning away
from the peeling window. Beyond the window's
ancient distortions, the Scavengers whooped and
laughed and chased each other from one shaval drift
to the next.

Daemen looked up glumly and said nothing.

Kirtn shrugged. If he had waited as long for a
decent meal as the Scavengers had, he would cele-
brate too. He picked absently at flakes of window
dangling from invisible fibers.

The material was very tough. Rheba had tried to

burn some of it. After a lot of energy, it smoldered
fitfully and softened. She could burn their way out
of the house, but it would take a long time and more
energy than she could easily draw from moonlight.
Sunrise would be a different matter. Energy would
be abundant and, she hoped, the Scavengers would
be comatose after a night of celebration.

If forced to, Rheba would tap the Zaarain core.
Neither she nor Kirtn wanted that. Zaarain energies
were highly complex, dangerous and difficult to channel. Even a master dancer with centuries of experience would hesitate to tangle with a Zaarain core.

There was also the fact that once tapped, the core
might go eccentric. The Scavengers who survived that
would live only long enough to die of starvation. Neither Rheba nor Kirtn wanted to be responsible for
more deaths.

On the other hand, neither one of them planned to
spend the next few centuries as Treats for a shapeless
God.

"Scuvee's coming," said Kirtn, turning away from
the peeling window.

"Probably wants you for the shaval pile," snapped
Rheba.

He smiled and wisely said nothing.

Fssa, still loosely knotted around Kirtn's neck,
extruded a dish-shaped listening apparatus and
pointed it at the door. He added a circle of metallic
red quills that quivered and combed the air as though
alive. Ripples of metallic colors coursed over his distended body.

Daemen stared, still unused to seeing Fssireeme
transformations. Rheba and Kirtn watched for a different reason. It was rare to see Fssa having difficulty
picking up Fourth People speech.

Fssa changed again, substituting a convex dish for the concave one. Quills vanished, only to reappear as a platinum ruff around the dish. Rheba and Kirtn looked at each other. They had never seen the Fssireeme in that shape. Whatever was beyond that door was something new.

Silently, Kirtn set Fssa on the floor and came to stand behind Rheba. She gathered energy, preparing for whatever the next minutes might bring.

The door opened. A battered Scuvee walked in. Her jaw was so swollen she could not talk. Her grunts and gestures were enough, though. She pointed to the porch, pushed the guard who had followed her into the room back over the threshold and slammed the door.

Instantly, Fssa changed back into a snake and began spouting long phrases in a language that was neither Universal nor Daemenite. Scuvee's face blurred and reformed into the colorless features of f'lTiri, the Yhelle illusionist Rheba had rescued on Loo.

F'lTiri smiled, changing his face from bland to slyly humorous. "Surprised?" he asked in soft Yhelle.

Fssa translated unobtrusively into Senyas. Although f'lTiri knew Universal, so did quite a few of the natives. It would be safer to speak Yhelle and not to be understood by eavesdroppers.

"How did you get here?" demanded Kirtn in Senyas. "Is the ship safe?"

Rheba visibly burned with unasked questions, but she waited to hear f'lTiri's explanations.

The Yhelle looked a little uncomfortable. "The ship is as safe as it can be without full power."

"I told the *Devalon* not to let anyone in or out without my express permission," said Kirtn flatly. "As long as the ship is intact, it obeys me. You're here, so the ship isn't intact."

F'lTiri looked even more uncomfortable. He sighed. "Ilfn told me you'd be difficult."

"Ilfn?" Kirtn's voice was sharp. "Is she all right? And Lheket?"

The illusionist knew what Ilfn and Lheket meant to Kirtn. As the only other akhenet team that was known to have survived Deva, the female Bre'n and male storm dancer represented the only future the races of Senyas and Bre'n had. "They're both fine," said f'lTiri quickly.

"Then how—"

"Kirtn." Rheba's hand subtly restrained the Bre'n. "Let him talk. When he's finished you can chew on him or whoever else has it coming. If they've done anything to the *Devalon,* I'll cook them and feed them to you myself."

F'lTiri shuddered and looked away from Rheba's eyes. "The ship is as you left it, with one minor change. Ilfn is giving the orders."

"Ilfn?" Rheba's voice was doubtful. "The only way she would disobey Kirtn was if Lheket's life was at stake."

"Exactly. The J/taals figured that out rather quickly. They told her that if she didn't open the ship and let them come after you, they'd kill Lheket."

"They don't speak Universal and she doesn't speak J/taal," said Kirtn, his voice cold. "How would they communicate?"

"Ever heard of sign language? A knife, for instance? Held at a boy's throat while two J/taals stand by the downside access?"

The Bre'n winced. He could see the J/taals doing just that. What's more, they would have carried out their threat. They had no compunctions about heaven or hell where Rheba's safety was concerned. "Go on," he said, letting his anger slide away.

The Yhelle drew a slow breath of relief. "Ilfn said if I survived the first few questions, you'd be reasonable." He looked sideways. "Your race is as short-tempered as it is strong. Ilfn was ... *angry* at the J/taals."

"Tell him something he doesn't know," suggested Rheba dryly.

"I decided to come along with the J/taals. Without your magic snake"—he gestured to Fssa—"communication is uphill and into the wind. Enough of the Seurs knew Universal for me to be useful."

"I hope they were grateful," said Kirtn.

"The J/taals?"

"No. The Seurs. The J/taals would have gone through them like a lightgun through pap, looking for Rheba."

The illusionist's smile was thin. "We lost a few Seurs on our way to Tric. They should have known better than to take on two J/taals and their clepts. Tric was smart. He loaded us onto a mover and shot us out of Centrins before the fighting started."

"Fighting?"

"Riot," amended f'lTiri. "Seems that something has gone wrong with their food machine: First it turned out unprocessed sewage, then it stopped entirely. Everyone blamed the Seurs. When the mover pulled out, Centrins looked like payday in Chaos."

"How did you get through the tunnel?"

"There wasn't much of the rockfall left." He made a gesture of admiration toward Kirtn. "Even the J/taals were impressed. I left them at the tunnel," he added. "I couldn't cover them with my illusion.

Then I listened around one of those native piles until I figured out what had happened. After that, it was just a matter of getting a look at Super Scavenger Scuvee." He smiled with an illusionist's pride. "Clever of me to figure a way around the language problem, wasn't it?"

The swollen face of Scuvee returned. F'lTiri grunted and waved his arms. The Scavenger face blurred into illusionist laughter.

"Very clever," agreed Kirtn, bending down and picking up Fssa. He knotted the snake loosely around his neck and pulled up the hood that was attached to the Scavenger robes the Treats had been given. Fssa poked out his head, sensors wheeling with colors. "Put on Scuvee's face again," said Kirtn. "The sooner we get to the tunnel, the safer I'll feel. Fssa, can you take care of the voice?"

"Right," said the snake, flawlessly reproducing Scuvee's rasping tone.

"Can you make the illusion of a rope around our wrists?" asked Kirtn. "We were tied when we came here. We should be tied when we leave."

Startlingly realistic ropes appeared around their wrists. "Like that?"

"Too good. The ropes here are dirty and frayed."

The illusion flickered, then reformed more convincingly.

"Good. 'Scuvee' will take the lead," said Kirtn. "If anyone asks, even unwilling Treats get a turn in a shaval pile. To make sure we don't get away, she's taking us to a small one where she can keep her eye on us. Got that?"

F'lTiri clapped his hands, agreement and appreciation in a single gesture. As he turned toward the door, his face changed. As far as the guards could see, it was Scuvee who walked out leading the three Treats.

"Shaval," grunted Scuvee to the surprised guards.

The guards hesitated, then stepped aside. "How about us?"

Scuvee pointed toward the nearest shaval drift. Clouds of the gold dust flew up as happy Scavengers groped and thrashed toward consummation. She grunted again.

The guards did not wait for a second invitation. They raced toward the drift, shedding clothes as they went. With loud whoops they vanished into the pile.

F'lTiri sniffed the fragrant motes of shaval that drifted toward them. He sighed. "If I were a trader, I'd sell that stuff and die rich."

Laughter and shrieks of pleasure punctuated the darkness as F'lTiri led the three Treats toward the tunnel. Once they heard a hoarse shout, angry surprise followed by curses. Kirtn speeded up until he was stepping on f'lTiri's heels. The illusionist, who had also heard the shout, redoubled his speed.

Several times they had to detour around shaval drifts that were filled to overflowing with benignly demented Scavengers. Until the shaval wore off, nothing much smaller than the end of the world would be noticed by many of the inhabitants of Square One.

Long before the escaping Treats reached the tunnel, the cliff face loomed over them, cutting off half the sky. Beyond the cliff mountains rose, stone piled on stone in dark abandon.

"Hurry," whistled Fssa around the gurgling sound he made while sloshing about Kirtn's neck. "Someone's following. I think it's Scuvee. She must have come back for Kirtn and discovered we were gone."

They moved as quickly as they could, but it was

not fast enough. Behind them came clear sounds of pursuit, shouts and curses and hoarse cries of encouragement.

The clepts found them before they reached the tunnel in the cliff face. The war dogs materialized out of the night, touched Rheba with their blunt muzzles and vanished. Almost immediately they returned with M/dere and M/dur. Both J/taals touched Rheba as though to reassure themselves that it was their J/taaleri in the flesh. Then they hustled everyone into the tunnel and posted a clept to guard the entrance.

From the trail came shouts, the real Scuvee's among them. A second clept leaped out to help the first. The war dogs stood slightly apart, silver eyes gleaming in the night, waiting for a command to kill. Beyond them gathered the Scavengers, at least sixty of them milling in the moonlight.

"Give me light!" said Daemen urgently, shoving past Kirtn into the tunnel. "I've got to get to the mover discs!"

Rheba gave Daemen a bright light and got out of his way. She scrambled after them through the narrow opening in the rockfall that the J/taals had made. The sounds of shouting acted as a goad. Scuvee had dragged enough people out of shaval drifts to make a mob.

"Have you found anything yet?" Rheba called to Daemen.

"Bad Luck!" swore Daemen. "These discs are cracked. We'll have to go farther into the tunnel and find others."

"Will it take long?" asked Rheba, glancing nervously over her shoulder. The mob sounded as if it was nearly at the tunnel.

"Depends on how fast you can run."

"Fssa. Tell the clepts not to hurt anyone if they can help it, but to hold off the Scavengers until you whistle. Then tell the dogs to run like the hounds of death."

Fssa uttered a series of grunts, clicks and gravel-like sounds that composed the language of the J/taals. The third clept vanished into the narrow tunnel through the rockfall.

Kirtn's hand closed around Rheba's arm, nearly lifting her off her feet. A clept's snarl echoed chillingly back down the tunnel. Rheba ran next to Kirtn, cursing the loose Scavenger robes that threatened to trip her with each stride. After a moment she realized that the J/taals had not followed her. They had gone back to the rockfall to protect their J/taaleri's retreat.

Daemen ran with surprising speed, his robe bunched in his left hand, legs flying. The illusionist was right behind, his breath coming hoarsely. Rheba and Kirtn followed, Fssa gurgling and thumping with each step.

The tunnel seemed endless. Finally Daemen skidded to a halt and began casting around frantically along both sides of the tunnel. Rheba doubled the light and leaned against Kirtn, panting with the violence of their run.

Daemen muttered up and down the tunnel and then pounced like a hungry clept. "Discs!"

Rheba and Kirtn crowded around him. Discs stretched across the tunnel. Daemen stepped from one to the next until he had activated nine of them, one for each person and three for the clepts.

"Stand next to me," he said, gesturing impatiently. "And call in the J/taals."

Fssa sent a punishing burst of sound back down

the tunnel. If there was an answer, only the snake heard it.

"Now what?" said Kirtn, standing next to The Luck.

"A mover condenses," he said. Then muttered, "I hope."

"Aren't you sure?" said Rheba.

"It's a Zaarain machine," said The Luck. "It usually works, but it's old."

Silently, they stood and waited for the mover to form. Nothing happened. They looked at Daemen. His eyes were closed. He seemed to be praying.

The J/taals and clepts appeared with the astonishing speed that was part of their deadly mercenary skills. Without being told, they formed a protective ring around Rheba. Daemen opened his eyes, approved the J/taals' positions, and resumed exhorting his gods.

From the tunnel came the sounds of the Scavenger mob. Daemen sweated and muttered but did not open his eyes. The sounds became louder. Rheba gathered what energy she could, but in the black tunnel she was as close to helpless as a fire dancer could be.

The mob burst into howls of triumph as they saw the group illuminated by dancer light. F'lTiri projected a monstrous image at the same instant that Rheba shimmered into flame. The Scavengers faltered, then rushed forward in a mass to reclaim their Treats.

A mover condensed silently, inexorably around The Luck and his friends, dividing them from the Scavengers. The last thing the Treats heard before the mover enclosed them was Scuvee's anguished wail.

XXI

Centrins was subdued, a city exhausted after an orgy of violence. There were no Seurs out, no robes or whips to be seen. Just small groups of people slinking from alley to alley, looking as battered as the buildings and as hungry as the shadows.

Rheba shivered and moved closer to her Bre'n. Their only comfort was the slender grace of the *Devalon* rising above the windblown streets. She was grateful for the mover's invisible barrier around them. The people of Centrins had the mean look of skinning knives.

Kirtn put his arm around her, sensing her unease. He, too, wished to be inside the *Devalon's* familiar protection. The Scavengers had been angry but not desperate. Centrins was another matter entirely. People huddled sullenly around the outlying feeding stations, ignoring the cold wind that chased tattered bits of cloth along cracked pavements.

The Luck looked unhappily at the view provided by the mover. If the Seurs had been gaunt, these people were skeletal. Centrins' Luck had run out the day they shipped his mother off planet. "Why?" he said hoarsely. "Why didn't they just let her stay?"

Kirtn looked at Daemen and said simply, "They wanted to change their Luck. They did."

"She wasn't *other*."

The Bre'n sighed and said nothing. Daemen's mother was dead, a variety of Luck that came to all living things. "They must have been desperate," he said finally.

Daemen made a strangled sound that even a Fssire-eme could not translate.

Centrins rose out of the gray city that later men had built in the shadow of Zaarain magnificence. Multicolored and as multilayered as a dream, the building's outer walls glistened with enigmas that had been old before akhenets were more than an evolutionary promise.

"I can see why they called it God's House," murmured Rheba. "Anything that beautiful can scarcely be human." She glanced at her Bre'n, whose beauty was as much an enigma to her as a Zaarain construct. "You should live there, mentor."

Kirtn smiled oddly, almost sadly. "Would you live with me, little dancer?"

She looked up and saw herself reflected in golden Bre'n eyes. For an instant she felt as beautiful as he, then he blinked and the instant passed. Tears came to her eyes, eyes that had wept only once since Deva died. "I'm not a god."

"Neither am I." His voice was gentle, but very final.

She looked at him, remembering his eyes glowing gold out of the tunnel's darkness as he lifted boulders nearly as large as himself, Bre'n power and beauty that no Senyas could equal. She looked at him and

felt like an awkward child stumbling in the wake of
perfection, awed and almost resentful.

*It's you who call fire, not me. It's you who burn with
inhuman beauty, not me. You are like flames, color and
grace and heat. Look at the Face you wear. See yourself as
you are. Or are you still so young that you want to worship
instead of love?*

Kirtn's voice in her mind was like a blow. She pushed
away from him, ending the touch that had made mind
dancing possible. Even then the intensity of his communication almost overwhelmed her, echoes of his emotions and her own seething through her so quickly that
she could not separate them into understanding.

Her hand went up to her earring, an object that
was both jewelry and teaching device. She touched the
Bre'n carving that turned with her every movement, a
Face hidden within the restless cloud of her hair. She
did not need to see the Face to remember it, Bre'n
profiles aloof and serene, sensual and laughing, changing and yet changeless as a sea. Once she thought she
had seen herself in the carving but the image was like
a wave breaking, gone before she could fix its reality.

Centrins closed around the mover, startling her.

"Where does the mover stop?" asked Kirtn, looking
at the courtyards and residences that were part of the
Zaarain building's colorful interior.

"In the Seur residence."

"I should have guessed," said Kirtn sourly.

Daemen turned to face the Bre'n. It did not take
a mind dancer to guess his thoughts. "Don't worry.
I'm The Luck. I'm coming back with my find. They'll
be glad to see me."

Kirtn stared. "If you believe that, you shouldn't be
let out of the nursery without a guard."

The Luck's skin darkened with embarrassment or

anger. "It's our way," he said tightly. "I don't expect you to understand."

Kirtn looked over Daemen's shoulder where the Seur quarters rose out of a ruined garden. Ragged rows of Seurs were gathered around the discs where movers condensed or dissolved. Neither the expressions on their faces nor the weapons in their hands looked welcoming.

"My understanding isn't the problem," said Kirtn, pointing toward the Seurs. "Save your arguments for them."

Daemen turned, assessed the waiting Seurs, and made a sound of disbelief. "Don't they understand? I'm here to save them. I'm their Luck!"

Kirtn's big hand closed over Daemen's shoulder, forcing the young man's attention. "It's you who don't understand," said the Bre'n gently. "You touched their food and it turned to shit. Remember?"

Daemen's mouth opened and closed soundlessly. He shook his head as though to rid himself of doubts. "When I explain, they'll understand."

Kirtn looked at Rheba, silently asking her to argue with The Luck.

She saw Daemen's confusion, his youth, his vulnerability. "We'll help you, Daemen. If it weren't for Rainbow you wouldn't be in this mess."

"The best way to help him would be to get his smooth ass off this planet," snapped Kirtn.

Daemen looked shocked. "I can't leave. They'll die. They need me. I am—"

"—their Luck," finished the Bre'n dryly. "I know. You've told us often enough." He measured the waiting Seurs. "You might be able to kill them, but convince them you're Good Luck? Even a Fssireeme wouldn't have enough mouths to do that."

"Then I'll have to get around them," he said stubbornly.

"That's a good idea," said Rheba. "Is there another entrance?"

Daemen hesitated. "Centrins isn't like Square One. Just the core area is the same. But once we get there, it won't take long to dump in the zoolipt," he added hopefully.

"What," said Kirtn distinctly, "is between us and the core?"

"Three doors. No, four. The first two don't fit very well and the last two are never locked."

Kirtn's whistle made Rheba's teeth ache. "That's all? Just four doors and all the Seurs Centrins can muster?" He smiled sourly. "You don't need us. You need a J/taal army!"

"He doesn't have a J/taal army," pointed out Rheba. Even the J/taals cringed at Kirtn's answering whistle.

Before Rheba could shape a retort, the mover dissolved. This time Kirtn was not caught unprepared. He steadied f'lTiri with one hand and Rheba with the other. Daemen, naturally, landed on his feet.

The Seurs moved only enough to let Tric come to the front. Behind him the ranks closed with seamless finality. It was obvious that nothing—particularly Bad Luck—was going to get through the Seurs alive.

Tric walked forward a few steps, then stood looking sorrowfully at his sister's son. "I'd hoped never to see you again."

There was little Daemen could say to that.

"Haven't you discovered it yet?" asked Tric.

"What?" asked Daemen, finding his voice.

"You're Bad Luck," said Tric, his tone gentle and terribly sad. "Bad. Luck."

"No."

"Listen to me," Tric said, his eyes pleading for understanding, for forgiveness, for a future free of Luck. "Your mother felt the way you do and for a long time I believed her. We thought that the problem might be a thinning of the heritage in her. It had been so long since a strong Luck had lived. None of her children showed signs of it. So we—"

Tric stopped, looked down and then aside, anywhere but at Daemen's bright young face, "We made you. Together. We were the only direct descendants of the First Luck. We thought if we—if we—" Tric stopped and this time did not start again.

Daemen stared, trying to see himself in Tric's wrinkled features. "I don't believe you."

Tric's smile was sad and swift. "You don't have to. You are what you are—The Luck. Very strong Luck. We were right. The heritage had thinned. But not in *you.*" He looked at his hands, then at his nephew and son. He sighed and forced himself to continue. "We were right. But we were very wrong, too. Your mother was going to kill herself and all her children. All but you. Then you would inherit the Luck and do for her people what she could not. She could not bring them Good Luck."

Daemen's lips moved in soundless denials. Whatever he had expected Tric to say, it had not been this.

"I couldn't let her kill herself," Tric said simply. "Yet I couldn't let her stay and kill us. Oh, she wouldn't mean to," he said, answering Daemen's unspoken objections, "any more than you meant to when you threw your necklace into the core. But unless our Luck changes we'll die just the same." He made an odd, helpless gesture. "So we put her and her family on our last ship and sent her to face her Luck alone among the stars." His voice thinned. "You were captured by slavers, weren't you?"

"Yes," Daemen's voice was a whisper. "You arranged for that, didn't you?"

"I?" Tric laughed softly. "That would have been redundant. Your mother's Luck was more than enough. But your Luck was stronger. You survived."

"Because I'm *Good Luck*."

"No," sadly, "because Bad Luck knows no end."

Daemen's face hardened, making him look older. His rain-colored eyes narrowed. "Get out of my way, Uncle or Father or whoever you are. I'm going to the core with my find, like every Luck back to the beginning of time."

The Seurs moved like grass stirred by wind. Tric stepped back until he was a part of them once more. "No."

"What have you got to lose?" said Daemen. "You told me you're dead already."

"Unless our Luck changes," corrected Tric. "It can only change if you die. Go away, Daemen. Please. Or do you hate us enough to make us kill you and be haunted by your Luck until even our souls starve?"

"I don't hate you at all!" exploded Daemen. "I want to help you!"

"Then go away."

"No." Daemen's voice was ragged. He gestured around him wildly, taking in the dead garden and trash blowing in the cold wind. "What are you afraid of? What could be worse than eating shit and waiting for your core to go eccentric and kill you?"

"I don't know," admitted Tric. "But if you stay, I'm sure we'll find out."

Kirtn watched The Luck struggle for arguments to change Tric's mind. The Bre'n knew it was futile. Tric and the other Seurs had nothing left to lose but hope. They would protect that hope any way they could.

Unobtrusively, Kirtn drew the illusionist aside. Rheba, standing slightly to the front with Daemen, did not notice. When Kirtn was sure that no one was watching, he leaned over f'lTiri and whispered in Universal, "Can you make both of us invisible long enough to get through those Seurs?"

F'lTiri measured the distance separating them from the Seurs. "I can try."

"If you can't hold it long enough, can you make us look like Seurs?"

"Of course!" said F'lTiri, obviously stung by what he took as a slur upon his abilities.

"Long enough to get to the core? Then I'll empty Fssa into the soup and we'll see what kind of Luck is with us."

"What if nothing happens?"

"Then Daemen won't have any reason to stay, will he?" said Kirtn, a snarl thickening his voice. "And my fire dancer won't be forced to kill just to stay alive."

"I'll make us invisible as long as I can." said f'lTiri, "and then I'll make us look like Seurs."

"Good." Kirtn hesitated. "If you can cover me with illusion from here, you won't have to come along."

"And be around when Rheba finds out I helped you sneak away?" F'lTiri shook his head ruefully. "I've seen what happens when she gets angry. I don't want to end up like the Loo-chim, burned so completely not even a smell is left behind."

Kirtn winced. "If things go well, she won't even know we've gone until we get back."

He did not add that little had gone well since The Luck had come home to roost.

XXII

Rheba looked from the stubborn, desperate Seurs to the young Daemen, equally stubborn. He and Tric glared at each other across stone pavements cracked by age. Like the stones, the Daemenites were locked in patterns so old their beginnings were a myth.

In the back of the ranks, near the badly fitted double door leading into Centrins' core, a Seur stumbled and fell on his neighbor, tripping him and sending him reeling against two other Seurs. They fell against the door, which popped open. A small scramble followed while the Seurs regained their composure.

The disturbance was brief, but it was enough to break Daemen's staring contest with his uncle/father. The Luck turned to Rheba. "I'll need your help to get in."

She measured the determined Seurs and the double door that was still slightly ajar. "Is that the only door?"

"No. There are three more. Only two of them close, though. The last two."

"Locks?"

Daemen made an ambivalent gesture. "They're only used on ritual days when non-Seurs aren't allowed into Centrins."

"But there are locks."

"Yes."

She gave a Bre'n shrug. "Then they'll be locked against The Luck."

She studied the problem before she said anything more. Zaarain buildings were hard to burn, as she had found out at Square One. First she would have to find a way past the Seurs, who would surely object to The Luck's presence. Then she would have to take out the locking mechanism on the last two doors. If the locks were energy-based rather than mechanical, she would have to flirt with the core that fed energy into the locks. She did not want to do that.

On the other hand, if Fssa and his cargo of zoolipt did not get into the building, the Seurs would die and so would the slinking, skeletal population beyond Centrins. Somehow she would have to find a way past the Seurs and their locks, a way that would not attract attention. She did not want to be put into the position of fighting and killing Seurs.

Then she remembered f'lTiri's skill. On Onan, he had projected an illusion that had saved their lives. Perhaps he could do the same for the Seurs on Daemen. She turned to ask the illusionist, but no one was there. She frowned and turned to her mentor.

Kirtn was gone.

She looked around. M/dur and M/dere, three clepts, and no Kirtn. Behind her was a series of interconnected courtyards, empty of all but shadows. Had

Kirtn gone to check for other openings into Centrins
or to see that no one ambushed them on their way
back?

"M/dere, did you see Kirtn leave?"

The J/taal woman recognized her name, but nothing else. She gestured apologetically.

Rheba swore. Without Fssa, she was reduced to
sign language with the J/taals, who understood no
language but their own.

"Well?" asked Daemen, who was waiting for her
answer.

"As soon as f'lTiri and Kirtn get back," said Rheba,
her cinnamon eyes searching every face and shadow
as she spoke, "I'll have f'lTiri create a diversion so
that I can sneak into the . . ."

Her voice thinned into silence as she realized that
was exactly what Kirtn had done, leaving her behind.
Her hair whipped and seethed with its own deadly
life, an incandescent warning of fire-dancer rage.

Daemen cried out and spun aside as Rheba burst
into flame. He did not know what had caused her to
burn. He was not sure he wanted to know.

J/taals and clepts ranged in fighting formation
around their J/taaleri, knowing only that she burned.
It was all they needed to know.

The Seurs gasped and drew together, sensing death
in the alien fire. They watched her burn, watched
her take their thin sunlight and condense it into
energy that blinded them. They retreated through
the door but could not pull it completely shut behind
them. They ran through the hall's blessed darkness
to the next door, where other Seurs waited.

The smell of scorched stone called Rheba out of
her rage. The ground she stood on smoked sullenly.
Nothing was left of her clothes but a fine powder

lifting on the wind. For an instant she was glad that her mentor was not there; Kirtn would have taken away her energy and scolded her for having a tantrum.

She damped her rage, controlling it as she had learned to control other kinds of energy. She did not release what she had gathered, however. She would need that to follow her Bre'n.

"Daemen." She turned toward him, her eyes burnt orange with streaks of gold pulsing, counting the instants until fire came again. "Kirtn and f'lTiri are inside. I'm going after them. Tell the Seurs to stay out of my way."

The Luck stared at her, fascinated and more than a little afraid. "How did they get inside?" he asked. But even as he objected, he moved toward the doors. He knew better than to argue when stone smoked beneath her feet.

"F'lTiri made an illusion. Invisibility," she said impatiently. "Now they're probably Seurs."

"Then why follow? We'll just call attention to them."

She looked at him with eyes gone gold in an instant. "Because f'lTiri can't hold invisibility for more than a few seconds," she snapped. "Projecting an illusion onto Kirtn and holding another illusion on himself will use up f'lTiri's strength too fast. They're going to need help to get out of there alive."

She ran toward the door.

M/dur moved so quickly that his outline blurred. Before Rheba could take another step, the J/taal wrenched open the door and disappeared inside. Two clepts followed in a soundless rush. M/dere stood in the opening, barring Rheba's entrance with a courage that astounded The Luck.

Curtly, Rheba gestured the J/taal woman aside. She did not move. Akhenet lines surged so brightly that

M/dere's grim face was revealed to the last short
black hair. Her stance told Rheba as plainly as words
that it was a J/taal's duty to protect her J/taaleri, and
protect her she would.

M/dur reappeared, ending the impasse. He and
M/dere exchanged a long look, mark of the species-
specific telepathy that was part of what made the
J/taals such formidable mercenaries. M/dere stepped aside.

Rheba went through at a run. Even so, she had
taken no more than two steps when M/dur brushed
by. She realized then that the J/taals did not want to
prevent her from finding Kirtn. They simply wanted
her to be as safe as possible while she looked. That
meant that M/dur went first and she did not follow
until he told M/dere that it was safe.

Very soon, two clepts cut in front of Rheba, forcing
her to slow down. Just ahead, the hall divided into
three branches. Rooms opened off the branches, Seur
living quarters. No one was in sight except M/dur.
He stood where the hall divided, obviously waiting
to find out which branch she wanted to follow.

"Which one leads to the core?" Rheba asked, turning to Daemen.

"Left," he said, pointing as he spoke.

M/dur spun and raced down the left hall. Rheba
waited impatiently, listening for any sign that their
presence, or Kirtn's, had been discovered.

There was no sound but her own breathing. From
all outer indications, Centrins was deserted.

She did not believe it. Silence meant only that
a reception was being prepared somewhere farther
inside the building. She prayed to the Inmost Fire
that it would not be Kirtn who was ambushed. Her
Bre'n was strong and fierce but the Seurs were many

and desperate. Without his fire dancer, he could be overwhelmed.

The thought of Kirtn struggling against a tide of Seurs sent fire coursing raggedly along her akhenet lines. Silently she fought to master her fear. Unchecked, fear would destroy her control. And without control she would lose energy and be helpless among her enemies.

By the time M/dur returned, Rheba's akhenet lines were burning evenly. Daemen looked away from her, preferring the J/taal's savage face to what he had seen in the fire dancer's serenity.

At M/dur's gesture, Rheba leaped toward the left-hand hall. She had gone no more than a few steps when the hall branched again. The narrow left branch was deserted as far as she could see. The right branch was wider—and barricaded.

She looked at Daemen. "The right one?"

"Yes," he said unhappily.

She approached the barricade, escorted by J/taals and clepts.

A long whip uncoiled with a deadly snap. Only J/taal reflexes saved Rheba. M/dur's hand flashed out, intercepting the whip before it could strike the J/taaleri. M/dur jerked. A Seur tumbled out of hiding, pulled by his own whip. M/dur twitched the whip. Its long body curled into a loop around the falling Seur. The J/taal yanked. The Seur's neck broke.

It happened so quickly that Rheba had no time to intercede. Then she saw the lethal glass shard that was the tip of the weapon. Without M/dur's speed, she would be bleeding to death from a slashed throat. She touched her forehead to M/dere in the Universal gesture of gratitude. Then she signaled everyone back from the barrier.

"Tell them to let us through," she said, measuring the barrier as she spoke to Daemen.

"It won't do any good."

"Do it."

The Luck yelled to his kinsmen beyond the barricade. If anyone heard, no one answered. He turned back to Rheba with a questioning look.

"Tell them to get out of the way," she said. "I don't want to kill anyone, but I will."

Daemen remembered Loo, and a stone amphitheater where the slave masters had died. He yelled a warning. There was no answer.

Rheba closed her eyes. She had enough energy stored to set the barricade aflame, but then what? The only energy in Centrins came from the core. She could tap it, yes, but without her Bre'n she might not be able to control the result.

She studied the barricade. It was a loose pile of furniture collected from living quarters and dumped in the hall. The speed with which the barricade had been built suggested that this was not the first time Centrins had been invaded. Apparently the city population had rioted in the past.

"Can't we just pull it apart?" suggested Daemen.

"What if more Seurs are hiding inside?"

"After what happened to the last one, I doubt if any stayed around," The Luck said dryly.

He walked up to the barricade and began tugging at a protruding chair. The J/taals did not interfere. Rheba was their concern, not The Luck. He pulled out the chair and began to work loose a table. No Seurs moved to interfere.

Rheba walked up and began helping Daemen. When they realized what she wanted, the J/taals set to work dismantling the barricade. Although the

J/taals were smaller than either Rheba or Daemen, they were far stronger. Beneath their small hands, the barricade came apart with astonishing speed. Soon they had made a path to the ill-fitting doors hidden behind the pile of furniture.

As Daemen had said, the second pair of doors was not locked. M/dur kicked them open. A clept leaped through, followed by M/dur and another clept. No shouts or sounds of battle came from the other side. Even so, M/dere waited until M/dur returned before she allowed Rheba through.

The delay irritated Rheba, increasing her fear for Kirtn. She had J/taals and clepts—and The Luck, whatever he was worth—while Kirtn had only illusion and a bloated Fssireeme.

"Hurry," muttered Rheba, her lines smoldering.

M/dur appeared, then vanished back behind the doors. Rheba did not wait for an invitation. She moved so quickly that M/dere had to jump to keep up.

Beyond the doors were signs of a hasty retreat. A partially built barricade had been abandoned. Doors on either side stood open, revealing rooms that had been ransacked of favorite possessions in the moments before Seurs were forced to flee. Pieces of clothing were scattered around, beds overturned, whole rooms askew.

There were no Seurs.

Rheba moved at a run that left Daemen behind. The J/taals ran with her, one ahead and one behind. Clepts led the race, their silver eyes gleaming in the twilight rooms as they searched for Seurs who might have stayed behind.

Fear built in Rheba with every second. It was too quiet in the hall, too quiet in the whole building. Where had the Seurs gone? What defense were they preparing? And most of all—was Kirtn still safe beneath a veil of Yhelle illusion?

The only answer to her silent questions was the sound of her own bare feet racing over ancient floors and the distant shuffle of The Luck trailing far behind. Ahead, the hall curved away.

Abruptly the clepts' claws scrabbled on smooth Zaarain surfaces as the animals swung to protect Rheba. M/dur spun in midstride, retreating down the hall with a speed that matched the clepts'. Behind him plastic knives rained onto the floor. A Seur ambush had been set where the hall curved. Once again, Rheba was grateful for the J/taals' presence.

Daemen ran up to her, calling a warning. "Beyond the curve—doors," he panted.

"And an ambush," she said, looking down the hall. She could see neither Seurs nor doors, but knew both were there, just beyond sight. "What are the doors like?" she demanded, turning her attention to him.

"Zaarain," he said bluntly.

"Weren't the other doors?"

"No. The outer one was added in my mother's time. The next one was a century older. You can tell by the fit," he added. "Seurs are archaeologists, not extruders."

"How do the doors lock?"

Daemen opened his hands in a gesture of emptiness. "They just . . . flow together."

"No seams? No bolts or other obvious mechanisms?"

"Nothing but a space for one of Tric's crystals. At least, I assume Tric has the key," he added bitterly. "It was mother's before they exiled her."

"I suppose it locks from the other side."

"Yes."

She looked at Daemen with something less than affection. At the moment she did not appreciate the quality of his luck. "Is there any other possible way to get to the recycler?"

Daemen's unhappy expression was all the answer she needed. She turned back toward the doors dividing her from her Bre'n. She glanced at M/dur, not wanting to ask him to risk his life for a quick look down the hall, but knowing he was better equipped than she was for the job.

M/dur cocked his head, pointed to his eyes and then around the curve of the hall. He cocked his head again, obviously asking a question. She made the J/taal gesture of agreement, a quick show of teeth that was both more and less than a smile.

Two clepts stole silently up to the curve, followed by M/dur. The animals vanished, M/dur only a step behind. Rheba felt her muscles tighten as she waited for screams.

Almost immediately, M/dur reappeared. He gestured curtly. Without waiting for M/dere, Rheba ran toward the point where the hall curved away. She dashed around the curve—and nearly slammed into a wall. Where the hall should have been, there was nothing but a seamless Zaarain surface.

She searched frantically for hidden joints, for cracks, any hint that the hall did not terminate right there at her fingertips. She pressed harder, trying to find where hall ended and wall began.

There was nothing but cool extruded surfaces, rippling colors, and silence.

With a sound of frustration and despair, she slammed her fist against the wall. There was no response, no change in the wall's seamless whole.

Dead end, and nothing in sight to burn.

XXIII

Rheba spun around when she heard Daemen approaching. "I thought you said this was the way to the core," she snarled. "You led us into a dead end!"

"I told you the door was Zaarain," he said simply.

"Door?" she said, turning to face the seamless extrusion. "Are you telling me this is a *door?*"

"Zaarain doors are different."

Rheba whistled several unpleasant Bre'n phrases. She reached out and ran her fingertips delicately over the door/wall that abruptly terminated the hallway. She sensed vague energies, pale shadows that made Daemen's thin sunlight seem like a voracious force. Gently, she leaned against the Zaarain door. Her hair lifted with a silky whisper and fanned out, seeking tenuous currents.

She remained motionless for long minutes, learning the exotic patterns that were the hallmark of Zaarain constructs. It was an exercise even more delicate than cheating at Chaos by controlling the Black

Whole's computer. Akhenet lines glowed hotly, beating with the rhythm of her heart. New lines appeared, faint traceries beneath the skin on her shoulders and neck, lines curling up her calves, lines doubling and redoubling until her hands and feet glowed like melted gold.

Finally she sensed hints of direction, of restraints and commands imposed by the placement of molecules within the extrusion. She pursued them with a delicacy that Kirtn would have applauded, but still could not locate any weakness within the door. The lock *was* the door, and vice versa.

Once she thought she had located a node where currents congregated. Yet when she sought its exact location, it eluded her. Without Kirtn's presence she did not have the precision she required. Nor could she simply burn a man-sized hole in the door using her stored energy. Zaarain constructs were far too tough for that.

She pursued the nebulous node indirectly, following the energies that fed it back to their source. Raw force exploded along her lines as she brushed a current that came directly from the Zaarain core. Quickly, she withdrew. Her hands smoked slightly, burned by the energy she had inadvertently called.

As she controlled the pain, she caught a shadow of movement within the construct. The motion was close to where she thought she had sensed the lock node.

"Is the key crystal put in about here?" she asked Daemen, pointing to an area at about eye level.

"I remember it as being over my head," said Daemen doubtfully.

"You were smaller then."

"Oh." He squinted, measuring the place where

her hand was against his childhood memories. "Yes . . . I think so."

"Stand back. It's going to get hot around here."

Daemen backed up hastily.

Rheba's eyes slowly changed from cinnamon to gold as she gathered the energy within herself. Her hair crackled wildly before she controlled it. Her akhenet lines blazed with life. For a long moment she held herself on the brink of her dance, shaping energies into coherence. For a terrible instant she missed Kirtn with an intensity that nearly shattered her dance.

Then she lifted her burned hand and let energy leap.

A line of brilliant blue-white light flashed from her fingertip to the Zaarain construct. Colors surged dizzily over its surface. The only constant was the coherent light called by a fire dancer, light that slowly ate into a door millions of years old.

Smoke curled up from the colors, an eerie smoke that smelled of shaval and time. It flowed seductively around her, sweet as Bre'n breath, warm as Kirtn's body against hers. She cried out and her hand shook, energy scattering uselessly.

The pain of her teeth cutting through her lip dispersed the smoke's enchantment. Her hand steadied. Energy condensed into an implacable beam of light.

The door sighed and dissolved back into the building so quickly that a Seur on the other side was pierced by the deadly energy flowing from Rheba. Surprise was more effective than any attack could have been. Seurs ran away, retreating down the hall, unable to face the alien who burned more brightly than their sun.

Rheba's dance collapsed as exhaustion sent her

staggering. She fell over the corpse of the Seur she had killed. With a muffled cry she rolled aside and braced herself on her hands and knees, too tired to stand up. Her hair hung limply around her breasts and her akhenet lines were no more than faint shadows beneath her skin. Burning through the Zaarain lock had cost every bit of energy she had stored, and more.

It was much harder to dance alone.

M/dur leaped across her and ran down the hall, followed by clepts.

"Rheba?" The Luck's voice was tentative, awed. "I heard the stories about how the Loo-chim died, but I didn't really believe . . ." He held his hand out to help her up, then snatched back his fingers, afraid to touch her.

M/dere brushed The Luck aside. Her small, hard hands pulled Rheba upright. Eyes the color of aged copper checked the J/taaleri for wounds. Then she cocked her head, asking Rheba a silent question.

In answer, Rheba pushed away and began walking after M/dur, using the wall as support for the first few steps. By the time M/dur and the clepts returned, Rheba was walking faster but she still occasionally needed the wall's support.

The J/taals exchanged a long silence. Not for the first time, Rheba cursed Fssa's absence. The snake would have told her what the J/taals had found.

"It's probably the second Zaarain door," said Daemen quietly.

She slumped against the wall and hoped he was wrong. She did not have the strength to battle another Zaarain construct alone.

M/dere touched Rheba's shoulder in a silent bid

for attention. Rheba looked up and thought she saw
compassion in the J/taal's green eyes.

M/dur stood on tiptoe and stretched his arms as
high as they would go. Then he sketched the outline
of a man, a big man. When he was finished, he
touched M/dere's fur and pointed to the imaginary
outline again.

"Kirtn?" Rheba straightened and felt fear like cold
water in her veins. "You saw Kirtn?"

M/dur grimaced in agreement.

Rheba pushed past the J/taals and ran down the
hall. If M/dur had seen Kirtn, f'lTiri was either hurt
or too tired to cover the Bre'n with an illusion. Either
way, Kirtn was in trouble.

The hall curved gracefully, left and right and then
left again, each change of direction marked by subtle
gradations in the colors that rippled over the walls
and floor. The hall curved right again. And ended.

Rheba was too tired to stop herself. She ran into
the Zaarain door with a force that made her see double. She leaned against the door, shaking her head,
trying to see just one of everything again.

Then she realized she was seeing the room beyond,
seeing it as Kirtn saw it, a swirl of enemies circling
around and beyond them the pale gleam of the recycler fluid.

She screamed Kirtn's name but he could not hear
her through the door, unless he was seeing as she
saw, not double but one of each, his view and hers.

Seurs swirled in a flurry of whips and knives. Kirtn
reached for Fssa, heavy around his neck. With a powerful throw, he sent the Fssireeme and his cargo of
zoolipt toward the recycler. The snake landed in the
midst of Seurs, scattering them. But instead of moving
toward the recycler, Fssa turned back toward the

Bre'n, screaming about enemies sneaking up behind Kirtn's back.

Pain exploded in Rheba's back, hammering her to her knees, taking from her even the ability to scream. But not Fssa. He disgorged the zoolipt with a shriek of Fssireeme loss that made even the Zaarain walls quiver.

Vision canted, slipped, and the floor came up to meet Kirtn, swallowing him in a darkness that had no end.

Rheba clawed herself back to her feet, seeing only the Zaarain door in front of her, feeling only the slashing pain that had hurled Kirtn headlong into unconsciousness. In one terrible instant she felt everything, saw everything, knew everything burned in patterns of energy across her mind. Seurs screaming hatred, a knife ripping through Bre'n muscle to the organs beneath, Fssireeme anguish, and Zaarain construct humming around everything with eerie immortality.

Kirtn was dying.

She could not light the darkness condensing inexorably around him, could not even touch him. She reached for him, reached for anything that she could hold, because he was slipping through her grasp like twilight.

And she touched the Zaarain core.

Lines of power exploded across her body, fed by the same energy that sent ships out to the stars. She writhed like a worm in a skillet as alien patterns scorched her brain. But she felt the pain only at a distance, for there was no greater agony than her Bre'n dying beyond the reach of her light. She gathered the core around her like a terrible cloak and reached for Kirtn once again.

The door vaporized in a cloud of shaval smoke, leaving her horribly burned wherever she was not protected by akhenet lines. The pain was so great it simply did not register. She was beyond its reach, beyond everything but the need to be with her Bre'n.

Through the smoke's scented pall she saw Seurs backed against the most distant walls, Seurs fleeing, Seurs fallen and glistening beneath an icy covering. It was the signature of a Fssireeme, a predator who sucked up even the energy that made electrons dance, leaving his victims so cold that moisture in the air condensed around them, becoming a shroud of ice.

Kirtn lay on his side amid the glistening corpses, a Fssireeme keening against his copper fur. In Kirtn's hand was the bloody knife he had wrenched out of his back as he fell.

She knelt beside him, ablaze with akhenet lines. Her fingers probed gently, seeking any pulse of life. She found a sense of distant pain, distant emotion, life sliding away beneath her raw fingertips, blood running down her burned body, blurring the gold of akhenet lines.

She found no pulse, though the slow welling of his blood onto the floor argued that he was still alive. She let energy flow into him.

There was no response.

She increased the flow of energy into him but it was like trying to power a spaceship with a candle. It was then that she tapped the Zaarain core, risking death almost casually, accepting the searing agony that came.

But the core was not enough, for even the Zaarains had not discovered how to transform dying into living.

Numbly, she let go of the core. She stroked Kirtn's face with hands that shook, hands as gold as his eyes staring sightlessly beyond her. She closed her eyes and felt coldness slide up her fingertips like another color of night, heard Fssa's keening coming from the end of time.

The cold feeling moved, flowing over her with a gentle sucking sound. She opened her eyes and saw the turquoise sheen of a zoolipt covering her hands and Kirtn's face. She was too numb to do more than watch dully, her skin cringing from the zoolipt's cool touch.

The zoolipt quivered, tasting the burned flesh beneath her akhenet lines. A queer tingling rose in her, starting from her fingertips and spreading through her body with each beat of her heart.

The zoolipt thinned even more, covering her burned body until it looked as though she wore a turquoise veil. The tingling spread throughout her body, a feeling of energy spreading, an energy that was both subtle and immense. She tried to move but could not, held in the zoolipt's blue-green embrace. It permeated her body cell by cell, multiplying and tasting her with a thoroughness that left her shaken.

Then, with a sound like a long sigh, the turquoise veil peeled away and dropped onto Kirtn. She stared, certain the zoolipt was darker now, more dense, with more shades of blue turning beneath its odd surface.

The zoolipt shivered, lifting a part of itself into the air like a clept questing for a scent. Before she could move, the zoolipt surged over Kirtn's back and poured itself into the Bre'n's deep, ragged wound. She made a futile gesture, trying to keep the zoolipt away from Kirtn's helpless body. But the zoolipt simply flowed between her smooth fingers.

Her fingers.

She stared at her hands, not believing what she

saw. There was no blood oozing, no raw flesh burned to the bone beneath akhenet lines. Her hands were as smooth and perfect as a baby's. She looked from her hands to the rest of her body, remembering the instant the Zaarain door had vaporized, burning her so completely that her mind had simply refused to acknowledge the messages of pain.

But there was no pain now, nothing except an odd tingling euphoria in every cell of her body. Every *healed* cell. She was as whole as she had been when she had crawled out of Square One's living pool.

This time it was different, though. This time the zoolipt had not been satisfied with merely tasting her. It had become a part of her.

She stared in horrified fascination at the zoolipt pseudopod that had remained outside of Kirtn's body. The zoolipt was definitely smaller now, but still dense, still with tones of blue turning beneath its surface. More blues than it had had a moment ago, and more greens. Currents were visible, shivers of deeper blue-green, vivid glints of turquoise like laughter moving across its face.

Sighing, sucking softly, the zoolipt slid off Kirtn onto the bloody floor. With amoebic patience the zoolipt advanced on a Seur's frigid corpse, leaving a clean floor behind. The zoolipt paused at the icy barrier, then seemed to flow through it.

Slowly, the ice became shades of blue, reflecting the zoolipt beneath. When the zoolipt withdrew, the ice collapsed with tiny musical sounds. The corpse was gone. The zoolipt was bigger.

And Kirtn's heart was beating beneath her hands.

XXIV

Kirtn shuddered and was on his feet in an instant, pulling Rheba with him, a Seur's knife still held in his hand. He remembered only that he had been under attack. A swift glance told him that the battle was over. Dead Seurs lay scattered around him. Living Seurs had retreated to the side of the huge recycler room, held at bay by J/taals, clepts, and an exhausted but otherwise unharmed illusionist.

Rheba's joy coursed through Kirtn like a shockwave, uniting him with her in brief mind dance. For a moment he lived what she had seen and felt from the instant of double vision on the far side of a Zaarain door. He buried his face in her hair, holding her close, trying to comfort her and convince himself that he was not dead.

"How do you feel?" she asked, tilting her head back and staring hungrily at his eyes, alive again.

"I—" He hesitated, then said with surprise in his voice, "I've never felt better." Turquoise flashed at the corner of his vision, startling him. "What's that?"

Rheba followed the direction of his glance. She could not help shuddering as the zoolipt condensed around yet another Seur corpse. *"That* is the zoolipt."

"Are you sure?" he asked, eyeing the zoolipt and remembering the amount that Fssa had swallowed. "Isn't it bigger than it was?"

"Yes," she said succinctly, "it is."

Another shroud collapsed with a musical tinkle. The zoolipt shook off random pieces of ice and flowed over to the nearest dead Seur.

"Fssa?" whispered the Bre'n, suddenly realizing just how the Seurs had died. "Did Fssa do that?"

The answer was a Bre'n whistle that vibrated with shame. The Fssireeme slithered toward Kirtn. Dark lines ran over the snake's incandescent body. The lines showed his shame at reverting to his ugly predatory heritage; the incandescence showed that he was replete with energy taken from Seurs.

Kirtn, knowing how Fssa felt, whistled extravagant praise of Fssa's beauty, followed by thanks for saving his life.

"I'm not beautiful," mourned Fssa, "I'm a parasite, and the zoolipt saved your life."

Rheba counted the bodies of Kirtn's attackers. "If it weren't for you, snake," she said crisply, "there wouldn't have been anything left for the zoolipt to save."

She knelt and scooped up the Fssireeme. He was so hot she burned her hands, making Fssa all the more ashamed of his nature.

"My fault," she said ruefully, shaking her hair over the snake. "I should know better than to handle you when you glow."

Fssa vanished into her hair, radiating heat as quickly as he could, though he knew her hair would not burn even with a Fssireeme's hot presence. Shedding the warmth that he so loved was a kind of penance for the way that he had obtained it.

She felt heat shimmer through her hair and knew what Fssa was doing. She also guessed why. She could think of no way to console him. Sighing, she looked at her hands, wondering how badly she had burned them.

As she watched, the last of her blisters shrank and disappeared.

"What . . .?" said Kirtn wonderingly, taking her hand. He ran his fingertips over hers and found only whole, healthy skin.

She bit her lip. If she had had any doubts that the zoolipt had left some of itself inside her, she had none now. "The zoolipt," she whispered, smiling crookedly at Kirtn. Then she shuddered. "I hope it doesn't get tired of my taste for a *long* time."

"And mine?" asked Kirtn. "Is it in me?"

"Yes," smiling, "but nobody could get tired of your taste."

He closed his eyes, trying to sense the alien presence inside his body. All he felt was a pervasive sense of health and a strength he had not known since Deva burned to ash behind their fleeing ship. *Thank you, zoolipt, whoever and whatever you are.* He thought he felt a distant echo of pleasure but could not be sure.

In silence, Rheba and Kirtn watched the zoolipt absorb another corpse. The Zaarain construct—plant, animal, machine or all three at once—flowed in tones of blue beneath the ice.

The Seurs also watched, horrified and fascinated at once. When the ice shroud collapsed and the turquoise-streaked zoolipt moved in their direction, the Seurs moaned and cursed their Luck.

A disheveled Tric stepped forward, placing himself

between the advancing zoolipt and the other Seurs. Visibly shaken, he waited to be devoured.

"It won't hurt you," called Daemen as he came forward to place himself directly in front of the zoolipt. It reared up slightly, fluttered its edges and flowed past The Luck. "See? It's a recycler. A machine. It won't hurt anything that's alive."

Tric looked at The Luck doubtfully. "Is this your gift? A new recycler? A recycler that won't starve or poison us?"

Daemen's smile could have lit a sunless world. "Food. A future. My gift to my people," he said softly. "I'm Good Luck, Uncle-and-Father. Perhaps the best Luck this planet has ever seen."

Slowly, the Seurs shuffled away from the wall, stretching their necks for a better look at their future. With a profusion of blues, the zoolipt engulfed the last corpse. The Seurs watched in silent appreciation of its efficiency.

Kirtn and Rheba looked at each other, remembering Square One, where the greater portion of this zoolipt presided over chaos. Healthy chaos, but chaos all the same. Not only presided, but *created*. Runners, burrowers, flyers, the zoolipt experimented with the abandon of an idiot—or a God.

And that same zoolipt was inside them, multiplying, echos of turquoise pleasure resonating through them.

Machine? They did not think so.

God? They most profoundly hoped *not*.

The last icy shroud collapsed in a shower of tiny crystal notes. Wordlessly, Kirtn and Rheba advanced on the engorged zoolipt. It was as big as she was now, and far heavier. Its surface danced with every tint of blue.

Kirtn hesitated, then bent over the zoolipt and

began kneading it into a sphere. She hesitated too, then went to work by his side. Neither spoke.

The Seurs muttered unhappily and advanced. Fssa's head appeared out of Rheba's hair. The snake let loose a malevolent hiss. The Seurs stopped. They had seen a Fssireeme in action. They had no desire to become ice sculptures carved by an alien snake. Yet they were not convinced that The Luck was their salvation, either. They stared at the zoolipt with the suspicion bred by years of being victims of a whimsical recycler.

"What are you doing?" asked Daemen, watching Rheba curiously.

"Rolling it into the soup," said Rheba, gesturing with a tendril of hair toward the depleted recycler pool.

"Oh. Can I help?"

"Have any cuts or scrapes?" she asked, grunting as she caught a slippery fold of zoolipt and tucked it into place.

Daemen looked at his hands and feet. As usual, he had come through the worst of it with little more than a few scratches. "One or two. Why?"

"Apparently, when we took a piece of this zoolipt we gave it an idea; it can live separately from the central mass. Then it had another idea. Living in us."

"What do you mean?"

Kirtn looked up from his work. "It's in us. Both of us." The zoolipt quivered under his hands like blue marmalade. "It came in through our wounds. Maybe it just liked our alien flavors too much to leave after it healed us. Or maybe it will use any broken skin as an excuse to take up residence. You're The Luck. Take your choice."

Kirtn bent over the dense, quivering mass and heaved. The zoolipt rolled eccentrically. Rheba deflected it toward the pool. In doing so, her hands sank up to her wrists in zoolipt.

Daemen looked at his modestly abraded palms and decided that just this once he would not push his Luck. When the zoolipt wobbled in his direction, he leaped back out of its way.

As Rheba, Kirtn and the lopsided zoolipt slopped toward the recycler pool, the Seurs' muttering increased. Their recycler was not much, but without it they would surely die.

"It's all right," said Daemen soothingly. He smiled his charming smile for Tric. "Really. The zoolipt kept Square One alive after their grid went eccentric. Our grid is intact. Imagine what the zoolipt will be able to do for us."

Rheba and Kirtn exchanged a long look. They were imagining, all right, and none of it was particularly comforting. "Be ready to run after we kick it into the soup," whistled the Bre'n sourly.

Fssa translated for the J/taals and illusionist, carefully avoiding any language the Seurs might understand. The J/taals withdrew into a protective formation. Fssa lifted his head out of Rheba's hair and focused his sensors on the restless Seurs.

The zoolipt quivered at the edge of the recycler pool. The contrast between the pale, almost invisible turquoise of the pool and the zoolipt's robust blues was startling. It did not seem possible that the two forms of quasi-life had any relation at all to each other.

Kirtn hesitated and looked at Daemen. "You're sure this is what you want?"

Daemen laughed. "Of course!"

Kirtn shrugged. "It's your planet."

He kicked the zoolipt into the soup.

Rheba held her breath, waiting for a repeat of the

disaster that had occurred when Rainbow was tossed into Centrins' core. Kirtn's hand closed over her wrist, ready to yank her back if anything happened. The zoolipt rolled to the bottom of the pool. And sat there.

The lights stayed on.

Rheba began to breathe again. Kirtn's grip relaxed.

The zoolipt exploded through the soup in a soundless blue shockwave. Tints and tones of blue, shades of blue, impossible variations on the theme of blue, all of them at once, shimmering, quivering, *alive*. And then the greens came, wistful and luminous, subtle and magnificent. The bottom of the pool vanished in emerald turmoil. When it was still again, the pool was a blue-green, translucent sea where emerald lights glimmered restlessly on turquoise currents.

Kirtn whistled a soft tribute to the zoolipt's uncanny beauty. The Seurs sighed and looked at their Luck with awe.

The lights went out.

Kirtn swore.

An incredible sunrise swept through Centrins, banishing its habitual twilight. Every Zaarain surface scintillated, throwing off light like enormous jewels. Sound condensed between the colors, a song so beautiful that it made Fssa tremble with joy. For an instant everyone lived in the center of perfection, suspended in uncanny brilliance.

Colors swirled across one wall, then cleared to reveal the rest of the installation. Like a ship's downside sensors, the wall enlarged one detail after the next, giving those inside an intimate view of what was happening in the city. Beneath the debris of time and ignorance, Zaarain pavements glowed, hinting at marvels just beyond reach.

The feeding stations came alive, singing of scents

and flavors unmatched in Seur history. Skeletal crowds milled from one station to the next, gorging themselves on food that went instantly throughout their systems, visibly healing and rebuilding starved bodies. Stupefied, they stretched out on pavement that sensed their need and became a bed. Smiling, they slept the sleep of the newly born.

Feeding stations became shaval fountains. Drifts of fragrant gold began to form, tenderly engulfing the sleeping bodies.

The wall changed, becoming a symphony of colors once more. Rheba blinked and awakened from Zaarain enchantment. She turned to ask the Seurs if they were satisfied with their Luck.

The Seurs were gone.

"I thought that last group looked familiar," said Kirtn. He turned hopefully to his left, but The Luck was not gone. The Bre'n sighed. "Still here?"

Daemen smiled shyly. "I wanted to say thank you."

"You're The Luck, not us."

"I couldn't have done it without you."

Kirtn could not argue with that. "You're welcome." He turned to Rheba. "Ready?"

"Wait," said Daemen quickly. "You saved my people from extinction. Let me do the same for you."

"What do you mean?" demanded Rheba.

"You're looking for more of you—and of him." He pointed at Kirtn.

"Yes." Her voice was tight, as it always was when she thought about the odds against finding more Bre'ns, more Senyasi, another world to build another akhenet culture. "Do you know where some of our people are?"

"No. But I'm The Luck. Take me along." Daemen touched her arm and smiled. "Let me help you. Please."

Kirtn looked at the young man whose smile was as beautiful and complex as a Zaarain construct. The Bre'n wanted to grab his fire dancer and run, but the Choice was hers, not his. He stepped aside, waiting and feeling cold. Daemen could not have made a more compelling offer if he had used all of eternity to think of one.

"But what about your own people?" asked Rheba.

"The machine will take care of them. They don't need me anymore."

She thought of Square One and wondered. Despite Daemen's assurances, she *knew* the zoolipt was not a machine. It was alive, and intelligent after its own fashion. Now it had its hands—or whatevers—on the most sophisticated technology known in all the Cycles of man. What happened next was very much a matter of Luck. His Luck. If she took him, used him to find her own people and in doing so caused the extinction of his . . .? That was too high a price to pay for akhenet survival.

And in the back of her mind there was always Satin's voice screaming, *Space him!*

Not that she agreed with Satin. Daemen was not bad luck. Not quite. But in his company she had been beaten, drugged, shunted off to die in a tunnel, fed to a voracious zoolipt; and worst by far, *she had felt her Bre'n die beneath her hands*. It had all turned out all right, of course. She was alive, and he was, both of them carrying their little cargo of God. . . .

She did not know how much more of The Luck she could survive.

"You belong to your people," she said slowly. "They bred you. They deserve your Luck." She kissed his cheek. "But thanks anyway."

Daemen let her hair slip between his fingers and

tried to smile. "Good Luck, beautiful dancer. If you change your mind, I'll be here." He took off Rainbow and handed it to Kirtn. "I won't need this, now."

They left The Luck standing by a pool brimming with improbable life, trying to smile.

Silently, J/taals and clepts scouted through the transformed city. There were no threats, no dangers, nothing but shaval drifting fragrantly on the wind.

Rheba was silent, looking neither right nor left as her Bre'n guided her toward the spaceship. When they were in the *Devalon*'s shadow, they could see power shimmering around the ship. The core drain was off. The *Devalon* would be ready to lift as soon as they were aboard.

Kirtn whistled an intricate Bre'n command. Shaval floated up as the ship extruded a ramp.

"Sorry you didn't take him?" asked Kirtn as he mounted the ramp, unable to stand her pensive silence any longer.

"What?" asked Rheba.

"The Luck. Are you sorry you left him behind?"

Her hair seethed quietly. "I don't think so. But I was just thinking—"

The ship opened, revealing an interior packed with former slaves impatient to be on their way. Rheba stopped, amazed all over again at the variety of beings she had promised to take home.

"You were thinking—?" prompted Kirtn gently.

"Look at them."

Kirtn looked. "And?"

"The Luck was just one. What will it take to get the others home?"

Kirtn smiled whimsically. "A fire dancer, a Bre'n and a Fssireeme—what else?"

The answer came in tiny echos of zoolipt laughter.

If you liked *Dancer's Luck*, be sure to look for *Fire Dancer*, available now from Pinnacle Books, wherever paperback books are sold. And be sure to watch for *Dancer's Illusion*, coming in April, 1996. Just to whet your interest, read on for a taste of *Dancer's Illusion*. . .

DANCER'S ILLUSION

I

The tension in the *Devalon*'s crowded control room was as unbearable as the air. The ship's life-support systems were overloaded. Passengers and crew were being kept alive, but not in comfort. Rheba wiped her forehead with the back of her arm. Both arm and face were sweaty, both pulsed with intricate gold lines that were visible manifestations of the power latent within her.

She looked at her Bre'n. Rivulets of sweat darkened Kirtn's suede-textured skin. The fine, very short copper fur that covered his powerful body made the control room's heat even more exhausting for him than it was for her.

"Ready?" she said, wiping her face again.

"Yesss," hissed Fssa, dangling his head out of her hair. His thin, infinitely flexible body was alive with metallic colors. He loved heat.

"Not you, snake," Rheba muttered. "Kirtn."

The Bre'n smiled, making his yellow eyes seem

even more slanted in their mask of almost invisibly fine gold fur. "Ready. Maybe it will be an ice planet," he added hopefully.

Rheba looked around the control room at the sweaty races of Fourth People she had rescued from a lifetime of slavery on Loo. Some were furred, some not. They had as many colors as Rainbow, the Zaarain construct that was at the moment a necklace knocking against Kirtn's chest.

All of the passengers had two things in common: their past slavery on Loo and their present hope that it would be their planet's number that would be chosen by the *Devalon*'s computer in the lottery. The winner was given the best prize of all—a trip home.

The owners of the ship, Rheba and Kirtn, were not included in the lottery. Their home had died beneath the hot lash of an unstable sun, sending the young Bre'n and his even younger Senyas fire dancer fleeing for their lives. They had survived, and they had managed to find two others who had survived. One was Ilfn, a woman of Kirtn's race. The other was her storm dancer, a blind boy called Lheket. Rheba had sworn to find more survivors, to comb the galaxy until she had found enough Bre'ns and Senyasi to ensure that neither race became extinct.

But first she had light-years to go and promises to keep. She had to deliver each one of the people on the ship to his, her, or *hir* home. The first such delivery—to a planet called Daemen—had nearly killed both her and Kirtn. Since then there had been several other planets, none dangerous. But each number the computer spat out could be another Daemen.

"You may be ready," Rheba sighed, "but I'm not sure I am."

She licked her lips, then whistled a phrase in the

intricate, poetic Bre'n language. Instantly the computer displayed a number in the air just above her head.

311:Yhelle

Kirtn whistled in lyric relief. That was the most civilized planet in the Yhelle Equality. Certainly there could be no difficulty there. Besides, the Yhelle illusionists on board had more than earned their chance to go home. Without them, Kirtn certainly would have died on Daemen, and Rheba, too.

On the other hand, they would miss the illusionists. It was piquant not knowing who or what would appear in the crowded corridors of the *Devalon*.

Fssa keened softly into Rheba's ear. He, too, would miss the illusionists. When they were practicing their trade, they had a fey energy about them that could appeal only to a Fssireeme—or another illusionist.

"I know, snake," Rheba said, stroking him with a fingertip. She sent currents of energy through her hair to console the Fssireeme. "But it wouldn't be fair to ask them to wait just because we like their company."

Fssa subsided. With a final soft sound he vanished into her seething gold hair.

Rheba stood on tiptoe to see over the heads of the people crowding the control room. "Where are they?"

Kirtn, taller than anyone else, spotted the illusionists. "By the hall."

"Are they happy?"

"With an illusionist, who can tell?" he said dryly. Then he relented and lifted Rheba so that she could see.

"They don't look happy," she said.

Kirtn whistled a phrase from the "Autumn Song,"

one of Deva's most famous poems, variations on the theme of parting.

"Yes, but they still should be happy," whistled Rheba. "They're going *home.*"

All of her longing for the home she had lost was in her Bre'n whistle. Kirtn's arms tightened around her. She had been so young; she had so few memories to comfort her.

And she was right. The illusionists did not look happy.

With a silent sigh, Kirtn put her back on her own feet. He tried to imagine why anyone would be reluctant to go back home after years of slavery. What he imagined did not comfort him. At best, they might simply dislike their planet. At worst, they might have been exiled and therefore did not expect to be welcomed back.

He pushed through the disappointed people who were slowly leaving the control room. Rheba followed, unobtrusively protected by two J/taals. On Loo, the mercenaries had chosen her as their J/taaleri, the focus of their devotion. They continued to protect her whenever she permitted it—and even when she did not.

"Congratulations," said Kirtn, smiling at the illusionists. "The ship is computing *replacements* from here to Yhelle. Are there any defenses we should know about?"

F'lTiri tried to smile. "Probably not. No one has fought with Yhelle for thousands of years. The last people who did conquered us. They retreated five years later, babbling." This time he managed a true smile. "Yhelle is hard on people who expect reality to be what it seems to be."

"Is that what you're doing?" said Rheba. "Practicing?"

I'sNara's confusion showed in her voice as well as her face. "What do you mean? We're appearing as ourselves right now. No illusions."

"Then why aren't you happy?" Rheba asked bluntly. "You're going home."

The two illusionists looked quickly at one another. At the same instant, both of them appeared to glow with pleasure. Rheba made an impatient gesture. She had been with them long enough to separate their illusions from their reality . . . some of the time.

"Forget it," she snapped. "Just tell me what's wrong."

"Nothing," they said in unison. "We're just overcome with surprise," added i'sNara. "We never expected to go home so soon."

Kirtn grunted. Their voices were as unhappy as their faces had been a few moments ago. "Fssa, tell everyone to clear the control room and get ready for *replacement.*"

The Fssireeme slid out of Rheba's hair into her hands. There he underwent a series of astonishing transformations as he made the necessary apparatus to speak a multitude of languages simultaneously. It was not difficult for the Fssireeme. The snakes had evolved on a hot, gigantic planet as sonic mimics, then had been genetically modified during one of the earlier Cycles. The result was a resilient, nearly indestructible translator who needed only a few phrases to learn any new language.

In response to the languages pouring out of the snake, people hurried out of the control room. When the illusionists turned to go, Kirtn stopped them. "Not you two."

He waited until only four plus Fssireeme were left in the room. He stretched with obvious pleasure, flexing his powerful body. The *Devalon* had been designed originally for twelve crew members and hurriedly rigged for the two who had survived Deva's solar flare. Even after dropping off people on five planets, the remainder of the refugees from Loo's slave pens seriously overloaded the ship's facilities. As a result, Kirtn spent most of his time trying not to crush smaller beings.

"Now," he said, focusing on i'sNara and f'lTiri, "what's the problem?"

The illusionists looked at each other, then at him, then at Rheba. "We're not sure we should go home," said i'sNara simply.

"Why?" asked Rheba, slipping Fssa back into her hair.

The illusionists looked at each other again. "We are appearing naked before you," said f'lTiri, his voice strained.

Rheba blinked and began to object that they were fully dressed as far as she could tell, then realized that they meant naked of illusions, not clothes. "That's rare in your culture, isn't it?"

"Yes," they said together. "Only with children, very close friends and sometimes with lovers. A sign of deep trust."

"I see." Rheba hesitated, knowing the illusionists were proud as only ex-slaves could be. "You didn't leave your planet voluntarily . . .?"

"No."

Rheba and Kirtn exchanged a long look. She slid her fingers between his. They did not have the intraspecies telepathy of the J/taals or the interspecies telepathy of master mind dancers, yet they sometimes could catch each other's thoughts when they were in physical contact. Once, on Daemen, telepathy had come without contact; but Kirtn had been dying then, too high a price to pay for soundless speech. Now there was no urgency, just a long sigh and the word *trouble* shared between them.

"Tell us." Rheba's tone was more commanding than inviting, but her smile was sympathetic.

"It's a long story," began f'lTiri, "and rather complex."

Kirtn laughed shortly. "I'd expect nothing else from a culture based on pure illusions."

"Don't leave anything out," added Rheba. "If we'd known more about Daemen, we would have had less trouble there."

F'lTiri sighed. "I'd rather be invisible while I talk," he muttered. "Holding invisibility couldn't be much harder than telling you. . . ." He made a curt gesture. "As you said, our society is based on illusion. Nearly all Yhelles can project illusions. Some are better than others. There are different categories of illusion, as well."

Rheba remembered the young Yhelle illusionist she had seen on Loo. His gift was appearing to be the essence of everyone's individual sexual desire. The result had been compelling for the audience and confusing for her—she had seen the appearance of Kirtn on the young illusionist, yet Kirtn was her mentor, not her lover. The image still returned to disturb her. She banished it each time, telling herself that it was merely her knowledge of legendary Bre'n sensuality that had caused her to identify Yhelle illusion as Bre'n reality.

"The result is that while other societies have tangible means of rewarding their members, Yhelle doesn't," continued f'lTiri. "What good is a jeweled badge when even children can make the *appearance* of that badge on themselves? What good is a magnificent house when most Yhelles can project the appearance of a castle? What good is a famous face when almost anyone can duplicate the appearance of that face? What good is beauty? Even poetry can appear more exquisite than it is. One of my daughters could project a poem that would make you weep . . . but when anyone else read the words, they were merely ordinary."

The illusionist sighed, and i'sNara took up the explanation. "He doesn't mean that everything on Yhelle is illusory. Our money is real enough most of the time, because we need it for the framework of real food and cloth and shelter we build our illusions on. But the elaboration of necessity that is the foundation of most societies just doesn't exist on Yhelle. We have nearly everything we want—or at least the *appearance* of having it." She looked anxiously from Bre'n to Senyas. "Do you understand?"

"I doubt it," said Kirtn, "but I'm trying. Do you mean that a Yhelle could take mush and make it appear to be a feast?"

"Yes," said i'sNara eagerly. "A good illusionist can even make it *taste* like a feast."

"But can't you see through the illusions?" asked Rheba.

Both illusionists looked very uncomfortable. "That's a . . . difficult . . . subject for us. Like cowardice for the J/taals or reproduction for the Lerns."

"That may be," said Rheba neutrally, "but it's crucial. We won't be shocked."

F'ITiri almost smiled. Even so, his words were slow, his tone reluctant. "Some illusions are easier to penetrate than others. It depends on your skill, and the power of the creator. But it is unspeakably . . . crude . . . to comment on reality. And who would want to? Who prefers real mush to an apparent feast? Especially as they are equally nourishing. Do you understand?"

Bre'n and Senyas exchanged a long silence. "Keep going," said Rheba at last. "We're behind you, but we're not out of breath yet."

I'sNara's laughter was light and pleasing. Rheba realized that it was the first time she had heard either Yhelle really laugh.

"You'll catch up soon," said f'lTiri confidently. "After Loo and Daemen, I don't think anything can stay ahead of either of you."

Rheba smiled sourly and said nothing. They had been lucky to survive those planets.

"We don't have much government," continued f'lTiri. "It's difficult to tax illusions, and without taxes government isn't much more than an amusement for wellborn families. There's some structure, of course. We are Fourth People, and Fourth People seem doomed to hierarchy. We're organized into clans, or rather, *disorganized* into clans. Each clan specializes— traders or artists or carpenters, that sort of thing. I'sNara and I belong to the Liberation clan. We're master snatchers," he said proudly. "Thieves."

Rheba blinked. The illusionists treated reality as a dirty word and thievery as a proud occupation. She sensed Kirtn's yellow eyes on her but did not return his look. She was afraid she would laugh, offending the Yhelles.

"And quite good at it," said Kirtn blandly, "if Onan is any proof of your skill. Without you two we'd still be stuck in Nontondondo, trying to scrape up the price of an Equality navtrix.''

F'ITiri made a modest noise. "We were out of practice. The only thing we've stolen in five years worth mentioning is our freedom—and *you* stole that for us." He sighed. "Anyway, we weren't good enough on Yhelle. We were assigned to steal the Ecstasy Stones from the Redistribution clan. We were caught and sold to Loo."

"I'm out of breath," said Rheba flatly. "You spent a lot of time telling us about appearances being equal or superior to reality, then you tell us that you tried to steal something. Why? Couldn't you just make an illusion of the Ecstasy Stones?"

"That's the whole point. Oh, we could make something that looked like the Stones, but no illusionist in Yhelle history has been able to make anything that *felt* like the Stones. That's their value," said f'ITiri. "They make you feel loved. That's their illusion."

Rheba looked at Kirtn, silently asking if he understood. He smiled. "You're too pragmatic, fire dancer. It's your Senyas genes. Think of it this way. The Yhelles have, or *seem* to have, everything that Fourth People have pursued since the First of the Seventeen Cycles. Wealth, beauty, power over their environment—if there is a name for it, the Yhelles have someone able to make it appear. Or," he added dryly, "*appear* to appear. The illusion of love is the only exception."

He looked at the illusionists. They moved their hands in a gesture of agreement. "Exactly," said the Yhelles together.

F'ITiri continued, "We create illusions, but we aren't deluded by them. Illusionists who fool themselves are, by definition, fools. So when it comes to love, we're no better off than the rest of the Fourth People."

"Except for the Stones," put in i'sNara. "Their fabulous illusion—if it indeed *is* an illusion—is love. They love you totally. The more Stones you have, the more intense is the feeling of loving and being loved."

"That would make them valuable in any society," said Rheba.

"Perhaps," conceded f'ITiri. "But in Serriolia, the city-state where we were born and the most accomplished illusionists live, the illusion of everything is available. Except love. In Serriolia, the Ecstasy Stones are priceless. Most of our history hinges on the masterful illusions that have gone into stealing one or more of the Stones. Master snatchers of each generation used to try their skills on whoever owned one or more Stones."

"Used to?" asked Kirtn. "What happened?"

"The Redis—the Redistribution clan—snatched almost all of Serriolia's Stones. You see, the Redis were formed out of the discontented thieves of various clans. That was hundreds of years ago. For generations, the clan trained and sent out platoons of master snatchers. In the beginning, the clan's sole reason for existence was to steal Ecstasy Stones from the selfish few who had them. The Redis hoped to combine the Stones into one Grand Illusion available to every citizen."

"That doesn't sound too bad," said Rheba hesitantly.

"It wasn't," agreed i'sNara. "But the Redis didn't share. Only Redis were allowed into the Stones' presence. And only a few Redis, at that. So another clan was formed out of unhappy snatchers, the Liberation clan. Besides," she smiled, "there were all those highly trained snatchers and nothing to practice on but their own clan—unthinkable. Stealing from your own clan is grounds for *disillusionment*."

"And you were caught stealing the Stones?" said Kirtn. "Is that why you were exiled?"

"We're Libs," said f'ITiri proudly. "It was our duty to snatch Stones from the Redis. But the Redis didn't have any sense of humor. It wasn't just that we were snatchers—our history is full of snatchers—but that our mere existence suggested that the Redis were not holding the Stones for the good of *all* Serriolians. The Redis Charter is quite specific about the Redis stealing Stones for high purposes rather than for selfish pleasures. The Redis Charter is posted in every clan hall. The fact that the Charter rather than the Stones circulates among the clans is attributed to the Stones' extreme worth."

"Or the Charter's extreme worthlessness," added i'sNara sarcastically.

Rheba rubbed her temples and wondered why she had urged the Yhelles to tell her everything. She was totally confused. Her hair crackled. Kirtn stroked the seething mass, gently pulling out excess energy. After a moment her hair settled into golden waves that covered her shoulders.

"What's the worst that can happen if you go back?" Rheba asked bluntly.

"That's just it," said i'sNara, her voice soft. "We don't know."

"Will your clan disown you?" asked Kirtn.

"No," answered f'ITiri. "Never."

"You haven't broken any local laws?" pressed Rheba.

"No."

"Then why are you reluctant to go home?"

"We may be sent after the Stones again, and caught again, and sold to Loo again. Or worse."

Rheba tried not to groan aloud. The more she heard of Yhelle and Serriolia, the less she liked it. She could, and should, just set down in Serriolia, sadly but firmly say goodbye to the illusionists, and then lift for deep space with all the power in the *Devalon*'s drive.

But without f'lTiri's masterful illusions, a fire dancer and a Bre'n would have died on Loo or Daemen.

"You don't know what will happen to you?" said Kirtn, his voice divided between statement and question.

"No, we don't."

Kirtn sighed. "Then we'd better go find out."

About the Author

Ann Maxwell lives in the Pacific northwest with her husband (and frequent co-writer), Evan Maxwell. She's best known for her many bestselling romances, written under her own name, and under her *New York Times* bestselling pseudonym, Elizabeth Lowell. She and Evan, writing as A. E. Maxwell, are responsible for one of the finest mystery series to hit paper since the invention of moveable type—the Fiddler and Fiora books, including the recent bestseller *Murder Hurts*. She has also written everything from historical fiction to non-fiction to thrillers. Her books have been nominated for virtually every award in the publishing industry, from the Romance Writers of America's *RITA* award to the Science Fiction Writers' Nebula Award, to the Mystery Writer of America's Edgar awards. Be sure to look for her recent release from Pinnacle, *Fire Dancer*, as well as the forthcoming futuristic romance *Dancer's Illusion*. Ann Maxwell's novels of romantic suspense include *The Diamond Tiger*, *The Secret Sisters*, *The Ruby*, and her forthcoming book, *The Silk Strategy*, which will be a December, 1996 Pinnacle lead title.

FOR THE VERY BEST IN ROMANCE—
DENISE LITTLE PRESENTS!

AMBER, SING SOFTLY   (0038, $4.99)
by Joan Elliott Pickart
Astonished to find a wounded gun-slinger on her doorstep, Amber
Prescott can't decide whether to take him in or put him out of his misery.
Since this lonely frontierswoman can't deny her longing to have a man
of her own, who nurses him back to health, while savoring the glorious
possibilities of the situation. But what Amber doesn't realize is that this
strong, handsome man is full of surprises!

A DEEPER MAGIC   (0039, $4.99)
by Jillian Hunter
From the moment wealthy Margaret Rose and struggling physician Ian
MacNeill meet, they are swept away in an adventure that takes them
from the haunted land of Aberdeen to a primitive, faraway island—and
into a world of danger and irresistible desire. Amid the clash of ancient
magic and new science Margaret and Ian find themselves falling helplessly in love.

SWEET AMY JANE   (0050, $4.99)
by Anna Eberhardt
Her horoscope warned her she'd be dealing with the wrong sort of man.
And private eye Amy Jane Chadwick was used to dealing with the wrong
kind of man, due to her profession. But nothing prepared her for the
gorgeously handsome Max, a former professional athlete who is being
stalked by an obsessive fan. And from the moment they meet, sparks
fly and danger follows!

MORE THAN MAGIC   (0049, $4.99)
by Olga Bicos
This classic romance is a thrilling tale of two adventurers who set out
for the wilds of the Arizona territory in the year 1878. Seeking treasure,
an archaeologist and an astronomer find the greatest prize of all—love.